# PURGATORY BEACH

## BY EDWARD J. MCFADDEN III

SEVEREDPRESS

# PURGATORY BEACH

## WWW.SEVEREDPRESS.COM

## *ISBN: 978-1-923165-48-9*

"Infernal punishments are purgatory and medicinal."
–Unknown Prophet

# 1

**Purgatory Beach, Liigei Too, northern California, U.S.A.**
**6:58 AM PST, September 21st, 2023**
*Twenty-two days until the scheduled start of The Funnel Big Wave Competition*

Mountainous waves arced through the grayness, their shadowy visages materializing from the gloom as frothing white lines marched toward shore. The hiss of breaking waves announced the towering swells as they exploded, erupting into a cascade of frothy whitewater that spread across the inky surface of the Pacific Ocean. Clumps of beach grass dotted the stony shore, and mist rolled off the ocean, the stench of rot thick in the air. The slap and crack of shells being dragged over stones echoed off the rolling hills, and the wind chanted through the boulders that marked the ends of the cove.

Connie Noll sat atop K2, a huge, wind-sculpted hill that towered over the beach. She peered through binoculars at the steep walls of water rising from the ocean like leviathans as she made notations on a pad—height estimation, track, wind direction, and force. In many ways, she was the most important person in the operation, though outside observers would assume it was Gerard. She set the tone for the day. Connie was the spotter, the wave whisperer, though she didn't ride, and never had.

Tentacles of tension massaged her shoulders, and she shivered, warning lights flashing across her mental control board. Someone... or something, was watching her.

She looked over her shoulder, but there was nothing there except the whispering grass and unforgiving hills. The vast dirt parking lot was empty, save for her Prius, but soon it would be filled with surfers, all of whom would want her report. From there word would spread like a virus, a disease that in less than a month all the best surfers in the world would want to contract.

Snowy Plovers tittered and argued, and a flock of dirty gray and white gulls picked at a tangle of seaweed filled with seed muscles that had broken away from a nearby rock. The sea roared and shrieked, but nothing bigger than gulls moved along the beach.

Connie peered through the binoculars as she made another notation on her pad. It was going to be a good day.

Early-season storms and strong winds had been churning up the middle of the Northern Pacific for weeks, creating huge rollers that traveled east unhindered until they met the continental shelf, where the swell rose dramatically, forming massive waves. Connie dipped her middle finger into her mouth to wet it and then held it up. A strong westerly breeze blew from the land toward the sea, which sculpted the wave faces into clean, organized peaks, which meant greater control and speed for the riders.

With modest temperatures, not a cloud in the sky, and a high-pressure system sitting fifty miles offshore, the table was being set for a strong session. There wouldn't be any record breakers, but everyone who needed to get wet in preparation for the competition would be able to do so.

Nice curlers rolled into the shallows and broke two hundred yards offshore. Connie estimated the average set measured twenty feet in height, which was nothing special for The Funnel break, where in season waves had reached sixty feet.

Connie rolled her shoulders and cracked her neck, her nerves dancing just beneath her skin. The weeks leading up to the competition were always stressful. Imagine trying to plan a wedding but having to give your guests a three-week range for the possible date of the nuptials, the final date being decided three days before the monumental event. Add to that, Gerard was in charge and unable to compete, and his normally calm demeanor transformed into the persona of a relentless taskmaster that she could barely live with, let alone love.

Her husband's fall from grace had been epic, and had it not been for Liigei Too, she didn't know where they'd be. As the de facto mayor of the revitalized town and the person who had changed its fortunes, her husband understood this better than anyone.

A flash of movement in her peripheral vision made Connie jerk her head to the right, but she saw nothing unusual. The faint rumble of a car churning over the rock-encrusted dirt road carried over the wasteland of dunes and hillocks.

She pressed the binoculars to her eyes as a shadow crawled amongst the tufts of beach grass, but with the sun still working its way over the horizon there wasn't enough light. It looked like a stone the size of a house cat—but rocks didn't have legs.

Connie got to her feet and jumped down the side of K2, an avalanche of sand chasing her. She took a path that ran through a tangle of detritus; logs, fishing nets, garbage pails, chunks of broken Styrofoam, paper, rope, and an uncountable number of unidentifiable pieces of trash that had been carried in by the sea during storm tides.

The tide sucked at the shoreline, and the crackling of shells being pulled over stones sounded like a broken wind chime. Tumbleweeds of dark seaweed rolled over the rocky beach, and as she approached the stone-like form scurrying across the sand, it froze.

Dusk pressed on the shoreline, and Connie pulled her flashlight without taking her eyes off the anomaly. The Maglite was cold to the touch, and as the tip of her finger found the on button, she sucked in a sharp breath but didn't light the torch.

Two bulbous orbs of light gleamed in the gloom.

Terror seized her, and Connie's stomach churned as daggers of pain stung the tips of her fingers and toes. The rational side of her brain, the side that was always in control—mainly because Gerard's rarely was—told her to turn and run and not stop until she was safe in her car. But that other part, the part that had drawn her to a man who had once surfed an eighty-foot wave, held her in place.

She flicked on the flashlight.

The lights were eyes, and they belonged to—Connie wasn't sure.

What looked to have once been a red rock crab had transformed into a grotesque amalgamation of its former form. The creature was five times the size of a normal red rock crab, and the mutant's swollen mantle was mottled with sickly patches of decaying flesh and gashes filled with red pustules. Its exoskeleton was rough and uneven with jagged edges protruding from its limbs like broken claws, and two shining golf ball-sized eyes sat above a mouth churning with maxillipeds that whined with an uncanny moan.

Connie shifted on her feet and took a step back. The creature didn't appear to fear the bright LED light, and suddenly she felt exposed alone on the beach.

As if sensing her fear, the massive crab scuttled closer, its huge forward claws clicking with a ferocity that made Connie take another step back. The mutant's segmented walking legs were disproportionately large and thick and looked capable of crushing stone, each limb ending in a serrated pincer. Oversized swim legs dragged behind the creature as it surged forward, whitewater foaming around it, a nauseating blend of rotting flesh and briny sea spray filling the air.

Connie picked up a baseball-sized stone and cocked her arm, intending to hurl the rock at the creature, but she held back.

The crab stopped advancing and watched her. Connie felt the thing's stare, sensed it appraising her, sizing her up, evaluating its chances of... what? Taking her down? Crabs are bottom feeders, and they ate anything and everything, but the idea of getting attacked by the biggest crab she'd ever seen made her rub her eyes with disbelief and confusion.

When Connie's vision cleared the mutant was ten feet away.

A finger dangled from a pincer at the end of one of the creature's walking legs.

In the harsh light, the finger looked black, and the crab seemed to have forgotten the digit as if the meat were being saved for dessert. The finger had been severed at the middle joint, and the digit appeared and disappeared as the creature's legs cycled around.

Connie was no stranger to the outdoors, and she and Gerard had been all over the world and had hiked in places most folks wouldn't dare to tread. She knew how to deal with testy wildlife. Be aggressive. Make noise. Let the beast know you're not afraid. This usually worked with bears and the like, but a mutated crab that appeared intent on stripping the skin from her bones? She didn't know, so why risk it?

She spun around and almost fell as she set off at a run.

A squeal of fury rose above the pounding waves, and Connie looked over her shoulder as she came to a stumbling halt.

The mutant was gone.

Connie scanned the beach, the undertow easing over the shore, the boulders... She rubbed her eyes again. Had that just happened? Had the thing held a finger in its pincer?

She'd seen many things she couldn't fully explain, but believing was hard. Shadows distorted only so much, and though daybreak played with the senses and dazzled the imagination, the phantoms that writhed therein were often nothing more than the mind's most depraved fantasies.

No, she'd seen the strange monster crab. And the finger. She was certain of that, but... Connie patted her pocket and felt the outline of her cellphone. Why hadn't she thought to take a picture? She'd photographed her breakfast, flowers along the side of the road, broken buildings, and forlorn bicycle wheels, but it hadn't occurred to her to document the appearance of a creature that could be an unknown species. She licked her lips. There wasn't enough light for a good picture, anyway.

Unexplainable things washed up on shorelines all over the world every day, and to claim humans were aware of every type of creature that called the ocean home was arrogance beyond belief, but still... What would Gerard think? With three weeks to go until the start of contest season? And the finger. She didn't recall hearing about any local losing a digit.

"Yo, Connie. That you?" carried a voice on the wind.

Connie spared a final glance at the ocean, searching for the creature, but of the massive mutant crab, there was no sign. She said, "Morning."

Tommy T appeared from the tangle of flotsam piled against the base of K2, his sculpted chest bare and already damp with the day's perspiration. His long blonde hair was pulled back in a ponytail, and as he approached, the keenness of his blue eyes, and the sharp line of his jaw made Connie think impure thoughts. The local was ten years her junior, but he never failed to make her feel good.

"Looking good," he said.

"With those storms churning up the northern Pacific I think we're going to have a good month."

"I was talking about you."

Connie chuckled. "I'll let Gerard know you said so."

Tommy T laughed and said, "He knows. How big today?"

"I think if you get on it right now you might catch a twenty."

The sun had worked its way over the lip of the world and faint light pushed away the grayness as the eastern horizon turned into an inverted sunset.

Tommy T's crew came down the path hauling a trailer holding a wave runner that would be used to tow Tommy T into the surf and provide the speed needed to ride the faces of monstrous waves.

"Is Gerard coming down today?"

Connie nodded. Her husband rarely rode these days. He claimed not being able to compete had killed the thrill, but he was still a fixture on the beach most days, preaching about waves, promoting the contest, and helping the younger surfers who didn't know how the business of surfing worked.

"Tell him I said hey, will you?" Tommy T said.

She nodded, her eyes straying back to where she'd seen the massive crab.

# 2

**Liigei Too, northern California, U.S.A.**
**7:19 AM PT, September 27th, 2023**
*Sixteen days until the scheduled start of The Funnel Big Wave Competition*

The stench arrived moments before the phone call.

Gerard sat on his porch, sipping his morning tea as dusk crept over the land, the sun fighting to burn through the morning mist. The rumble of children getting ready for school leaked from the small house, and yellow light angled through windows and cast columns of light across his prized flower garden that was doing its best to push away the deep scent of rot but was failing miserably.

Decay danced with the wind, assaulting Gerard's senses and destroying the flavor of his Earl Gray. He imagined the sour stench of forgotten leftovers left to fester in a neglected fridge, mingling with the acrid aroma of damp, decaying wood in a forgotten cellar. It was the odor of life extinguished, of once vibrant existence reduced to nothing but a festering mess of decomposition.

Gerard closed his eyes, and he could almost taste the rot on the back of his tongue. His phone chimed and vibrated as it inched over the wrought iron table. Connie's face appeared on the screen. She was smiling, the ocean in the background, her aqua bikini top dirty with sand, her lips white with sunblock. He tapped accept call and said, "Yo."

"Hey, the kids getting ready?"

"That's not why you called," Gerard said. He didn't dignify her poke with a response. He usually got the kids off to school because the wave whisperer left for Purgatory Beach before sunrise most days.

"No, it's not," Connie said. "Derrick is here, and he thinks you should come down."

Gerard sat forward in his seat and put down his cup of tea. Derrick Manvale was the town sheriff. He was an ornery sort and wasn't one to call meetings without a good reason. It was a courtesy, one that Gerard appreciated. He'd been elected to no office, held no town job, and received no paycheck, yet most who called Liigei Too home considered Gerard the town's leader. It had been him, after all, who had brought the place back from the dead.

He said, "Why does he need me?"

"An orca washed up on the rocks north of The Funnel."

"And I need to see it?" he said. A dead orca was bad for the dwindling population of sea wolves, but he didn't see what he could do other than call the state conservation folks who would want to see the corpse, and Derrick could do that.

"I haven't seen it, Gerard. He said you should come down. That's all I know."

"Got it," he said. "See you after I drop the kids."

Gerard wrangled Willow and Sage, dropped them off at the K-12 school that educated the ninety-three permanent resident minors that lived in the area, and headed for the beach.

In the dusk of early morning, the town held some of its rustic charm. The old buildings encroached to the edge of the stone road, which had been covered in so many layers of blacktop nobody had seen the ancient Mattole Indian thoroughfare in years. As the sun came up more metal gleamed and glass shined, stripping away the old-school charm and revealing Gerard's most important life's work.

He was a man who had once danced on the razor's edge of monstrous waves, but when Gerard found Liigei Too he was teetering on the precipice of losing everything—even his family. The place had been nearly deserted. There was a café, a mini-mart, and that was it. Everything else was closed or out of business. But something magical happened that day as he drove through that forgotten town. The waves were ripping.

That led to the idea of The Funnel Big Wave Competition, and thanks to him, and the hard work of Connie and many others, the revitalization of Liigei Too had been a tremendous success. The contest brought international recognition to The Funnel break and Purgatory Beach became a hot tourist destination.

Gerard recalled his first time at the beach. He'd been perplexed by the size and quality of the waves, which had led him to research the geology of the area. The cove that cradled Purgatory Beach was the result of powerful tidal forces that ran through a series of seamounts and an underwater canyon.

Seamounts play a vital role in the ocean's circulation patterns, influencing nutrient cycling, climate regulation, and wave phases. As the underwater mountains rose from the depths, they disrupted the Pacific's currents, creating eddies and upwellings that drove seawater through an underwater canyon that opened onto Purgatory Beach like a garden hose. It was these unique geological features that made The Funnel break unique.

The parking lot was full and several people wearing wetsuits and carrying boards waved as he found a spot and made his way down to the beach.

Sea grass whispered and sighed, and the scent of decomposing flesh lingered in the salty air despite the offshore breeze. The rhythmic pulse of the ocean, once soothing, now sang a siren's song as Gerard trekked north along the windswept shore to where Connie waited with a knot of surfers. Three wave runners were pulled up onto the beach, and Derrick's police Tahoe, its single red light spinning, sat atop the jetty of tumbled boulders that marked the northern end of the cove and separated the beach from the rocky cliffside shallows beyond.

"Morning," he said as he pecked his wife on the cheek.

"Be more unenthusiastic," said Bongo.

Connie punched the twenty-eight-year-old kid who was Liigei Too's best shot for a local contest champion. "Sorry about the stink," she said.

"Not your fault his mother had indiscriminate taste," Gerard said.

Bongo licked his lips, tossed his hair with a jerk of his narrow head, and shifted on his feet as he tried to decide if he'd been insulted. The top half of his wetsuit was pulled down, the arms tied around his waist, and his cut abs made Gerard think of the bicycle tire inflating around his waistline.

The crowd of surfers was subdued and there were no riders in the water.

"Did Derrick ask everyone to get dry?" Gerard asked.

Connie shook her head no. "The corpse is chewed up, but they deployed the drone, and everything looked clear."

Gerard nodded. "Be right back."

He climbed the jetty slowly, planting each foot and shifting his weight gradually as he tested the stability of each stone. Whitewater washed over the shallows and filtered through the rocks splashing Gerard with sea spray.

A steep vine-covered cliff face and a jagged shoreline of boulders zigzagged north, and as he climbed off the pile of rocks and picked his way from boulder to boulder, he was assaulted by the thick scent of decomposing flesh.

Derrick stood with his deputy, Nayeli Stonetree, and two dolphin detectives from the state dressed in army green. The sheriff stood in the shallows, water washing over his chest-high waders as the undertow pulled shells, seaweed, and stones through his legs. The others were perched on boulders.

Among the debris and foam, a dead orca lay sprawled on the sand like a giant rotten slug. Its colossal, once majestic form was twisted and contorted, and it bore the scars of an unnatural existence. The creature's skin, a sickly shade of blotchy gray, was stretched taut over its massive frame, displaying an array of bulging veins and lesions that oozed a foul, black ichor. Patches of decaying flesh hung loosely from its body, exposing the underlying sinew and bone beneath.

Gerard gagged.

Derrick chuckled and said, "Not freshly baked bread and roasting bacon, is it?"

Gerard said nothing. He had no words. Death and the ocean were wicked sisters, and he'd seen what sharks and other apex predators could do. But this...

The orca's once sleek and streamlined body was distorted almost beyond recognition. Its tall dorsal fin resembled a shard of broken glass, twisted and deformed into a grotesque mockery of its natural shape. Tendrils of seaweed and debris clung to rotting flesh, entwined like a malevolent parasite feeding off the decay. Ribbons of red pustules, like poison oak, cut across the corpse like scars. Flies drawn to the promise of flesh and a rot-filled miasma of sea spray permeated the air.

But it wasn't the decay that held Gerard's attention and silenced the chatter of the sheriff and crew, it was the bites.

The orca looked to have been chewed on by everything and anything with claws and teeth. There were several deep crescent-shaped tears with multiple puncture wounds that said massive shark. The tips of the sea wolf's pectoral fins and tail fluke had been shredded by crabs and carnivorous fish like Pacific jack mackerel and rockfish, their tiny penetrating bites easy to identify all along the dead orca's flanks.

Gerard's phone vibrated, but he ignored it.

The dead orca's mouth, frozen in a grotesque rictus of death, revealed rows of jagged teeth stained with blood and gore. Orca eyes are normally dark and barely perceptible, but the dead beast's eyes were engorged and red as if irritated by toxic smoke. Waves lapped against the bloated corpse, and Gerard's heart raced, a sheen of sweat forming on his brow despite the breeze.

A hollow thumping hid just below the hollering of the waves closing-out.

Chiming phones, rubber boots squeaking on stone, and Derrick's shouts pulled Gerard from his reverie. His phone was ringing also. It was Connie.

He swiped accept call and said, "Yo."

"We've got company."

Then he heard it. The steady thumping of helicopter airfoils beating the air rising over the thunder of the waves.

Men in black wearing full body armor poured over the jetty like ants. The sea reflected in their dark face shields as the force charged forward, jumping from boulder to boulder and crashing through the shallows. The soldiers held futuristic-looking rifles, and though none of the guns were pointed at him there was still a sense that one false move could be his last.

"Please evacuate the area!" the lead stormtrooper screamed.

A black Apache helicopter streaked over the lip of the cliff and swooped in low as it buzzed the shoreline.

Derrick pointed at his chest as he verbally frothed at the mouth, Nayeli Stonetree and two conservation officers falling in behind him. Badges were brandished, egos flexed, and before Gerard's normal hearing returned, he was being led over the barrier of boulders to Purgatory Beach.

The whirlybird circled and came in low and Gerard peered into the copter's ballistic glass-enclosed cockpit. A man with dirty-blonde hair and wearing a navy-blue suit and a blue tie sat in the gunner's chair. He stared at Gerard and the men locked gazes for a heartbeat. Gerard had seen the man before... On T.V.? The news?

A gust of wind scoured Gerard's face with sand as he climbed over stones. He looked back every couple of seconds and the soldiers were forming up around the carcass. The sheriff had given up arguing and he appeared to be taking orders from the lead stormtrooper.

Gerard's breakfast soured in his stomach. What was so important about a dead orca that the feds—had to be feds because only they could mobilize so fast—were expending valuable resources to retrieve it? He didn't know, but he needed answers. Soon, because with the start of contest season only a couple of weeks away the timing couldn't have been worse.

# 3

Seventeen minutes later a black Chinook tandem-rotor helicopter arrived to retrieve the orca carcass.

Soldiers arrayed in black wearing full body armor kept watch from atop the jetty as vehicles streamed from the parking lot. No one was being forced to leave, but they were being asked nicely, which didn't matter much to some of the riders. Twenty-foot rollers were coming in and folks were going to surf, regardless of what it took, the risks, or whatever rules and edicts had to be broken. And intimidating a surfer was like trying to talk sense into a wolverine.

"Come on. They can't stop us from climbing up K2 for a better view," Connie said. She led the knot of surfers, including Gerard, up the path to the top of K2, which provided a good view of what was happening beyond the jetty.

Derrick stood at the edge of the cove, staring at the stormtroopers like a child at the top of the stairs on Christmas morning. Nayeli stood at his side, but the rabbit rangers had retreated to their vehicles, content to inform their superiors that the buck had officially been passed.

The Chinook's rotor wash flattened the whitewater rolling into the shallows and churned the sea spray into a dense salty mist as the bird settled in and hovered over the dead orca. Built for heavy lifting and transport, the CH-47 had a long history of doing the world's dirty work. The craft had multiple options for loading cargo; doors running the length of the fuselage, a wide loading ramp located at the rear, and three external ventral cargo hooks to carry underslung loads. Capable of a top speed of one hundred and seventy knots, the craft could travel four hundred nautical miles without refueling and carry a maximum payload of fifteen tons.

"Gerard, have you ever seen anything like this?" Bongo asked. He stood with Tommy T, Glenda, and several other hardcore boarders.

Gerard shook his head no.

The Apache was circling at a safe distance as the Chinook dropped a supply crate. With waves crashing and thick carpets of whitewater spreading over the shallows, the soldiers worked like ballet dancers who had performed the same dance routine together their entire lives.

Due to the sheer size and weight of the orca corpse, coupled with the necessity to maintain the integrity of the carcass and minimize ecological impact, the process was slow going.

The ground crew opened the supply crate and removed harnesses, a folded sling, ropes, and chains. Then they set about preparing the corpse to be lifted by pulling the large sling beneath the dead beast and rigging it with the ropes and chains.

As the soldiers worked, the helicopter prepared to receive its payload. The Chinook's pilot maneuvered the aircraft into position, the heavy craft steady in the turbulent coastal winds as chains were affixed to the copter's lifting hooks.

The lead stormtrooper on the ground signaled everything was ready, and the helicopter dropped slowly before holding three hundred feet above the churning sea, lift lines dangling beneath the behemoth.

With rotor wash turning the shallows into a hurricane of mist and sea spray, the soldiers attached the rigging lines connected to the lifting hooks that were strategically positioned to balance out the weight.

When all rigging connections were secured and triple-checked, the lead man gave a thumbs-up to the pilot.

The Chinook gradually ascended, slowly taking the weight of the orca as it transitioned from static to flight. Heavy load pilots, like crane operators, were a patient lot, and the flyboy piloting the Chinook maintained a steady, slow lift as he adjusted the craft's controls to counteract the additional weight.

As the copter gained altitude and turned, the huge bundle containing the orca carcass swung at the end of its tethers. The Chinook's engines cycled up, and the bird wheeled away and headed north, the *womp womp* of its airfoils slicing the air rising above the driving waves.

The Apache spun in the air, dipped its nose toward shore, and took off after the Chinook.

Gerard wondered what the corpse's final destination would be; a research facility, laboratory, or a disposal site? Given what he'd just witnessed, he figured the corpse was destined to be picked apart until there was nothing left but bones.

With the decaying orca went the stench, and business turned to more practical matters.

Surfing.

A crowd had formed on the beach, anxious riders who had decided going home wasn't an option on this day.

Foot soldiers poured over the jetty onto Purgatory Beach. Derrick and the stormtroopers' leader had a brief conversation before the soldiers double-timed it to the parking lot, piled into their SUVs, and left the scene.

"Thank you for your service," Bongo mocked as he watched.

Derrick made his way across the beach and Gerard, Connie, and the others climbed down K2 to meet him.

"What's the deal?" Connie asked.

Derrick gripped the brim of his hat as if preparing to tip it, but instead let his hand fall back to his side. Gerard felt the man's frustration rolling off him.

"They..." He hiked a thumb in the direction of the retreating soldiers. "They'd prefer that no one surfed today."

"Well, I'd prefer they—" Bongo started.

"Bongo!" Gerard rarely raised his voice, so when he did it resonated. "Is the beach closed or not Derrick?"

Creases formed on Derrick's face, lesions of pain that twisted and pulled at his features. Gerard knew the look well. The sheriff was trying to balance his tendency to exercise authority and control, with the idea that if The Funnel Big Wave Competition didn't happen, neither would his raise.

"This place has always been surf at your own risk, hasn't it?" asked Tommy T.

Derrick's gaze shifted to the sand, and he said nothing.

"How concerned can they be?" Gerard asked. "They didn't leave anyone behind." There was nothing left of the men in black except the dusty wakes of their vehicles hanging in the parking lot and the faint warble of the helicopters.

Gerard cracked his neck as he eyed the three wave runners drawn up on the beach.

"That red ski Mario's ride, Bongo?" Gerard asked. Mario was Bongo's tow partner. He drove the wave runner and put Bongo in the best position to catch the biggest waves.

Bongo sucked on his lips, then said, "Yeah? Why?"

"You've got nothing else to do today?" Connie asked, reading her husband's mind.

"Aren't you always the one telling me to get wet?" Gerard argued.

"And you choose today of all days?" Connie said.

"You said it yourself," Gerard said. "Derrick's crew patrolled with the drone and saw nothing."

"Nothing!"

"I have to agree, Gerard. Just because we didn't see anything doesn't mean something weird isn't going on," Derrick said. "The government just spent a ton of money to retrieve a dead fish."

Gerard said nothing.

"You're needed around here, Gerard," Derrick said. What the sheriff left unsaid was that Bongo, Tommy T, and the others weren't.

With that, the offshore breeze picked up and pushed the conversation out to sea. The group stood there for a time, the undertow sucking at their ankles, the arguing gulls, crackling waves, and the steady push of sand scraping over stones filling the silence.

Derrick sighed and said, "I assume you're all going out?"

Nodding heads, murmurs of affirmation, and a chorus of "hell yeahs."

Derrick nodded. "Unlike the feds, I care about what happens on this beach." He hitched his gun belt the way they teach recruits in cop school and tipped his hat at Deputy Sheriff Nayeli Stonetree. He said, "Do you mind hanging around, Nayeli? At least until the morning session is over?"

The young officer shook her head. "No problem. I like watching them."

Derrick's face soured. "I'll head back to the office and make some calls," he said. "Maybe I can find out what just happened. I'll let you know if I learn anything useful."

"Thanks," Gerard said. All eyes were on him now.

"What about press inquiries?" Derrick said. "There were plenty of curious people here this morning."

"I know," Gerard said. "Advance teams and spotters are already arriving so they can feed information to their surfers. My phone is already blowing up."

"Mine too," Connie said.

Derrick hiked his shoulders. "So… what do you want me to say?"

Heat spread through Gerard. There had been a time when he'd deserved little—or no respect, and now the sheriff of Liigei Too was deferring to him. It made him proud and scared at the same time. He didn't want to let anyone down.

"Say nothing," Gerard said. "Refer them to conservation."

"They won't even pick up the phone," Bongo said.

Derrick nodded, the faint trace of a smile leaking over his face as he left.

"Bongo, do you mind if I take Mario's spot for the morning session?" Gerard asked. "I do know the break pretty well and I'd like to keep an eye out."

Bongo looked to Mario, a small Italian who had once been a big wave champion in his own right. The man hiked his shoulders.

"Great," Connie said.

Derrick left as Nayeli repositioned her patrol car, so she had an unobstructed view of the beach. She, along with Connie, would keep both eyes on the surfers and surrounding ocean, not only to prepare the riders for the choice sets, but to keep an eye out for any unwanted beasties.

Tommy T, Bongo, Glenda, and the others pushed the skis into the shallows as Gerard pulled on his wetsuit and a life preserver. He wore a comm headset under his hoodie that allowed him to speak with Connie who would advise him. Then Gerard would do his best to put Bongo on the biggest and cleanest waves.

The jetty on the northern end of Purgatory Beach split into a fork, and a line of large boulders allowed access to the open ocean, which made getting through the breakers much easier.

Bongo and Gerard pulled his Honda into the shallows as Connie watched with her hands firmly planted on her hips.

The ski started right up, and as the engine gurgled, he checked the rescue sled attached to the back of the wave runner that would allow Gerard to collect Bongo should he wipeout and get caught in the snarling soup bowl that was The Funnel.

Gerard waved to Connie as he hopped on the ski, and she tossed him a frustrated half-wave before heading for K2.

"Testing. Testing. Connie, do you copy?" Gerard said.

Static in his earpiece, then, "I hear you, Gerard."

"Heading out." He turned to Bongo who sat in the water, his feet in his board's footholds, the ski rope's grab bar in his hands. "You ready?" Gerard asked the young competition hopeful.

The kid nodded. Gone was the sly smile that perpetually played over his face, and the aura of self-confidence that usually surrounded the kid like a storm cloud had dissipated. People had died surfing The Funnel, and it was time to get their game faces on.

Gerard goosed the throttle, and the ski leaped from the water, jerking the towrope taut and pulling Bongo into standing position. Gerard piloted the wave runner through the boulders and cut along the edge of the crashing waves as he headed for deeper water beyond the break.

When the ski was dipping in and out of wave valleys Gerard brought the wave runner to a stop, the tension in the towline slackened, and Bongo slipped into the sea.

"Get comfortable," came Connie's voice through the comm. "Nothing for a bit."

Like a T.V. show, book, music—any pleasurable experience, consumers and spectators only saw the wonderous jaw-dropping rides as men and women risked life and limb to surf waves not meant to be surfed, except maybe by dolphins. What folks didn't see was all the preparation, failure, and frustration. In the case of surfers, waiting was the hardest part, and the longer one waited, the more eager one became, which lowered the standards of wave selection.

Patience and trusting spotters were the keys.

The ski bobbed with the roll of the ocean, the sun glared down, and gulls shrieked as they speared small fish that dared swim too close to the surface. Ten minutes slipped away, Bongo lying on his board and sunning himself before Connie called and said there was a large set coming in.

Gerard raised a fist and Bongo gave a thumbs up. It took years of practice and experience to be able to choose the perfect wave, and as the rollers eased by Gerard picked his target and twisted the throttle control to full. The wave runner streaked forward, and Bongo was jerked from the sea.

Bongo was up and cruising, a wall of dark water rising like a monstrous specter behind him, a towering aqua-mountain of blackness taking form out of the vast ocean.

"Get out of there, Gerard," said Connie.

Gerard spared a glance over his shoulder and Bongo gave a thumbs up as he let go of the towrope and plunged down the face of the wave.

Bongo disappeared behind a hissing tangle of whitewater as the wave broke and Gerard jerked on the handlebars, turning the ski sharply as he shot through the raging sea and launched off the back of the wave.

The wave runner screamed and came down with a crash. Gerard was engulfed in a watery cloud as the ski plowed forward onto calmer seas.

"Rider at completion," Connie said. "He's over by the chute, Gerard."

This process was completed six more times, and Connie estimated that Bongo had caught a twenty-five-footer.

After the seventh ride things went off the rails.

Bongo nosedived from the crest of a twenty-five-footer and Gerard had to go into the breakers to rescue him. It was dicey business, but the partners executed perfectly. Gerard raced in between closing-out waves and paused just long enough for Bongo to heave himself onto the rescue ski.

As they waited for the eighth ride of the day, Connie called. "Gerard. Are you seeing that?"

The sun painted the surface of the Pacific silvery white, the glare creating shadow valleys and distorting distances. As he looked around, he asked, "See what, Connie? Over."

"Two o'clock."

Gerard shielded his eyes with his hand as he studied the northwestern horizon. There, under the klieg light stare of the midday sun, a field of dimpled whitewater the size of three ball fields moved across the heaving surface.

# 4

"Bongo!" Gerard screeched. "Get on the sled. Now!"

The approaching wave was dappled with whitecaps and silvery scales glinted like diamonds.

"Gerard, I think you should come in," came Connie's voice over the comm.

Understatement of the year. "10-4. Collecting my rider."

Bongo was on his board and coiling the towrope with one hand while using the other to paddle toward the sled.

Bluefin tuna surged from the face of a rolling wave, their sleek and muscular torpedo-shaped bodies shimmering metallic blue. The creatures' heads were crowned with large, piercing eyes that were tinged crimson, and the beasts' powerful jaws churned, revealing pointed teeth sharp enough to grip and tear through prey.

"Hurry, Bongo!" Gerard had seen schools of bluefin tuna do serious damage and Gerard's skin tinkled and stoked his urgency. He twisted the ski's handlebars and gunned the throttle. The water cycle surged from the sea as it spun around, the rescue sled cracking like a whip.

Bongo let go of the towrope and dove for the sled as the ski streaked past him. "My board!" Bongo yelled.

Gerard ignored his plea. Boards were a dime a dozen. He gunned the throttle and sped away from the oncoming wave, the face of which was filled with an epic sea battle unprecedented in nature. The wave rose behind the ski, and when Gerard looked back, he saw that he wasn't being pursued by one school of fish, but two.

With synchronized precision, fish surged from the rolling mountain of water, their sleek forms cutting through the sea like torpedoes. Blue metallic tuna glinted as they attacked smaller, green-scaled Pacific jack mackerel. Gerard had never seen anything like it. As the fish dove and weaved through the face of the wave, they fought, with the tuna dominating the mackerel because they were much bigger. Bluefin tuna and Pacific jack mackerel are predatory fish, but neither was known to attack other schools or similar species. What he was seeing couldn't be happening… yet, it was.

Though Pacific jack mackerel were no strangers to conflict, they dispersed as they evaded their larger adversaries with agile twists and turns.

Slashes of red pustules ran along the gills of both species, and Gerard thought the wounds looked similar to the poison oak-like gashes covering the dead orca.

Bongo held on to the rescue sled as the ski was lifted on the cresting wave, the fighting fish exploding from the water all around the wave runner, the ocean's surface stippled with miniature whitecaps.

The tunas' skin was almost iridescent under the play of sunlight filtering through the water, and each of their finlets was tinged with the same blue hue as their backs. Powerful crescent-shaped tails propelled the beasts through the water with astonishing force, leaving rooster tails of bubbles in their wake.

Though just as tough, the Pacific jack mackerel were small by comparison compared to the tunas. The fish had streamlined bodies perfectly adapted for movement through the water, their elongated forms covered with shimmering silver-green scales that shined like molten metal.

Fish thrashed and fought, and blood filled the water. In a chaotic dance of death, the beasts surfed the rolling wave as the schools launched coordinated strikes. Jaws snapped and ripped, tearing away chunks of white flesh. The warring fish appeared to have no interest in the ski.

Gerard ran parallel to the incoming wave, and with a jerk of the handlebars, the ski skipped over the crest of the fish-filled wave as it broke. The hiss and snap of seawater rose above the splashing of the fighting fish as the mêlée was washed away with the wave.

He slowed the wave runner and asked Bongo if he was O.K.

"I… I'm fine," Bongo said, but it didn't take an expert in human psychology to recognize the kid was shaken.

With the fighting fish gone, Gerard backtracked so Bongo could retrieve his board, which floated free beyond the breakers.

"That was something," Connie said. "Are you guys O.K.?"

"Fine," Gerard answered via the comm. "What are they doing now?"

"It's crazy, Gerard," Connie said. "Both schools are in the shoals ripping each other up. I've never seen anything remotely like it."

He hadn't either, but he knew it couldn't be a coincidence that an orca had washed up on Purgatory Beach on the same day.

"We're done?" Bongo asked. It wasn't a question, but a plea.

"Yeah," Gerard said. "I need a drink."

**The skis were hauled**, equipment packed, wetsuits dried out, boards stowed, and by 4 PM Gerard and most of the other local surfers were moving on to nightly chores and pleasures.

Connie was up for a drink, but as responsible parents there was the issue of the children to be dealt with first. Bribes were negotiated and promises were made, and in the end, Sage agreed to go to his friend's place for dinner, which would've been his choice regardless unless Connie was making spaghetti and meatballs. Willow, who was always happy to break from the routine, even if it meant hanging out with her brother, tagged along.

Jolene's was sacred ground, and only the bravest tourists not accompanied by a local dared enter. The bar was Liigei Too's unofficial town hall, and there was always a debate in progress on a wide range of topics, most of which usually fell outside the town's sphere of control.

But not on this day.

The original Jolene had passed away several years ago but her daughter, Joey, kept the place running and had even made some improvements. There was a lot of open space where the tables could be pushed aside for dancing or seating, and a long bar ran along one wall. A hallway in the back led to the bathrooms, kitchen, and the rear emergency exit beyond the stockroom.

Jolene's was packed, the events of the day having spread via the coconut telegraph faster than fiber-optic cable carrying winning lottery numbers. Everyone had heard about the orca, and how the men in black had swooped in and taken it. Theories abounded that ranged from the sea wolf being an alien to it being a governmental conspiracy to kill all the wildlife in the ocean.

Gerard and crew had agreed to keep their encounter with the battling fish to themselves for the present, but he was sure Bongo and the others were already spreading the tale far and wide.

The crowd at the bar parted like the Red Sea and Gerard was Moses as he and Connie took up their customary positions at the end of the bar. Drink orders were taken, pleasantries exchanged, and Gerard settled in to take the temperature of the room, which he could already tell was running a fever.

As he listened like a teenager to a group of whispering parents, there appeared to be no real information. Derrick was nowhere to be seen and Gerard couldn't blame the man. Nobody liked being asked questions they didn't have the answers to, and the way the feds rolled in had left the sheriff in a difficult position.

Gerard felt a tap on his shoulder, and he turned to see Roxy Templeton, Liigei Too's real mayor, a former real estate investor and champion surfer who had moved to town to assist in its revitalization.

"That didn't take long," Gerard said as he sipped his vodka martini.

"Sorry. I heard you had a rough day," Roxy said as she glanced around. The conversations in the immediate vicinity were already dying away and the crowd was pressing in.

Gerard felt the heat of those stares, and he knew what was coming.

The mayor handed Gerard a sheet of paper. "Do you remember this?"

It was a printout of an article from the Seattle Times, and its headline read: "Diseased Orca Lay Waste to Friday Harbor".

Gerard nodded. "A bit of overzealous headline writing, but I remember." This wasn't what he'd expected. He hadn't remembered the incident up in the San Juan Islands until that moment, but there it was. The article documented a series of attacks by diseased orca, and how conservation officials, with the aid of the federal government, had succeeded in trapping some of the creatures for study. "You're thinking the one that washed up here is related? An escapee?"

"It would be an amazing coincidence if there wasn't some connection."

Crazy things happened all the time that proved the universe was a random cacophony of events that rarely appeared logical, but in the end usually were. There was order there if one knew how to see it.

The music faded, the crowd murmured, and everyone was doing their best to try and pretend they weren't eavesdropping on Gerard and Roxy's conversation.

"O.K. Let's get this over with." Gerard drove to his feet. "Listen, everyone," he said in his speech voice.

The bar fell still. A cough, a sneeze, the tinkle of glasses as every patron in the joint stared at Gerard.

"I don't know any more than you all do," he said. "Yes, I was there. I can confirm what everybody is saying. A dead orca washed up on shore. It was pretty chewed up and diseased. The feds choppered in and took it away, and the sheriff is trying to find out what's going on. That's it. That's all I got. The beach isn't closed, and the contest is moving forward as planned. Specific questions can be directed to Derrick, who is going to refer you to conservation. Because we just don't know what else there is to do."

Outside a gull squawked, an earsplitting screech that spoke for the entire crowd. They knew Gerard. Trusted him. So even the most obnoxious among them stayed silent.

Slowly the buzz of the crowd returned, and everyone settled in for a night of drinking. Gerard sat, sipped his martini, closed his eyes, and took a deep breath. With that over, maybe he could concentrate.

The mayor moved on, and Gerard and his wife were on their second round when Connie leaned in and whispered in his ear. "That woman sitting next to Tim Ingram. The blonde. Do you know who she is?"

Gerard was lost in a prioritization of scenarios that all ended in the cancellation of The Funnel Big Wave Competition. He shook the cobwebs free as he peered down the bar. The woman was maybe thirty-five, bleach blonde, and average-sized. She wore jeans, yellow rubber boots, and a fishing vest. Gerard had never seen her before. He said, "I don't know her. Why?"

"Is that a bandage on her right hand?"

Gerard licked his lips as he tried to focus, his head pounding, ears ringing, alcohol superheating his chest. "Yeah. She's got a bandage on her right hand. So?"

Connie looked down at the bar as she worked her pint between the palms of her hands.

Gerard knew that look and posture. She was about to drop a bomb.

"Can we step outside for a second? I need to talk to you, and I don't want a thousand ears listening in."

Oh shit. "Sure. You better not be pregnant."

She punched him but chuckled.

Gerard took a long pull on his drink to steel himself as he got up. He followed his wife down the short hallway, through the storage room, and out the rear entrance to a parking lot wasteland that stretched to an open field.

"I know you're dealing with a lot of stress right now, and I tried to pretend it wasn't important. But with the dead orca, the odd behavior of the tuna and mackerel, and now someone is missing a finger..."

Hearing all the oddities stacked up like that made his stomach grow hot. "How do you know she's missing a finger?"

Connie laughed. "Lucky guess." Then she told Gerard about the massive red rock crab she'd seen, how the creature appeared diseased, and the way the thing came at her. "Then I noticed the finger. It was crushed in a pincer on one of its rear walking legs."

"Red rock crabs don't have pincers on their rear walking legs," Gerard said.

Connie said nothing.

"And you didn't think this was important?"

"Gerard, how crazy does my story sound? I wasn't sure what I'd seen myself. It was so odd I thought maybe my mind was playing tricks on me. But with a nine-fingered woman standing in Jolene's... I was thinking of the contest. You've been through so much."

He nodded and said, "Sorry. As always, you did the right thing."

Connie's eyes narrowed and she spun on her toes and headed back into the bar, leaving Gerard alone with his muddled thoughts.

# 5

**Liigei Too Marina, northern California**
**4:12 PM PT, October 3, 2023**
*Ten days until the scheduled start of The Funnel Big Wave*
*Competition*

The commercial fishing boats and tourist charters started streaming into the harbor around 4 PM. All the charters were full for weeks, and half the boats wouldn't be fishing, but sitting outside the competition zone watching the best of the best in the world tear it up. Same went for the commercial vessels, many of which had given up their pursuit of halibut, lingcod, and rockfish in the coming weeks to accommodate safety personnel, film crews, and avid spectators for a hefty premium that would get the ships' captains through the lean months. The marina, which had once been a small bay used by the indigenous population going back a thousand years, had been expanded and fortified over the years with jetties. It only held a hundred boats, but temporary floating docks had been installed to accommodate the additional boats and skis.

Gerard recalled the first time he'd seen the place. There had been six broken-down fishing boats—the main source of employment for the town, and one pleasure craft that hadn't moved in years and was really a houseboat. Time, success, and necessity brought changes and jobs to the marina, and most days it buzzed with life.

"How do you intend to approach this woman?" Connie asked. She'd made a few phone calls and learned that the nine-fingered woman's name was Ms. Clara Monde, and she was an avid angler from San Francisco. She'd booked a week of charters with Tim Ingram, a latecomer to the party who had setup shop after the town had gotten over the hump. Gerard didn't mind bandwagoners. The guy had money and brought value to the town, even if the word on the street was that he was kind of an ass.

Gerard said, "What do you mean? I'm going to introduce myself and ask how she lost her finger." It had been verified that Clara had indeed lost a digit, though the clinic explained that they couldn't release any of the woman's medical information and that they were breaking the rules by telling Gerard what they already had. The clinic hadn't existed when he'd arrived, so it was as if he carried a badge, and figuratively, he did.

"I mean, the woman might be embarrassed. Or she might not want anyone to know for a bunch of reasons; she wasn't supposed to be here, and she didn't want her job or husband or girlfriend or lover to know what she was up to. Who knows?" She sighed.

Gerard understood but didn't appreciate her frustration. Connie was far more intuitive than he was, and sometimes she rushed several steps ahead on the logic-path before Gerard realized he'd fallen behind.

"I'm asking if we're doing the good cop, bad cop thing?" she said.

Connie and Gerard had mastered the old interrogation technique by honing their skills on Sage and Willow. "I'm not going to press her. It's not that important."

"Really?" She licked her lips and gave him a look that made Gerard feel like he had an IQ of fifty. "What if she tells her story when she's sitting at the bar with Ingram? Like she was the other night when I saw her? T.V. people are crawling all over the place already, Gerard, what if one of them—"

"Got it. Message received," he said. "I'll go slow and see what happens. That O.K. with you?"

"We'll see."

The Top Fish, captained by Tim Ingram, inched through the harbor mouth at 5:17, and as Gerard and Connie prepared to meet the vessel, Gerard's cellphone buzzed.

"Deputy Sheriff Stonetree," Gerard said to Connie as he swiped accept call. "Hello? Deputy Stonetree? You're on speaker and Connie is with me."

"Yes, hi Mr. Noll... Mrs. Noll. Do you have a minute?"

"Sure, but call me Gerard."

"And call me Nayeli."

The Top Fish's horn sounded as the vessel slowly eased into its slip.

"I was wondering if you had a few minutes to meet with my father, Chief Stonetree?" the deputy asked.

The perpetual knot in Gerard's stomach tightened as he glanced at his wife, who hiked her shoulders. Though primarily a ceremonial position these days, Stonetree was the head of the local Mattole tribe, ancestors of the indigenous peoples who called northern California home, and who had named Liigei Too, which meant 'white water' in Athabaskan. The largest local community of Mattole people lived in and around Petrolia, a community six miles inland where the very first Californian oil well had been drilled and where marijuana had replaced wood as the area's cash crop.

Gerard asked, "What does your fa—Chief Stonetree want to talk to me about?"

Tension leaked over the invisible line that connected the cellphones via a long pause. "My father, as you would imagine, is... traditional. He's seen signs, things that tell him a terrible storm is coming."

"A literal storm? There's nothing on the long-range radar," Gerard said.

"Not that kind of storm."

The tourists were disembarking from the Top Fish, some holding their wrapped filleted catch, others hauling only disappointment.

Feeling the need to wrap-up the call, Gerard said, "Where and when?"

"He can meet you at the overlook in, say, an hour?"

Gerard glanced at his watch, Connie nodded, and he said, "Sure. I'll be there."

"Thank you, Mr. N—Gerard."

He killed the connection and Gerard and Connie hurried down the dock to intercept Ms. Monde.

The dock was packed with people, most of whom were happy and smiling, and it took a few minutes to get to the Top Fish. Captain Ingram was filleting a customer's catch on a white plastic table, and when he saw Gerard approaching, he put down his knife and stripped off his gloves.

"Gerard," he said as he held out a hand. "To what do I owe the pleasure?"

With a reluctance formed during the COVID pandemic, Gerard thrust out an elbow and the two men bumped. The slight smirk on Ingram's face didn't go unnoticed. "I need to speak with Ms. Monde."

Ingram looked over his shoulder, and said, "She's already left."

"No, she hasn't," Connie said.

"Hi, Connie," Ingram said.

Connie pursed her lips and waved curtly.

Ms. Monde appeared at the top of the gangway that led down to the dock.

"There she is." Gerard headed for the bottom of the gangway.

Ingram stepped in his way. "Are you going to cause trouble for me?"

Gerard pulled up short and leaned in so close he smelled onions on the man's breath. "Well, I don't know. Step aside or I'll move you."

The two alphas stood chest to chest, six inches of fury and millions of years of evolution—or lack thereof—separating them.

Connie pushed through the men and approached Ms. Monde.

"Ms. Monde. Clara Monde. May I have a word?"

The woman paused when she heard her name. Introductions were made, and as the tourists filtered away, Gerard, Ingram, Connie, and Ms. Monde stood before the Big Fish, the sun starting its drop to Earth on the western horizon.

To say Ms. Monde wasn't helpful would be an insult to unhelpful people everywhere. Connie asked how she'd lost a finger, and the woman said she'd accidentally cut it off while cutting carrots. Complete bullshit that even the daftest person would smell. Even with a razor-sharp knife, it would take a few slices before taking off a finger. After each question, she looked at Ingram, who simply stared at her with angry eyes, but said nothing.

When the conversation was over, the captain and Ms. Monde left Gerard and Connie standing alone shaking their heads.

"Well, that was a waste of time," Connie said. "Why would she lie?"

"Who knows? You're the one with all the theories. Insurance? It seemed like Ingram didn't want her to talk."

"Clearly, they share a secret, but why?"

Gerard could think of a hundred reasons, and many of them overlapped with the reasons his wife hadn't told him about the giant crab. "The real question is, do we tell the sheriff?"

That question sat out there like an overdue tax bill as the couple retreated to Connie's Prius and headed for the overlook.

Perched atop a cliff, two miles north of Liigei Too, the overlook was nothing more than a dirt lot surrounded by a border of boulders and marked with an unofficial monument of stones, driftwood, and beach garbage. Nayeli's patrol car was facing the ocean and she and her father sat on a stone nestled in beach grass watching the sun settle on the horizon, the blue sky blurring to orange-white.

Chief Stonetree was a grizzled man who looked to have spent most of his days under the sun. He wore jeans, a flannel shirt, boots, and a ceremonial beaded necklace that marked him as chief. Gerard had met the man and found him patient, knowledgeable, well-thought-out, and kind.

"Thank you for meeting with me," the chief said.

Gerard nodded.

"I'll get right to it," the old guy said. "Do you fish, Gerard?"

He hiked his shoulders. "If I have to."

Chuckles from the assembled, including Connie who knew fishing was one of her husband's least favorite pastimes.

"I only ask to gauge your experience," the chief said. "I know you know waves, but do you know the sea?"

Gerard said nothing.

"My people have an intimate bond with the Pacific. It has shaped our culture, identities, and livelihoods. The ocean is not a geographic feature, but a living entity, revered as a provider of sustenance, a pathway for trade and travel, and a source of profound power. We feel the rhythmic pulse of the waves. The salty air is infused with spirits, and beyond mere sustenance, the sea holds deep spiritual significance for my people."

"I understand, but—"

The chief held up a hand. "When you spend as much time out on the sea as I do, you fall in rhythm with its cycles, learn its tendencies and preferences. All the creatures that call the ocean home have this deep connection and it usually guides their behavior."

"But?" Gerard said.

The chief shook his head. "I've been seeing some very odd things lately. Things that tell me something is very wrong with the ocean and its creatures."

"Can you be more specific, Dad?" Nayeli said.

The old man sighed long and hard as if he were the only person on Earth who saw what he did. "There has been an ill scent on the breeze, and it's more than the stink of the dead orca. A disease permeates the ocean. I can smell it. I've seen odd slicks of what I can only assume is animal waste floating on the surface, and the bones, blood streaks, and entrails mixed within speak of an unorthodox food chain."

"He means things are eating other things that shouldn't be," Nayeli said.

Connie and Gerard exchanged a glance.

"Understand," said the old man, "I'm not just talking about things I've felt and sensed. I have seen many oddities in recent days. Octopus attacking small sharks, huge blood-red muscles that opened and closed like mouths, and a variety of fish acting, well, damn strange. The balance is off, and something..."

Gerard sucked on his lips and said, "I can't say I... we, haven't experienced similar..." Words failed him.

"Anomalies," Connie finished.

"I see," the chief said.

"My question is: what are we supposed to do with this information?" Nayeli said.

Chief Stonetree hiked his shoulders. "The obvious solution is, of course, the most difficult."

"Don't let anyone go in the water," Nayeli said.

Connie chuckled. "As if that would be possible without special forces lining the shoreline."

"And the contest," Gerard said. Ultimately, it was his decision when… and now, if, the competition was held. There was no vote. No meeting. It was all him. "As your daughter asked, what do you want me to do? You know how things work, Chief Stonetree. Nobody worries about fixing anything until said thing breaks. Until I have real proof of the danger… or God forbid a surfer was attacked, then I would have justification. Now." He shrugged. "The losses for the town would be significant."

"And possibly permanent if someone is killed," Nayeli said.

To that, Gerard had no response. The deputy sheriff was right. But so was he.

Goodbyes were exchanged, and everyone agreed to stay in touch. When the patrol car was gone, Connie said, "This is getting serious."

He nodded. Anything to do with the ocean was always serious. He watched the taillights of the patrol car disappear around a bend.

Pressure built in his chest, a painful worry that threatened to push him over the edge. An edge he'd gone over before, and he had no wish to repeat the mistake. He said, "I'll speak with Derrick. I think at a minimum we need to tell the competition committee."

Connie harrumphed.

Gerard went to her, took her in his arms, and kissed her.

"What was that for?"

"Being you," he said. "And for sticking with me through all this. Most women would have bailed."

"Yeah, well, I'm not as smart as I look."

Gerard laughed, but he was only going through the motions. A deep sense of worry and dread wormed its way toward his heart, and for the first time since he'd started The Funnel Big Wave Competition, he considered canceling it, the chief's warning like a rotten cherry atop a nasty sundae.

But that decision was for another day. A day that he hoped would never come.

# 6

Two days later there was a scheduled meeting of the competition committee. In five days, Gerard would have to make the first call and then continue to make the call every day thereafter until the word was given for all the competitors to drop what they were doing, hop on a plane, and be ready to compete in three days. The way the weather was looking, the competitors were going to be chomping at the bit.

Gerard gave the group an update on everything he knew, only leaving out the finger. With little evidence and with Ms. Monde claiming accident by carrot, it was purely speculative that the missing digit was related to the sea creatures, even though it had wound up in a crab's claw.

Not much of the news was new to the committee members and Gerard's report was met with general malaise and mixed concern. Denial is a powerful thing, but some questions were asked. The topic of pausing or canceling the contest wasn't raised.

"I will be monitoring the situation closely. But, as always, be ready for delays, and possibly a cancellation," Gerard told the assembled. That last word was blasphemy, but at this point, it needed to be said as much as it pained him to say it.

Silence filled the room, but with the bad news delivered he gave the committee the red meat. "All the B&Bs, hotels, and temporary housing are full. Restaurants are staffed, stocked, and ready for the onslaught. Even Jolene's will be opening its doors more than usual.

"On the wave front, the building swell only seems to be getting better as the North Atlantic continues to get pummeled by early-season storms. Long-range radar looks good, and Connie estimates the wave height on the first possible day of competition at a clean thirty feet." Rarely did the competition start on the first day of the season. Last year, Gerard had held off for three weeks as he patiently waited for a strong swell to build.

Not that any of the locals cared. The longer Gerard waited the more money the town made. The logistics of the competition were monstrous. Liigei Too had a permanent population of just under two thousand, and another thousand transients who lived down south in San Francisco or Los Angeles and had vacation homes on the outskirts of town. During The Funnel Big Wave Competition, the town's population almost doubled.

All this put a tremendous strain on local services. Extra garbage companies were contracted, and a tent village was set up to accommodate temporary workers who came from all around the country to see the contest and pay their way by waiting tables, raking the beach, or helping clean and maintain the lodgings packed with competitors, their entourages and support staff, all the ancillary media, corporate sponsors, and fans. It was a tangle of responsibilities and Gerard was the heart of it.

The meeting adjourned, and Connie and Gerard were cleaning up the coffee service when his phone chimed. He pulled the device, swiped, and said, "It's Ray."

Connie's eyebrows lifted.

"Hey, Ray, thanks for getting back to me."

Lieutenant Raymond "Ray" Tantillo was a close personal friend. He was also a Divisional Officer on the fast response cutter USCGC Robert Ward out of Los Angeles, and he coordinated backup support for the contest. Typically, this wasn't a task the coasties performed, but with Ray campaigning from the inside, the cutter was usually scheduled to be in the "general vicinity" of Purgatory Beach during the competition, just in case they were needed, which they never had been.

"Gerard, what's up buddy? Are you pulling your hair out yet?"

"I wasn't but—am I going to be?"

Lt. Tantillo laughed, but Gerard could tell it was forced. "Listen, I'm off the coast. I'm going to drop a Zodiac and take a look around. Do you want to come with me? I'd like to talk to you."

Gerard licked his lips as he looked at his wife for guidance.

Connie hiked her shoulders and said, "I can grab the kids. No biggie."

"Sure. When?" Gerard said into his phone.

It was 3:30 PM and there was plenty of daylight left. Ray said, "4:30 at the marina?"

"See you there."

Gerard dropped Connie off at home and answered a few emails—surfers all around the world, many of whom were friends, were pumping him for information and asking about the final invite list. Though he didn't get specific, he did spread rumors about how the surf was looking good. That would draw the competitors like dogs to food

When he arrived at Liigei Too Marina a Coast Guard rescue Zodiac was tied to one of the floating docks. Ray sat on the vessel's orange inflated gunnel, the tiny gray spaceship-like pilothouse behind him. His friend looked the same as the last time he'd seen him, which had been the prior year at the contest. Ray was a surfer from California, though he'd never been on anything bigger than ten feet, which he argued was a big wave, and for normal people, it was. He wore an orange windbreaker and reflective sunglasses, his short blonde hair hidden beneath a blue CG ballcap.

A coastie stood behind a heavy-duty machine gun mounted on a tripod in the bow, and another seaman sat behind the command console. There was no outboard motor, and Gerard saw that the craft was waterjet-propelled. This made rescuing people easier, especially in rough surf, because the ship's pilot didn't have to worry about a propeller tearing up the person in need of rescue.

"Wow," Ray said as Gerard approached. "You look younger every time I see you."

The two men shook hands. Ray smiled and so did Gerard. Some folks still deserved a handshake and a smile.

Like a married couple that had been together so long words weren't necessary, Gerard and Ray climbed aboard the Zodiac and sat on the bench seat before the pilothouse, which was nothing more than a large covered center console with a small head and storage area underneath.

The coasties were dressed in work blues and wore their customary orange life jackets. The seaman manning the gun tossed a life preserver to Gerard, and he put it on. He hated the things. One of the questions that always set his stomach ablaze was when amateurs asked why surfers didn't wear life jackets. Explaining to a non-surfer that being on the surface after a wipeout was the last place one wanted to be was usually met with blank stares, but when he added that the jackets limited mobility, that resonated. People were so much work.

With a splash of churning water and the hum of the boat's motor rising above the gentle wind, the helmsman, whose name badge read "Ensign Rider", put the vessel in gear, and it eased slowly through the calm water toward the marina exit.

The sound of exploding waves grew as the boat passed the extended jetties into a channel that led through the breakers to deeper water. Gulls shrieked and harbor seals barked as the ensign dropped the hammer, and the boat surged from the water, throwing spray, the engine droning.

A mile beyond the break sat the cutter, its distinctive white hull emblazoned with the red, white, and blue racing stripe of the United States Coast Guard.

The Zodiac arced south toward The Funnel Break, the cutter off the starboard bow.

Commissioned in 2019, the USCGC Robert Ward was one of the newest vessels in the Coast Guard fleet. Named after Coast Guard hero

Robert Ward, who served as a keeper of the Charlotte Harbor Light Station in Florida during the late 19th century, the fast response cutter was one hundred and fifty-four feet in length, was equipped with state-of-the-art navigation and communication systems, and was powered by twin diesel engines that allowed the cutter to reach speeds of up to twenty-eight knots. The V hull vessel had advanced surveillance and detection capabilities, such as radar and infrared cameras, which aided in law enforcement as well as search and rescue operations.

But somehow on this day the ship was sitting off Purgatory Beach, and though that should have brought Gerard comfort, it only raised another red flag.

The rolling waves got larger as the Zodiac powered over the ocean, the hull slapping the sea. Gerard searched the surface, focusing below the waterline and expecting to see disparate species fighting, but there was nothing but bubbles and white foam.

A cloud of surfers and skis floated just outside The Funnel, and Ray ordered the helmsman to patrol around the outskirts of the competition zone.

Gerard leaned in close and asked, "Is the Ward here for the contest?"

"I wish," Ray said. "We'll be patrolling the entire west coast from Baja to Vancouver Island."

The mention of Vancouver Island made Gerard think of the orca attacks on Friday Harbor. "Do you know anything about the orca that was whisked away from Purgatory Beach?"

Ray hiked his shoulders and looked at the ground. That was the man's tell that he was about to lie. "No..." He shook his head. "Not really, anyway. What I do know is classified." His gaze strayed toward Ensign Rider, then to the gunner. "But something is afoot."

Gerard waited.

"There's been a lot of odd chatter. The sea creatures seem to be on edge, if that makes any sense."

It did, but Gerard said nothing.

"It's almost like there's some new threat they're struggling with. Have you seen anything odd?"

Gerard stayed silent.

"Heard anything out of the ordinary?"

Gerard bit his tongue. He was trying to get information from Ray, and now he got the feeling Ray was trying to get information from him.

"Sir, we've got something here," said the helmsman.

Ray and Gerard pushed to their feet and eased behind the command console so they could see the displays.

Ensign Rider pointed at the SONAR screen, which showed an elongated red dot getting larger as whatever the thing was ascended. "Looks like a whale, sir."

"Bring us to it," Ray said.

Ensign Rider slowly moved the boat an eighth-of-a-mile to the west, then shut down the engine.

A dark shape grew in the rolling clear water and a humpback whale floated into view.

The beast was fifty feet long, and its colossal frame faded from dark bluish-gray to black on its dorsal side. All along the beast's length jagged wounds filled with red pustules marred the smooth skin. The pronounced hump on the whale's back was bloody and shredded, and large crimson barnacle-encrusted knobs known as tubercles dotted the length of its jawline.

Mottled white and black flippers stroked the sea. Humpback whales usually sported tail flukes covered in a unique pattern of black and white markings, akin to a fingerprint, which allowed for the identification of individual whales. But the markings on this humpback were blurred by open wounds filled with pustules.

But it was the beast's eyes that truly unnerved Gerard. The whale hung just below the surface, and two tiny black eyes gleamed from within a mound of swollen red flesh, the creature's eye sockets engorged.

Ray got on the radio and called the cutter. He explained the situation and when he was done, he said to Gerard, "We're going to use all our fancy new tech to get some pictures of that bad boy. He—"

The whale was gone.

Everyone stared at the SONAR and the whale's image was getting smaller as it swam south.

"We're going to get some documentation on that guy," Ray finished. "We need to…"

"What?" Gerard pushed.

"You saw that thing, Gerard," Ray said. "Don't act like you didn't. That fish was diseased, and who knows what will happen if it spreads."

Suddenly Gerard felt his own world shrinking at a precipitous rate.

# 7

Gerard sipped beer, the past two weeks marinating in his head like a toxic stew. The pressure he felt wasn't alleviated by the fact that the town sheriff knew everything he did and hadn't rung the alarm bell and called in the staties, though Gerard doubted that would've accomplished anything. The Coast Guard had moved in, and they were more in the know. Ray's tell had told him so.

The sheriff was down the bar a ways, chatting it up with a few locals, who were bowing to the God of the blue religion. Derrick was a straight arrow, and bribery was out of the question, but kissing ass worked pretty well. The sheriff was holding court, telling everybody to get their acts together because the crowds were coming. And soon.

Gerard swirled beer around in his pint glass. Crowds. Soon.

Canceling the tournament at this point would be Earth-shattering, but he needed to make the call soon. But keeping people out of the water? That would be impossible, so if safety was the main concern, the powers that be would have to put patrol boats out in The Funnel with guns on their bows like the Coast Guard Zodiac. Even that wouldn't keep the locals out of the water, competition or not.

"Hey."

Gerard jumped and turned to see Derrick, who had managed to make his way down the bar unseen.

"Sorry. Are you alone?" the sheriff asked.

"No worries. What's up?"

As if the sheriff possessed some magical force, the person on the stool next to Gerard got up and the sheriff sat.

"I just got a call," Derrick said, his voice low but filled with frustration. The sheriff's eyes were spidered red, but the guy was a professional drinker, and he wasn't slurring his speech.

"And?" Gerard said. He was still nursing his first beer, but he was exhausted, not so much with the day's events, but with life.

"I know I'm starting to sound like a broken record, but this one sounds a little unusual. I thought you might want to come with me?"

Gerard looked up at him and said nothing.

"It's late, and Nayeli is probably asleep and..." He looked down at the bar.

"Fine. I'll come with you."

The sheriff settled his tab and Gerard's, and the pair shuffled off to Derrick's pickup. The first thing the lawman did was dig his gun belt out from under the truck's front seat and put it on.

Gerard opened the pickup's passenger door but didn't get in.

"This is fine. I'm not going back to the station house to get the Tahoe. Come on. Get in."

The moon glared down like an accusing eye as darkness pressed in on the winding road that led down to the sea. There were no streetlights, and the rolling hills stood in the darkness like silent sentinels covered in dried-out devil grass.

"What makes this call so weird?" Gerard asked.

Derrick took his eyes off the road and looked at Gerard for a second. "You know I respect you, right?"

Gerard nodded.

"You're a surfer, and you know I have a strange relationship with surfers. But I trust your opinion. I want you to see this with virgin eyes just like me, and then we'll compare notes."

"Sounds like a plan," Gerard said.

"It worked for Mulder and Scully."

"Can you at least tell me where we're heading?"

"The Bondie place."

The Bondie family were fashion titans that lived in half a building in the middle of San Francisco. They were around a lot in the spring and summer but usually left town until Christmas, but Gerard figured they were back for the contest. The Bondie vacation home was one of the many mini-mansions that had sprung up in the hills around Liigei Too after the town climbed from the muck, the local inhabitants unable to resist offers for slices of land at well above market value.

Gerard had never been to the Bondie place, but he knew the compound was on a cliff with a path and stairs that led down to a rocky un-swimmable beach. The tiny cove was nothing more than a cut in the cliff face where the sea rushed into a sharp gully of black stone speckled white with gull shit.

A driveway appeared in the thick foliage that ran along Mattole Road. The Bondie's gate was open, and the sheriff pulled his pickup through, drove around a circular stone driveway, and stopped before a large decorative portico made of natural timber.

There was only one car in the driveway. A two-seater Mercedes, which meant the children most likely weren't in attendance and were probably off at school.

Derrick shut down the truck and said, "Let me do all the talking. Yeah?"

Gerard licked his lips and nodded.

Xavier Bondie and his wife Tracy reeked of money. They were dressed for bed but looked like they were ready to go out for a night on the town. She wore a silk robe as fancy as an evening gown and her hair was up in a tangle that looked like one of those designs that took hours to make look casual. He wore two-piece pajamas that were one notch below a business suit and leather flip-flops that would've passed muster in church.

"Sheriff Manvale, thank you for coming. And Gerard, I didn't expect to see you," Mr. Bondie said. The man didn't offer a hand or coffee or anything, but he did seem more stressed than his wife, who appeared more aggravated than upset.

"What's the problem, sir?" the sheriff asked.

"Trixie. She's missing and we think she's been taken," Mr. Bondie said.

Derrick nodded slowly but didn't speak. Gerard could tell the man was trying to mine a memory from his marble quarry brain.

Gerard jumped in and saved him. "Your dog?"

Mr. and Mrs. Bondie nodded emphatically.

Then the woman of the house spoke, her voice silky and provocative. "Why don't we show you?"

The foursome trailed through the house, decorated in a beach motif, but dripping in money and the city. There were plenty of pieces of engraved and decorated driftwood, rock art, and great paintings of the sea and the creatures that lived therein. But the polished hardwood floors, high-end antique furniture, and the lack of a foot wash stepping pool on the back deck said the Bondie residence was anything but a beach house.

"I let her out to take care of her business. Like I always do. She's such a good girl," said Mr. Bondie. "But when I called, she didn't come back. She always comes back." He slid open a huge sliding glass door that led out onto the patio. Tropical foliage surrounded a blue kidney-shaped pool, and beyond that was the cliff's edge and the dark expanse of the Pacific Ocean.

The pool light was on, and the glow attracted bats that swooped in from the surrounding trees. Mrs. Bondie paused when the group reached the end of the patio. She crossed her arms over her chest and said, "I'll wait here."

Mr. Bondie didn't break stride as he left the patio and crossed a thin patch of turf that separated the refinement of the Bondie backyard and the wilds of the surrounding vegetation. As the house and pool lights faded Bondie stopped short and Derrick almost bumped into him. "I am a scatterbrain tonight," he said. "I forgot a flashlight."

LED light illuminated the area as Derrick pulled a Maglite from his utility belt and turned it on.

Spidery shadows frolicked within the swaying foliage, the breeze rustled leaves, crickets sang, and frogs bellowed.

A thin natural stone path ran through the border of plants to a staircase that led down to the sea. When Bondie reached the start of the path he stopped, dropped into a crouch, and pointed. "When I saw this, I called 911."

Under the harsh glare of the LED light, the drips of blood were black, but there were no doubts it was blood. Two small puddles had coagulated, and several of the stones had been spattered crimson.

Derrick drew his Glock and said, "You didn't go any further?"

Bondie looked at the ground, then out at the ocean. "No," he forced out.

Putting the man at ease, Derrick said, "You did the right thing."

Bondie hiked his shoulders.

"Wait here. We'll be right back." Derrick flashed Gerard a look that said "Watch my back" as he eased down the path, gun up like he was expecting to get jumped.

Gerard didn't blame him. His stomach was a knot of worry and fear.

The blood trail continued down the pathway, and when the pair reached the stairs, Derrick killed the flashlight. The duo waited at the top of the steps for a minute as their eyes adjusted, and then they started down to the shoreline, being careful not to step in the drips of blood that stained each stair tread.

A vicious bark, like a dog being tortured, carried over the crash of the waves and the moan of the wind.

Derrick looked over his shoulder, the whites of his wide eyes standing out in the darkness.

The wooden steps creaked and bitched as the partners descended, and when they reached the bottom the bite of the chill breeze made Gerard hug himself.

Huge wet boulders glistened in the moonlight, and the riotous sound of stones being dragged over stones echoed off the cliff face like a battle in progress.

"Oh, shit," Derrick muttered. He clicked on the Maglite and it drove away the darkness.

Atop a flat boulder half-submerged in the churning undertow, a piece of skin four inches long and an inch wide and covered in white fur and blood sat in a dark puddle. The sides of the large rock were spattered with blood and tiny chunks of fat, and there were odd slash-like prints in the stone.

"A harbor seal?" Gerard said.

"Not one in its normal state of mind," Derrick said. "I'm no marine biologist, and I know seals can be very aggressive, but I've never seen one climb a staircase and infiltrate a backyard to get a dog."

"I don't think we need to be marine biologists," Gerard said. What he left unspoken was this was just another warning of bad things to come.

"Come on," Derrick said. "I'm going to see if I can find…" He trailed off and shook his head. "A big enough piece to—"

A bark of raw emotion and animalistic instinct carried over the stones, and a low rumble that built gradually like the swell of a wave made Gerard ball his fists and Derrick raise his Glock. The croaking barks grew in strength, like a warning, a crescendo of guttural roars interwoven with deep grunts that reverberated with primal intensity.

The barking ended with a growl that was replaced by what sounded like the crunching of bones and the tearing of meat.

Derrick swung the flashlight, and its beam caught a massive harbor seal perched atop a boulder, the remains of Trixie hanging from its dog-like mouth.

Gerard stood transfixed, not that there was anything he could do.

With a grunt, Derrick aimed the gun.

The seal launched off the rock into the churning sea and disappeared beneath the inky surface.

Waves crashed as the wind picked up. Derrick holstered his weapon.

The duo stood in silence for several minutes because they both knew that much depended on their next conversation.

Suddenly the moonlight felt bright, and the sea spray pelting Gerard's face felt like acid. Ten minutes slipped away before a flashlight bloomed at the top of the staircase.

Gerard asked, "What are you going to tell them?"

Derrick hitched his gun belt and said, "The truth."

"Which is?"

"Trixie was taken by a harbor seal."

Gerard nodded.

"The next few days will tell the tale," Derrick said. "No need to shout fire just yet."

He nodded again, but the heat burning his stomach increased, and Gerard realized the fire was already raging.

# 8

**Liigei Too, northern California, U.S.A.**
**4:18 PM PT, October 13th, 2023**
*Day One of The Funnel Big Wave Competition season*
If no news was good news, Gerard had an excellent week.

His biggest issues were the final invite list and dealing with anxious sponsors who were prepared to move people and mountains five minutes after Gerard gave the word.

That word wouldn't be coming on this Friday the thirteenth. The wave heights were building, and things had quieted down. Gerard saw no reason not to let the swell develop a little more... and let the town make more money.

The Funnel Big Wave Competition was an invitational. That meant contest organizers—mostly Gerard, put together the list of competitors who were invited. There were backups, and backups to backups, and extra slots were given to locals, but ultimately the goal was to have the best big wave surfers in the world compete.

Gerard used a complex matrix of number of competitions, related placements, experience on big waves, age, and a smattering of opinions that he combined to come up with the list of invitees. Everyone knew how he did it and yet every year there was still a surprise or two when the list was posted.

This year wasn't all that difficult. Typically, thirty-six to forty surfers, half male, and half female, were invited to compete, and Gerard intended to fill out the entire forty-slot field this year. He'd already reached out to Kai Nenny, Keala Tennelly, and Twiggy Barker, the South African surfer who'd won the prestigious Mavericks Invitational. There were other names, but these were the main three the sponsors cared about most, and Gerard was relieved when all three riders said they planned to attend if invited, which was nothing more than a formality.

The hardest part was picking which locals would be invited. Bongo, Glenda, and Tommy T were in, but that left three open slots for roughly fifteen surfers who were running neck and neck. He needed to spend some time down at the break because ultimately those last three wildcard entries would be at his discretion.

Dealing with sponsors was a different matter altogether. They were a constant hair-tangle of aggravation that never went away, not even when the event was over. Gerard got emails in January—January!

When even he wasn't thinking about the contest. There was a lot of money at stake, and it wasn't just the winners who received a purse of $50,000. There were revenue sponsors, product sales, commercials, print ads, and documentaries, and it all hinged on the competition.

When he'd first started doing the contest, Gerard didn't know how to balance these things. He was a surfer, and back then he didn't think beyond tomorrow's wave. But Liigei Too changed all that, and now he had to think about waves that hadn't even formed yet and storms that would create them that were still nonexistent. He'd learned a lot, and most of it centered around money. What else was new?

Gerard answered sponsor email inquiries, his cellphone vibrating every few seconds. Like helicopter parents, the sponsors paid a large portion of the costs associated with the contest, and they expected their fair share of the limelight. Fights about banner placements, who was drinking what from what cup and where and when... he had little patience for any of it. But he'd learned patience wasn't what was necessary. Having answers, no matter what those answers were, never failed to quiet the chatter.

His phone vibrated again, and he picked it up intending to turn the device off, but when he saw it was Brian from PowerTime Hydration Supplements he answered the call. PT Power energy drink was this year's main sponsor, and if anyone deserved his time, it was them.

"Brian, what's up? I'm actually sipping an Arctic Wave at this very minute." That was a lie. Gerard hated the swill, but...

"Nice. I love to hear that," Brian said. "Don't forget to hook up with one of our photographers. I want a picture of you with our bottle to your lips."

Not happening. "Count on it," he said. "What can I help you with today?" If someone had told him ten years ago those words would flow from his lips he would have laughed.

Brian sighed. "Calling for the brass."

Gerard held back a chuckle. He and Connie weren't the only ones who played good cop, bad cop. "Yeah? What's got their knickers in a twist?"

"Two shipping containers of drinks, a four million dollar ad campaign, and... well, they're bigwigs. Shaking trees is really all they know how to do."

And what do you know how to do, Brian, pick up the fruit? Gerard kept his thoughts to himself. He wasn't a huge fan of salespeople, but everyone had to make a living, right? Gerard sighed long and hard, playing the game now. He had to give the man something to pass upstairs to his bosses or he'd keep hounding Gerard until he did.

"The swell in the northern Pacific is still churning things up," Gerard said. "Ask your bigwigs if they want small waves now, or monsters later." That always shut people up. The bigger the waves, the bigger the ratings, the larger the payday.

Brian said nothing.

"I thought you'd put up more of a fight," Gerard said.

Still Brian stayed quiet. Smart man.

"I'd say we're less than a week out," he said, and meant it. The feeling that he was experiencing the calm before a terrible storm kept nagging at him, pushing him to get the contest over with before the truly smelly poo hit the fan. But he had no live threat, and the restaurants, charters, tours, surf schools, hotels, bars—everything, was raking in the cash.

"I can work with that, Gerard. You're the best."

"Make sure you tell Connie when you see her."

A laugh, then silence. Outside, a gull screeched and the breeze rattled palm fronds.

Sensing there was something else on Brian's one-track mind, Gerard said, "Was there something else?"

Brian manufactured a sigh. "The CEO, Cindy Olritch—you met her last year."

Gerard searched his memory but couldn't find the woman.

"She heard that the Coast Guard was up your way. She said her folks told her the Ward was anchored outside the break all day and that you met with them."

"So? The coasties keep an eye on things every year."

"I know... We know, but... Is there anything out of the ordinary?"

Understatement of the decade. Gerard had to tread lightly because he couldn't lie, at least not completely. "They were... are, just doing due diligence." Gerard loved using legal terms, especially ones that could mean several different things.

"Ah... Got it. Nothing to worry about then?"

Gerard said nothing. Presumption was a powerful weapon.

"Great. Good. I'll let Cindy know."

Now I can sleep. "Are you coming this year?" Gerard asked in an attempt to change the direction of the conversation.

"Wouldn't miss it."

"Great. See you then." He clicked off.

Sunlight angled sharply through the office window, dust motes dancing in the air. The day was winding down as he finished his administrative work. Connie was running errands, and the kids were getting out of school soon, but they had plans with friends. He was free and it was time to head down to Purgatory Beach to take a look at the local crop of surfers, three of which would love him very soon while the others would look at him with betrayal, disappointment, and derision.

The old G-wagon had boards strapped to its roof, and the back cargo hold was packed with boxes of t-shirts and other swag, along with posters, flyers, and an assortment of nametags and staff hats that he used to recruit volunteers. His ski sat on its trailer, and he unhitched it from the wagon's hitch coupler before jumping in the vehicle. No way he was getting wet today.

He'd been considering inserting himself into the contest as a tow partner for one of the locals. Any of the locals—even Bongo—would trade their partners for Gerard. Nobody knew The Funnel better than the man who had discovered it, and whoever he drove for would have an instant advantage. An advantage that included Connie, the wave whisperer. Finding someone to partner with wouldn't be the problem, Connie would be.

The wagon whined as its engine churned and sparked to life.

Connie wouldn't want him out there, and not only because she was always concerned about his safety. Gerard hadn't ridden a big wave since the incident, and though she didn't say it, his wife was afraid Gerard would freeze up at a pivotal moment. As a tow partner that could endanger his surfer as well as himself. He knew all this, but still… His gut told him he needed to be out there this year, and his gut rarely cried wolf.

He opened the windows. The sweet salt air was invigorating. Beach grass whispered and sighed, and the pop and crack of rubber rolling over the blacktop soothed his growing angst. The closer the start of the competition got, the more his nerves danced. Gerard scratched an itch and left a red mark on his arm, which led to thinking about the gashes filled with red pustules that covered the orca corpse, how he'd seen the same wounds on the fish, the whale… The whale.

Gerard pulled out his phone and called Ray, who picked up on the first ring.

"What's up? Is today 'the day'?"

"No," Gerard said. "I'm calling to see if there's any word on our whale?"

"We were able to get some good images, and we put a tracker on it."

"Really? And?"

"It hasn't gone far, and without a bio sample there's not much our folks can do, so we're preparing to get a sample."

"At least you know where the thing is."

"And that's not all," Ray said. "While we were hunting the whale we came across..." He sighed. "Some serious shit."

"What?"

"Shit. We found a huge pile of waste floating on the surface, and we took a sample."

Gerard recalled what Chief Stonetree had told him. What had he called the stuff he'd seen? An unorthodox food chain?

"The bigheads are saying the waste is like nothing they've ever seen before, and they can't even tell me what type of animal waste it is."

That didn't sound good. "Where are you?"

"Up the coast off Lincoln City."

That was only a couple of hours away. "We're getting close here, Ray. I'll call you first. I'd love for the cutter to be out there on the first day. It would make me feel better about... well, better."

Ray harrumphed. "I understand. I'll do my best."

Gerard pulled into the Purgatory Beach parking lot, parked, and killed the engine.

"Have you made the final list?" At his core, Ray was a fan.

"Not the final one, but I think it's safe to say that you're not on it."

A chuckle. "Talk soon." Then Ray was gone.

Gerard was mobbed as he got out of his vehicle. He was a surf God and there was never a shortage of worshipers.

The big kids were still in the water, and as the sun settled like an egg yolk above the horizon, Gerard watched several runs, the scream of skis rising above the crashing waves. Bongo grabbed a thirty-footer and then joined him on the beach, followed by Glenda, and they pointed out particularly good tricks and gave their unsolicited advice. Gerard trusted these kids—but not today. Bongo and the others were competitors, and they'd do anything to get an advantage, including talking up weaker surfers.

Gerard made some notes, and he thought he had the final three slots narrowed down to six possibilities as the riders took their last rides. He needed two females and a male, and he'd settled on Jennifer Daniels, a relative newcomer for one of the last two female spots. Jenn had only lived in town a couple of years, but she was the best of what remained, and Gerard thought she'd give Glenda a run for her money. He had a few more days to think about it a bit more, but watching a few runs had settled his nerves and helped him get closer to final decisions.

Everyone was back at the parking lot imbibing, stripping out of wetsuits, and loading boards onto roofs when Gerard saw the bite mark on Glenda's thigh.

"What got you there?" he asked, pointing. "Toby's got a big mouth, but…"

Glenda didn't laugh and neither did Toby.

Gerard looked around at the assembled and suddenly everyone had clammed up. "Glenda?" He raised his voice just a hair.

"Something bit me when I got rolled earlier. No big deal."

"Let me see."

Glenda sighed as she stuck out her leg like a model and put her hands on her hips in the traditional pose.

Gerard dropped to a knee and used his cellphone light app to get a good look.

The bite was ragged and crescent-shaped with serrated edges, akin to a half-moon cut. The teeth punctures appeared deep, revealing layers of torn flesh, and thin trails of blood leaked from the surrounding tissue which was bruised and inflamed.

"You didn't get a look at whatever it was?"

Glenda studied a pebble on the ground as she shook her head no.

Gerard let loose with a frustrated cry of a sigh. She was lying. She knew he knew she was lying—everyone there did, but still, she stuck to her story.

"You can tell me," Gerard said, but they really couldn't. These kids had the contest. That's it. It was their life, and not a single one of them would do anything to jeopardize that for themselves and their friends. "Fine!" he hissed when he realized no real answer was coming. "Go to the clinic, now, and I'll—"

Glenda tried to protest but Gerard put up a hand.

"I know you're lying to me," he said. "I understand why, but if you don't go to the clinic, I'm going to bounce you from the list with a medical."

Glenda's mouth fell open, her head jerked back, and all signs pointed to a protest, but instead, she just nodded. It was never a good idea to anger a god.

The crowd dispersed and Gerard loaded into the G-wagon, its rusted door hinges creaking. His thoughts were dominated by the crescent bite on Glenda's leg as he drove, and he wondered how much longer he could keep his head in the sand.

# 9

Mattole Road twisted and turned as it left the shoreline and climbed into the brown hills that towered over the ocean. The darkening blue sky was clear, and faint pinpricks of light appeared on the gray canvas. Evergreens and undergrowth of weeds encroached to the edge of the blacktop, roots spidering under the road's thin shoulder, cracking and lifting it in spots. The air was redolent with the scent of pine mixed with marijuana, the sharp tang of ripe buds carrying through the forest.

The more he pondered, the more nervous Gerard became. This wasn't unusual with the contest days away, but with all the strange stuff that had gone down recently, he felt the weight of the entire town on his shoulders. As Connie had so eloquently once said, "You lifted this place up and now it's your job to keep it there."

Traffic was heavy, tourists and workers heading to Petrolia for the evening, and taillights filled the growing darkness ahead. He rolled his shoulders as the wind brushed pine needles and pushed dust clouds across the road. The last light of the dying day angled through a tall line of Ponderosa pines that ran along the edge of the road, and shadows frolicked in the undulating underbrush.

Had it not been for the Hampton farm materializing out of the gloom on the right side of the road and jarring him from his thoughts, Gerard would have missed his turnoff. He jerked the wheel, and the G-wagon fishtailed a little as the truck slid and Gerard made the left onto Old Mattole Road.

The street was deserted as it ran through a tunnel of greenery. Darkness filled the truck's cab, and Gerard turned on the headlights as he slowed, the road so narrow there were turns where only one vehicle could make it through at a time.

A solitary redwood tree marked a sharp bend in the road, and as the G-wagon rattled around the turn red taillights appeared in the darkness ahead.

"What's this now?" Gerard asked the empty car. As he got closer, headlights stripping away the gloom, he saw a Tahoe with a light rack on its roof wedged into the vegetation on the side of the road. It was the sheriff's ride.

Gerard pulled in tight behind the Tahoe, cut the engine, and put on his emergency blinkers. The G-wagon and the police vehicle were partially blocking the road.

As he got out of the truck a coyote call pierced the night.

"Hey, Gerard," Derrick said. His words weren't slurred, but they weren't rock steady.

"What's the problem? Did you break down?"

Derrick clucked. "I wish. Naw, Greasy... I mean, Mr. Langstein, called about Rippers."

Gerard sighed. Humboldt County was one of the largest marijuana producers in the country, and the Humboldt Harvest Festival ran the entire month of September. The Funnel Big Wave Competition was a big supporter because what went better together than surfers and pot? Gerard didn't smoke anymore, but the festival provided a big economic boost because there were several harvest festival events around Petrolia. Though the celebration was in September, many varietals of marijuana weren't harvested until after the first couple of fall chills.

With all this green came thieves, and with so many people in town and law enforcement stretched to its limits, Rippers attempted to steal local crops. Gregory "Greasy" Langstein was one of the largest farmers in the area, and he was a big contributor to the competition, funding several events and giving away free "Funnel" pre-rolls to everyone who was of age.

"What are you waiting for?" Gerard asked.

Derrick sighed. "Nayeli isn't responding. Not surprising. She's off tonight. I could call for support from Eureka, but that'll take time, and everyone and their brother will know the situation, which I'm thinking isn't the headline you're looking for going into the start of the competition."

"Have you seen the Rippers?"

"I chased away their getaway car and a cliff face runs the entire length of the eastern side of the fields. Greasy's... Mr. Langstein's compound is on the northern end, so they have to come out this way."

"Unless they know the area well or they scouted the location," Gerard said. He'd never seen the farm, but he knew the surrounding land well. Several streams could be followed, there was more than one cave to hide in, and there were old-growth trees that could hide even the weakest of climbers.

The darkness grew thick, and Gerard could almost hear the seconds ticking away.

"Shit," Derrick said as he shifted on his feet, his hand falling to the butt of his Glock. "I'm not for weed, but Greasy pays taxes, and the law is the law and..."

"Greasy is a good guy. You know that."

"Yeah. For a stoner."

As if on cue, the rumble and pop of an all-terrain vehicle lumbering down the road filled the forest.

Headlights drove away the darkness as a quad came into view. Greasy was sixty, but he looked fifty. On this night his long dreadlocked hair was pulled back into the never-popular man-bun, and he wore a bathing suit, a silk bathrobe, unlaced work boots, and a shotgun was in its sheath on the side of the ATV.

Greasy skidded to a stop and said, "What are we doing? Having coffee?"

Derrick licked his lips but said nothing.

"He deputize you, Gerard?"

Gerard bit his lip and smiled.

"Do you know how much money I'll lose if these assholes damage my fields? I don't even care if they steal a few buds, but I can't have them traipsing through my crop. Are you going in or not? Because if you're not, I—"

"You're doing nothing," Derrick said.

Greasy shutdown his ride, pulled the shotgun from its sleeve, and pumped a shell into the firing chamber. "I'm not sitting around waiting for something to happen."

"Yeah, you are," Derrick said. He went to his Tahoe and retrieved his shotgun. He held the weapon out to Gerard and said, "You up for this?"

He wasn't, but what choice did he have? Gerard understood the risks involved with letting citizens seek their own justice, and the last thing the town needed was Greasy shooting and killing an unarmed Ripper. He nodded and accepted the gun.

"He can go and I can't? It's my land, Derrick. Who the—"

Derrick padded the air and Greasy was smart enough to shut it down. "This is my job, and yeah, Gerard is like a deputy. Wait here and watch our backs. If they come out this way don't do anything stupid."

"And if they're armed?"

Derrick shrugged. Typically, Rippers didn't carry guns—unarmed theft of property and armed robbery held drastically different sentencing guidelines in California, but it always made sense to prepare for the worst. "If they're armed, which they probably aren't, do what you must. Just keep in mind what you'll have to deal with if you shoot one—doesn't matter the situation."

Greasy bounced on his feet like he was going to explode. "Whatever."

"Discretion, Greasy. Do you know what that means?"

"Fine! Fine! I won't shoot nobody unless they shoot at me first. Now come on!" Greasy said. "They're probably getting away with my green, literally and figuratively."

Derrick drew his Glock and said, "Settle down. Kill those lights."

The ATV's lights winked out and Derrick and Gerard killed the vehicle lights. A faint glow still filtered through the trees from the west, but blackness filled the forest beneath the dense tree canopy. Derrick and Gerard waited a couple of minutes to let their eyes adjust before plunging into the woods and leaving Greasy behind.

"What do I do if they come this way? Do we need a signal?" Greasy whispered.

Derrick sighed and said nothing.

Gerard said, "Chirp like a wren."

Derrick looked at Gerard stone-faced and didn't smile.

"What? You don't think that would be funny?"

Pine needles crackled beneath their feet as the partners threaded through the forest. It was slow going and they were loud. The undergrowth was dense, and pricker vines grabbed and tore at the duo's clothes as they worked their way deeper into the woods surrounding the fields.

Derrick raised a fist and Gerard stopped. He'd never been in the military, but he'd played paintball, so he knew the basic hand signals. Derrick's eyes flashed white in the darkness as he dropped into a crouch and peered through the dense foliage.

A coyote barked and howled, and the call was answered by a much closer series of yelps. Tree branches cracked and the pounding of footsteps echoed through the trees.

"Sounds like they're heading south," Gerard said.

"We need to cut them off, but..." Derrick's words sputtered out.

Gerard saw the dilemma. The partners could only cover one of the two possible escape routes—unless... "I'll take the southern route, and you continue straight."

"We shouldn't split up. That's backup 101."

Gerard nodded. "I know. But they might not know their getaway car is gone, which would mean they're heading this way. I would just be covering all our bases."

"Sounds good, but I call bullshit," Derrick said. "They've got cellphones, no? And even if there's no service, which there probably isn't, direct walkie-talkie apps are available for even the weakest of phones."

The sheriff had a point. "We can't just let them get away," Gerard said.

"I know, but… There would be much less of a mess, and how much weed could these guys be carrying?"

Based on what Gerard had seen, quite a bit. Enough to cripple Greasy? Not a chance.

"You're right, though. We can't let this stand. If word gets around—and it will, that Greasy's crop was ripe for the taking the Ripper problems will grow like a fungus." Derrick cracked his neck and shifted on his feet. "You go straight, and I'll go south. Call me—loudly—if you see or hear anything. Got it?"

Gerard nodded. The shotgun felt good in his hands and built his confidence. He'd never fired a Benelli pump action, but it looked similar to his Mossberg. He was a good shot, and he thumbed off the weapon's safety and chambered a round as he ducked under the boughs of an evergreen.

Sharp needle-like leaves scratched at his arms and face as he pushed through the trees, the shotgun serving as a battering ram. He heard snapping branches and knew he was getting closer to…

Then everything went still except the murmur of the wind, the rustling leaves, and the snap and pop of swaying tree branches.

Ahead in the darkness, two yellow-green eyes that looked almost gold stared at him from beneath a bush.

Gerard pulled up short, slipped in bronze pine needles, and almost dropped the shotgun as he came to a halt.

A low growl crept through the forest followed by a prolonged gurgle.

Columns of moonlight cut through the tree canopy, painting the forest floor in spots of pale light. Humboldt County had a large population of cougars, but rarely did the beasts do more than steal chickens and scare hikers.

As the cat sauntered into a column of moonlight Gerard's breath caught.

The beast's streamlined, muscular body was covered in tawny fur, its head broad and rounded, with a short muzzle housing powerful jaws filled with sharp teeth. Its ears were small and curved, and they were adorned with short tufts of fur, but it was the piercing eyes that froze Gerard's feet to the ground. He knew the cats could run up to fifty miles per hour, and in the densely packed forest running wasn't an option. Cougars had retractable claws for climbing as well as weapons, and though the cats rarely attacked humans, they were known to be feisty if their young or home was threatened.

The cat roared as it bounded forward, a dark formless shape surging through the darkness.

Gerard remembered he had the gun, and he brought it up and fired without thinking about how the blast would give away his position.

Turkey shot peppered the trees and undergrowth, but Gerard was off the mark.

But it was enough. The thunderous boom sent the cat scampering into the forest without looking back.

Blood heaved through his veins, his head ringing with tension and fear. He heard footsteps, then shouts, and a single gunshot pierced the night.

He lurched toward the sounds, slowly working up his speed as he wove between trees, avoided boulders, and did his best not to get snagged by prickers.

When he reached the edge of the marijuana field, he stopped. The Rippers had gone south, they'd slipped around him, or they were still in the field.

There was movement in the rows upon rows of densely packed marijuana plants that filled the huge field. The plants were varied in size, with some reaching heights of six feet or more, while others were compact and bushy. Each plant featured a central stem with an elongated Brussels sprout-like cola packed with dense buds. Shadowy leaves with serrated edges and multiple pointed lobes that Gerard knew were tinged with hues of purple looked black in the moonlight.

An earthy stink, reminiscent of pine and citrus crawled up Gerard's nose and he almost sneezed. Bees, butterflies, and other insects buzzed over the field as he stared.

Moonlight painted the world in harsh black and white and the entire field was dusted white with what appeared to be a light sheen of snow.

# 10

The white dusting atop the plants that glowed in the moonlight wasn't newly fallen snow, but sticky glands called trichomes, tiny, crystal-like structures that covered the surface of mature cannabis buds. Gerard understood why stoners paid fifty bucks for a group guided tour that allowed for photo-ops in the greenery. The field was impressive. Folks took thousands of pictures with grape vines down in Sonoma and Napa and with a giant mouse further south, so why not ganja?

Unlike a vineyard, there were no central trellises. Cannabis was a traditional plant with a main stalk, but like a tomato plant, side shoots were an integral part of the plant's health and production. Instead of traditional trellises, a series of stakes held plastic mesh in place over the plants which served as support as the saplings grew through the one-inch square holes.

Many of the plant's colas were so laden with dense buds that they bent and sagged almost to the point of breaking from their stems. Another chilly night and these plants would be harvested.

The coyotes were back, and it sounded like the two opposing groups had joined forces. Barking, yelps, and whining came from the direction of the cliff face that towered over the field to the south, and it sounded as though something had riled the beasts up.

Gerard's nerves crawled, but then he remembered he had the Benelli. As he eased between two rows of plants, he put the weapon's stock to his shoulder and listened hard. He tried to eliminate the night symphony of crickets, the cooing birds, and the singing amphibians that rang in his ears.

The crackle of footsteps crushing dried leaves carried from the forest and a cloud of light bloomed to the south. There was yelling that sounded like Derrick issuing orders, then the *boom* of another gunshot.

Gerard slipped into the shadows along the tree line as he worked his way toward the light, his heart hammering in his chest, sweat stinging his eyes as he jogged. The Benelli was getting heavy. He'd never run with a gun before, and he had to admit it didn't feel right. He slowed, his breath coming hard and reminding him just how out-of-shape he was. There had been a time when he could swim fifteen feet to the ocean floor, pick up a fifty-pound rock, and march it twenty yards before swimming back to the surface. Those days were gone, nothing but a lingering wound of unfinished business and the regrets of old age.

The blow came from his right, a shadow like a giant bat descending from its perch on an evergreen branch.

Gerard twisted and brought the Benelli around as protection, but his assailant gripped the weapon and drove Gerard to the hardpan.

The pair landed in a tangle, both men's hands gripping the shotgun between them. Gerard bucked and heaved as he tried to shake his attacker free, but the man was like a spider. The Ripper wore all black, a pulled-down knit cap covering his face except for two angry, brown, bloodshot eyes.

A shotgun blast thundered through the forest and the Benelli jumped as the weapon discharged and the undergrowth was sprayed with turkey shot. Gerard hadn't meant to fire the weapon, but his attacker was pressing hard. Time to take things up a notch, all over weed.

Gerard pushed with his legs and heaved himself upward, driving the shotgun into the man's chest. The fighter's faces were inches away, and Gerard smelled smoke on the man. He tried to knee the guy in the groin, but the Ripper saw it coming and rolled to the side. Gerard used the leverage to pull free of the man and bring the shotgun to bear.

"Hold up or I'll—"

The man bounced to his feet and bounded into the darkness.

Gerard aimed the Benelli at the man's back, his thoughts chiming between his ears; all over weed? He bit his lip, lowered the Benelli, growled at the cloud of light to the south, and gave chase.

The forest was dark, and Gerard slowed. The ground was uneven, there were large stones strewn about, and pricker vines and evergreen branches constantly threatened to snag him. With the competition on the way, the last thing he needed was to get hurt.

He paused to get his bearings and listen. The faint chatter of an argument rose just above the hum of the night creatures, but he no longer heard pounding footsteps, or the crack and pop of vegetation being stepped on and pushed aside.

Moonlight angled through the gap in the tree canopy where a dead pine had given up the ghost and taken down a few of its mates. Shadows danced across the open area, and weeds swayed in the gentle breeze, the tangy sweet scent of cannabis replaced with the sharp scent of pine.

"Derrick!" Gerard called out.

The voices stopped.

"Derrick!" he called again.

"Over here. You alright?"

Was he? Gerard had lost his man, he was going to have a nice knot on his head, and he'd let himself down.

Gerard spared a glance in the direction of his fleeing assailant and followed Derrick's voice south. He hadn't gone far before he was forced to work his way through a thick copse of evergreens, and when he emerged covered in spider webs with pine needles stuck in his hair, the cloud of light was much closer.

A rock smacked into a tree trunk to Gerard's right, and he was pelted with bark and splinters. Gerard swung the Benelli and aimed, but there was nobody there. Shadows played tag with the moonlight filtering through the canopy, and tiny eyes sparkled in the underbrush. Gerard's heavy breathing was swallowed by the hush of the forest, the night creatures holding their breath in anticipation of the clash to come.

A figure appeared like a specter materializing from the night itself.

Gerard aimed the shotgun, his muscles tensing as he prepared to fire, but he didn't pull the trigger.

The man lunged forward with a sudden burst of speed, and Gerard sidestepped, evading the strike as adrenaline coursed through his veins. If he couldn't shoot the guy, he sure as hell could pistol-whip him.

Using the gun as a club, Gerard let his right hand slip down the forestock as he released the pressure on the stock, and the gun swung free. The blow missed, but his assailant was forced to move away to avoid the strike and that gave Gerard enough room to bring the gun around for another swing.

The gun caught the guy on the shoulder, but the dude was tough. Maybe tougher than Gerard, because he absorbed the blow, grabbed the gun, and tore the weapon from Gerard's hand.

Both combatants froze for a heartbeat as if both competitors couldn't believe what had just occurred.

Not interested in going to prison for manslaughter, or worse, the guy tossed the Benelli into the underbrush and came forward like a boxer at the start of a round.

Gerard stepped back as he brought up his fists, his mind spinning as he searched for the last time he'd been in a fight. It had been a while— surfers did a lot of squawking, but little fighting.

The black-clad man threw himself forward, his left arm cocked and ready to deliver a colossal blow.

Gerard brought up his arm and blocked the punch, but the man's momentum drove him back and Gerard's feet got tangled. For a gut-wrenching instant, Gerard thought he was going down, but he pirouetted and managed to stay on his feet.

The Ripper delivered a rabbit punch to Gerard's jaw that jerked his head back like a PEZ dispenser, tiny sparkling stars filling the air.

With his vision going blurry and darkness creeping in at the edges of his vision, Gerard countered with a series of rapid jabs, but his attacker was fast and he slipped effortlessly out of reach.

As darkness pressed in on them, and the cloud of light in the south got larger, the duo's dance continued amidst the silent sentinels of the forest. Gerard felt the weight of each blow reverberate through his body as the men fought toe to toe, Gerard straining against the onslaught. But he refused to yield. He was too stubborn.

If he got hurt Connie just might finish him off. He could almost hear her admonishing questions: why did you get involved in the first place? What will you do now? You chased the guy even after he ran? With a gun!

Guilty on all accounts. He'd once plunged down the face of an eighty-foot wave, and he got angry when he lost to his children at checkers. Losing wasn't something he liked to do, regardless of a victory's importance, or, sometimes, its cost.

With a surge of determination, Gerard launched himself forward, his fists a blur of motion as he unleashed a volley of strikes. His attacker staggered under the assault, his defenses faltering for the briefest of moments.

It was the opening Gerard needed.

He drove his knee into his opponent's midsection and the man doubled over, gasping for air as Gerard delivered a devastating uppercut that sent the guy sprawling to the forest floor. But even as he fell, the man lashed out with a desperate swipe, his hand finding purchase on Gerard's ankle with a vice-like grip.

A sudden tug threw Gerard off balance, sending him crashing to the ground beside his assailant. They grappled in the dirt, locked in a primal struggle, the air thick with the scent of sweat and earth.

With a grunt of effort, Gerard managed to break free from the man's grasp and scramble to his feet.

The Ripper also stood, never taking his eyes off Gerard.

Heat pulsed through Gerard, an unquenchable anger. He was supposed to be home, relaxing with his family, and this Ripper—

With a final burst of energy, Gerard bounded forward and unleashed a devastating flood of blows; one, two, three fast punches, a roundhouse kick, each strike fueled by the fire of his rage.

The man in black covered his face as he staggered, his defenses crumbling.

But the guy was playing possum.

Gerard moved in for the death blow and the guy fell back, Gerard's punch going wide as he tilted off balance, all his force and momentum in the errant punch.

A blow to his chest jarred his bones and knocked him back, but Gerard never said he fought fair.

He brought up his knee intending to crush the guy's package, but the man twisted, and the glancing blow missed its mark but spun the man around.

The fighters circled, Gerard's fatigue spreading through him like poison. At that moment he wanted to give up. What the hell was he doing?

But in the end, there could only be one victor, and he couldn't change that even if he wanted to.

Gerard's attacker appeared to be flagging, and the right side of his body slumped as if something was broken. The guy's eyes darted around as he looked for the best direction to run.

"Don't do it. I'll—"

For the second time, the man in black ran, and for the second time, Gerard gave chase.

The way ahead was dark. Derrick's flashlight beam had grown closer, but he was still a ways off. If this Ripper was going to be caught, Gerard would have to do the catching.

He picked up his pace, his mind straying to the Benelli that lay on the forest floor. No matter, he hadn't been able to shoot the unarmed man, and the gun hadn't proved very useful in hand-to-hand combat.

Pain knit his spine into a rope of arguing muscles, his nerves shrieking, the tips of his fingers and toes stinging. Lichen hung like gray beards from the tree branches, the evergreens giving way to a loose forest of Valley Oaks. The majestic trees were tall, their tops lost in the darkness.

Gerard entered a field of massive trunks with gnarled and deeply furrowed bark, golden-yellow needles carpeting the ground. Acorns encased in fuzzy caps littered the hardpan waiting to be eaten by one of the forest's many chipmunks or squirrels, and here and there large ant hills dominated the ground like miniature volcanos.

The land pitched down, and Gerard's right foot sunk into soft earth as the forest floor gave way.

An intense buzzing, like the largest swarm of bees ever to cloud Earth's air, rose above the night symphony and drove out all other sounds.

He stumbled forward, his foot pulling free of the ground.

A cloud blacker than night surged from the hole he'd made, the shape undulating and twisting and forming like a sentient storm looking for a target.

Gerard regained his balance and plowed forward, his mind's eye picturing a broken open beehive with a labyrinth of tunnels and chambers carved out of soil, their walls glistening with moisture. Despite the darkness, the destroyed hive pulsed with life, the flutter of the bee's wings creating a gentle hum. The air was heavy with the scent of beeswax and honey, and it turned Gerard's stomach.

He almost laughed as he ran, the comical image of a raging queen bee screeching about her destroyed hive filling his panicked mind. Gerard saw himself doing interviews, his face covered in red welts. He heard the restrained laughter as folks asked him what had happened.

Then a truly nasty thought came to him. Was he allergic to bees? He didn't think so, but... Gerard had been stung many times, but it had always been a single sting. He saw a friend almost die from wandering into the beach grass to take a leak only to stumble on a nest and take multiple stings.

The air filled with yellow jackets, and Gerard flailed his arms, fighting through the beasts as he ran blindly through the forest.

Gerard had gone from being the hunter to being hunted.

# 11

Yellow jackets are vicious little buggers.

The air vibrated with the collective hum of angry insects, engulfing Gerard in a frenzy of motion and sound as the bees swarmed with relentless aggression. He ran blindly through the woods, stepping in holes and tripping over roots as he fought to escape the assault.

Gerard beat at his clothes as he ran, trying to scatter the bees. A yellow jacket alighted on his cheek, and before he could slap it away, he felt the sharp pain of the insect's stinger impaling his skin. The bee dropped from his face and Gerard swiped at it as the creature buzzed away, but he missed.

The gurgle and pop of water sliding over smooth stones echoed through the forest.

Cheek throbbing with pain, sweat dripping into his eyes, Gerard changed direction. He cut left and knifed between two thick oaks, the sound of trickling water getting louder.

The forest droned with life, pine needles crunching beneath his feet. His chest hurt, not from the exertion of running, but from the stress. Not much rattled Gerard, but messing around in the woods in the dark with Rippers running around didn't sit well with him.

He broke free of the trees and a silvery stream snaked through the dark forest, moonlight angling into the gap in the dense canopy. In the dark, with no flashlight, judging the depth of the stream was difficult. He knew that if he could get into the water the bees would leave him alone, but the shallow brooks that flowed from the hills were often no more than a foot deep, and finding a spot to submerge himself quickly was going to be hard, but he couldn't outrun the buggers.

A cloud of yellow jackets buzzed his head and divebombed his body. The swarm had thinned, but there was still a bunch of determined wasps desperate to avenge the destruction of their hive.

If it had been during the day he would've run down the center of the stream, not caring about slipping on stones, but in the darkness, the smallest of rocks threatened to take him down, and that would be worse than a few stings.

A yellow jacket landed on the back of his right hand. The insect's hairy legs planted themselves in his skin, and then the sharpness of a sting surged through him.

This one wasn't so lucky, and Gerard crushed the bee against the back of his hand with a firm slap, the sound rising above the cackling water.

With no time left, Gerard slid down the short stone-encrusted embankment into the stream and flopped into the cool water. As he'd feared, the stream was only a few inches deep, and Gerard crawled through the shallow water, slipping on slime-covered rocks as the last of the bees ranged around him, searching for a place to land and plant a sting.

He rolled in the shallow water, his clothes getting drenched, his face scraping on stones, stars wheeling overhead.

Then he was dumped over a short waterfall into a shallow pool, and he saw his opportunity. Gerard pushed all the air from his lungs, bubbles surging through the dark water as he sank. He didn't go far, but three feet was enough.

He lay on his back, stones digging into his spine as he stared up through the gurgling push of rushing water that blocked out all sound. Gerard couldn't see the bees swarming in the air above the stream, but he could sense them and knew their violent energy hung just above the surface of the water.

Willing his body to conserve oxygen, Gerard closed his eyes, pressure building in his lungs. At the height of his surfing career, Gerard could hold his breath for upwards of three minutes. These days it was more like a minute. He'd been underwater for twenty seconds and his lungs were already burning.

Gerard's mind shifted to one of his epic wipeouts at Mavericks as he tried to distract himself from the pain knifing through his head. He was tossed from a fifty-footer that churned him under a mountain of whitewater and pulled him deeper than he'd ever been sucked before. It had been a challenge resisting the power of the wave as he felt himself being forced deeper and deeper, but if there was one golden rule among surfers it was you never fight the ocean.

The surface had seemed so far away. His eyes stinging, pressure threatening to pop his head as it squeezed his brain, his muscles rebelling, his body going weak from lack of oxygen, Gerard had stroked up, dragging himself through the water. His arms felt like they were filled with cement and he feared he wasn't going to reach the surface in time.

He'd been seconds away from sucking in water when he broke the surface like a dolphin and flopped onto his back. As he floated, he stared up at the blue sky, not caring about the mountain of whitewater that was about to roll him under again. He had fun after that as he got pummeled six more times before walking out of the ocean to a chorus of cheers and clapping, his tow partner out in the deep water with the ski.

Gerard's head ached as the memory faded, the stream rushing around him. When he could take it no more, he thrust his head above the water, took a deep breath, and submerged himself again. In the brief instant he was exposed Gerard saw that there were still bees clouding the surface. Not many, but a few brave souls still waited to attack him.

Another minute slid away, and when he popped up the second time all he heard was singing crickets and bleating frogs.

The bees were gone.

He crawled from the stream and lay on the muddy bank, sucking in air, his head beating in rhythm with his heart. In addition to the multiple bumps, bruises, and cuts he'd sustained, he'd been stung on his cheek, and the back of his hand, and two ambitious insects had gotten his right ankle. The stings were already red and swelling, and he felt lightheaded and dizzy.

Gerard wasn't allergic to bees, but he was feeling the effects of the four stings. As he took deep breaths the nauseousness faded, and his heart rate steadied. He knew that as the bees' venom spread through him, symptoms such as nausea, vomiting, dizziness, and headache were to be expected, so he wasn't worried. But he also knew these types of conditions could turn on a dime. In severe cases, anaphylaxis shock can occur, and many stings can overwhelm the body's immune response, leading to a toxic reaction.

An owl hooted and stirred Gerard from his reverie. The river gurgled, and he could see the glow of Derrick's flashlight in the distance and he realized in his frenzy to escape the bees he'd run east, back toward the cannabis field.

He pulled his phone to see if there was any word from Derrick and to use the light app and he found the cellphone crushed, its case smashed, its screen spidered. Gerard cocked his arm in frustration intending to hurl the dead device, but then remembered his entire life was on the SIM card, and he pocketed the phone.

The night was young, the moon low in the sky, and thin rays of moonlight angled through the tree canopy. Using the position of the moon as a guide Gerard chose what he believed to be west and started his trek to the road.

If the Rippers wanted to take a shot at him, they could go for it. He was done—shoot, he'd never really started. Besides, the Rippers were probably halfway to Vegas by now.

Gerard brushed himself off as he threaded through the oaks. Ahead, evergreens packed the forest, and he angled south to avoid them. He'd had enough scratches to last a lifetime, and he could already hear Tommy T and Bongo's jokes. "You get into a fight with a cat, dude?" And, "That's a pretty big zit on your cheek, man." He cracked his neck. Did he deserve what happened to him tonight? No. Did he deserve to get ripped for his performance? Maybe.

The road appeared out of the darkness like an oasis. Cracked and graying blacktop wound into the trees in both directions, Derrick's police vehicle and the old G-wagon nowhere in sight.

He took his bearings. Gerard drove Old Mattole Road every day of his life—almost, and though there were no real landmarks, a close inspection of the roadside vegetation revealed the stump of a massive redwood tree that he drove by every day on his way home.

Had he passed the stump on this night? He didn't think so.

Gerard started walking south, the buzz of the forest his only companion.

The first sign of life was the glow of Greasy's flashlight. The pot guru stood in the center of the road peering into the forest.

"Yo!" Gerard yelled as he approached.

Greasy swung his shotgun and aimed at the darkness. "Who's there?"

Gerard put up his hands and said, "It's me. Gerard."

Light bloomed around Gerard as Greasy turned the flashlight on him. "You're alone? What happened to you?"

Gerard had given zero thought to how to spin his romp in the woods, but he decided spin wasn't the way to go, so he told the truth. All of it.

"Well, shit. You look like a drowned rat," Greasy said. "Are you alright?"

"I'll live."

A flashlight bloomed in the darkness on the road to the south. Greasy called out and Derrick approached with not one, but two Rippers as prisoners. The sheriff drove the thieves forward at gunpoint, and as the criminals got closer Gerard saw it was a man and woman, neither of which he'd ever seen before. That was a relief. If the thieves had been locals the problem would have been much bigger for him.

As it was, the couple clammed up and asked for their lawyers.

Greasy's frustration boiled over. "You shits got nothing to say? You come on my land, screw with my weed." He lifted his shotgun. "I should put an end to it right now."

Derrick's hand shot out and he pushed down Greasy's gun. "We'll have no vigilante justice in my town. Do you understand?"

Greasy frowned as he lowered his weapon, and said defiantly, "You know how this goes, sheriff. These losers will say they were hiking or some shit and got lost."

Derrick and Gerard said nothing. The prisoners wore backpacks and weren't carrying guns, and though both men knew that was part of the plan, there were no other options except to take the pair in and let the law deal with them, or not.

Greasy sighed and stalked to his ATV, holstered his shotgun, and said, "Let me know if you need me to come down to the station house and sign anything."

When Greasy was gone, Derrick said, "What the hell happened to you?"

Gerard went through it all again, Derrick doing his best to contain his laughter, but when Gerard got to the part about hiding in the stream a giggle leaked from the sheriff.

"Nice," Gerard said. "I help you, and what do I get?"

"Easy, Gerard," the sheriff said. "I'm just joshing with you."

"What about my guy... Or guys that got away?"

Derrick shrugged as he stuffed the two Rippers into his Tahoe. "Not much we can do. I assume your guys were covered up like these dipshits were?" He motioned toward the Rippers.

Gerard nodded.

"So you don't have a description?"

"No, but what about their partners there?"

"You said it yourself," Derrick said. "They claim they were hiking and didn't know it was private property. Say they were alone."

"And they didn't see the private property signs posted on half the trees along the property's border?"

"That's for a judge to decide," Derrick said.

Now Gerard felt like a total fool. He'd known how this was going to end and never gave it a second thought as he bounded forward blindly. Now he was stung up, bruised, embarrassed, and he'd accomplished nothing.

"The damage to Greasy's field was minimal," Derrick said. "Clearly he wasn't happy that some of the thieves got away, but since there was no significant damage to his crop, he agreed not to push the issue and even promised to retrieve my shotgun at first light."

A frog bellowed and the sheriff's phone trilled. "It's your wife," he said as he answered the call. "Hi, Connie, what's up?"

Gerard went to Derrick's side, the two men locking eyes. After a long moment, Derrick said, "He's here with me, Connie. He's fine. His phone got smashed and—" Derrick bit his lip then said, "Let me put him on and he can explain."

As Gerard accepted the phone, he realized what an ass he'd been—again. Connie was probably worried sick because he was due home an hour ago. "Hey, babe."

"Oh, boy. That doesn't sound good. Are you O.K.?"

Gerard smiled. "Fine, but I got myself into a bit of a snag."

Connie said nothing.

He told the story a third time, leaving out some of the details that made him look less than stellar.

When he was done Connie harrumphed and said, "Well, get on home then. We'll get you a new phone in the morning. I saved you a plate and you must need a hot shower."

He did. "The kids good?"

"Homework."

With that, he told his wife he'd be home soon, arranged a time to meet with Derrick the following day to sign a statement, and waved at the two Rippers as he jumped in the G-wagon.

His bruises throbbed and the bee stings thumped, but they didn't sting as much as his pride. His wet socks chafed his feet, his soaked underwear had inched up the crack of his ass, and he was sure he felt ants crawling over his skin. Gerard rolled his shoulders, focused on the road, and tried to turn his mind back to the contest, which was coming on like a freight train, but he found that harder to do than usual.

Three days passed, the swell building, and amazingly the events out at Greasy's farm didn't make it onto the coconut telegraph. He was thankful for that, and though he had to answer for the bee sting on his face, the rest of the embarrassing story stayed locked in Derrick's vault.

The Rippers were released on bail—two gang members from down LA's way, and Derrick said there was no way they would show for their court date, and nobody would chase them. What a country.

Gerard's frustration and patience ran out two days later when the first forty-foot wave rolled into The Funnel and broke over Purgatory Beach.

It was time to let the dogs out.

# 12

**Purgatory Beach, Liigei Too, northern California, U.S.A.**
*6:32 PM PT, October 18, 2023*
*Three days until the start of The Funnel Big Wave Competition*
Dusk settled over the beach, the sun nothing but a thin orange slice on the western horizon, the sky a glorious display of orange-purple that faded into gray as it stretched east. Gulls argued, the sea raged, and the scent of salt and rot filled Gerard's nostrils.

The email invitation with the final invite list had been sitting in his queue for days, but as Gerard tapped his new phone and hit send the knot in his stomach didn't untangle as it had in the past. The chime of the message being sent sounded, the crash of the waves driving it under. It was done. The trigger had been pulled and cellphones chimed all over the world as the surfers got their invitations and prepared to make the journey to Liigei Too.

Gerard's bee stings and bruises throbbed, but his ego had mostly recovered. His ego being crushed hadn't been the worst thing in the world. He was treated like royalty wherever he went, hadn't paid for beers in years, and accepted his share of free dinners and stays in luxurious seaside mansions. It was an unsustainable life. He knew that even as a young man, especially when he met Connie, and knew she was the one he wanted to spend the rest of his life with. From that day forward, he looked at life differently. Suddenly, he wasn't so careless, so reckless, and he wasn't so eager to put his life on the line for the sake of a thrill. For money...

The kids being born had been the final nail in the coffin that had been in the process of being sealed since the incident.

Gerard and Connie walked along Purgatory Beach, moonlight angling through gaps that looked like doorways to another world, dusk slowly fading to darkness. The couple walked hand in hand, as they often did. The sea had brought them together and served as a constant reminder of how their world had almost been pulled apart.

"Feel better now?" she asked.

He didn't, but he said, "Yeah, I suppose."

"You suppose? You've been stressing about the final invite list for weeks."

"I know, it's just..." It wasn't that he couldn't mold his feelings into words, it was that he didn't want to.

Connie, the ever-accurate reader of her husband's mental temperature, didn't push. She knew everything Gerard did—he'd told her, so she understood his angst.

He said, "When the contest is over, I'll feel better."

She squeezed his hand. "It sucks that it's become such a burden, but it's worth it. You're doing important work here."

The bee sting on Gerard's face stung with phantom pain.

A massive set rolled through the darkness, clouds of mist and whitewater thunder mounding over the inky sea as the waves broke. The air reeked of low tide, and the smell of death and decay jogged his memory. Then he was there again, the memory so strong he could taste the fresh Costa Rican air and feel the warm ocean spray on his tanned face. Darkness pressed in around him, and in that blackness, he saw his past.

**It wasn't a monster** wave that got him, but a temporary loss of concentration coupled with shitty luck.

A sweet breeze pushed over the water, and it had been a perfect morning at Potrero Grande. The legendary surf spot was located on the northwestern coast of Costa Rica, in the Guanacaste province. It was a remote and pristine break that was renowned among surfers worldwide for its fast, powerful, and consistent waves that broke over a rocky reef. The spot earned its nickname "Ollie's Point" from American soldiers during the 1980s, who named it after Lieutenant Colonel Oliver North, a key figure in the Iran-Contra affair, as the area served as a drop-off point for supplies.

The Pacific sparkled and Gerard closed his eyes as he floated just beyond the breakers, waiting for a big set to come through. The waves were only fifteen feet on this day, but Gerard loved free surfing when the pressure was off. He could turn off his brain and just have fun.

Connie sat on the beach surrounded by lush tropical foliage. She loved coming to Potrero Grande because it required a hike through the dense jungle, which was her favorite part of the day.

The waves at Potrero Grande are renowned for their consistency, breaking throughout the year, particularly during the dry season when offshore winds prevail, creating ideal surfing conditions. Gerard was a right-hand surfer, and the powerful right-hand point break produced long, hollow rides, making it a paradise for barrel riders. Despite its gentle appearance, Potrero Grande produced fast, powerful waves, and the rocky reef bottom posed significant risks if one lost concentration, as Gerard had.

A lapse that had almost cost him a leg.

The sun's glare made judging wave height difficult, and Connie wasn't spotting on this day, so Gerard tried to be patient, but he was getting hot sitting on his board, the warm Pacific cycling over his legs. A large set rolled in roughly ten waves back, and he chose his target and flopped onto his board, the thick layer of Sex Wax pulling at his rash guard.

He lifted his right ankle and made sure his leash wasn't tangled as he stroked forward, the roll of smaller waves lifting him on their swell. Gerard's neck was sore from looking back while lying flat on his board, and the sunburn didn't help, but that was the price of paradise.

Five waves rolled by as Gerard stroked the sea with no sense of urgency. He was on the razor's edge of the break, and if he came too far forward, he risked getting tumbled. He eased up, buying time as he strained his neck looking back.

The first wave of his set came through, a ten-foot roller with a blown-out top. Gerard never rode the first wave of a set. In his experience, the middle waves of a set were usually the largest and cleanest, though wind, tides, depth, and the contour of the sea bottom also played roles.

Gerard spied his wave, and he swam as if his life depended on it. The board hissed through the sea, a wall of water building behind him as if Godzilla was rising from the depths.

When he felt the board get pushed as the momentum of the wave grabbed him, he drove to his feet with the fluidity of a soldier being screamed at by their drill sergeant.

The crackly static of the wave breaking carried over the water, and Gerard was propelled forward, the surface of the ocean receding as the board cut into the face of the wave.

Gerard's eyes shifted to Connie, who was standing at the edge of the water, watching him. He waved at her.

His foot slipped, and then he was cartwheeling down the face of the wave, the leash tugging on his leg as his board got thrashed.

With an explosion of raw power the wave closed-out on Gerard, thousands of pounds of whitewater burying him and jerking his body around as if the sea was intent on ripping him apart.

Gerard went slack, releasing all the tension in his muscles, his arms and legs hanging loose as the ocean jostled him like a piece of trash.

He hit the reef with bone-jarring force.

Gerard's left leg twisted, crumbled, and snapped. He screamed, the force of his rage and the blast of his outgoing breath keeping water out of his mouth for a heartbeat. But when he sucked his lips closed, he took in water and swallowed a mouthful of briny sea.

A normal person would've panicked and gasped for air or choked in an attempt to expel the nasty fluid. But Gerard had been here before. He had been tumbled by the ocean many times and they had an understanding. Half a mouth full of water surged down his throat.

He closed his eyes tightly, willing himself not to breathe, not to hold his breath. Nothing. He was a rock falling through the sea, a flexible piece of trash that the ocean could do with as it willed. As he was tossed, his mind wandered, pain splitting his head, his leg hanging and twisting in the surging water like a broken wing.

When he was a boy, his old man had gotten into a bad car wreck, with him sitting in the front seat. Seatbelts and airbags had saved the day, but that was the first time Gerard experienced time slowing down.

He'd already known that time could speed up. That happened all the time. Like when he was riding his bike while playing with his friends or watching his favorite TV show. Though there were school days that dragged out, family gatherings, and other things he hated doing, it was boredom that really made time stretch.

But being in mortal danger elicited a different time speed.

Gerard heard individual bubbles popping, counted the pulses of pain spidering from his destroyed leg, and heard Connie's voice in the back of his mind telling him to hang on. Just hang on.

As his father screamed and jumped on the brakes, tires screeching, Gerard was thrust forward against his seatbelt.

And time paused.

He would later describe the sensation to his mates as his vision froze for a second, but in reality, his world had slowed—or his perception of it—to such a significant degree that he saw each thing happen before it occurred.

Gerard opened his eyes and another section of reef rushed up to meet him, gray stone spidering beneath it. He wiggled, thrashing in the turbulent sea as he rolled away from the spikes of white coral that threatened to impale him again.

Whitewater swept him away, and as he tumbled in the angry surf, the air in his lungs pulling him toward the surface, a thin ray of sunlight knifed through the whitewater and he felt relief. Pure peace. It was over, and though it would take a long time for him to come to accept that reality, he'd known at that moment that his career was over.

He broke the surface and choked up water, his leg dead weight. Gerard coughed and gagged for what seemed like forever, his head splitting with pain, sunlight an enemy of his eyes.

Then Connie was there. Like she always was.

When rescuers hauled him from the ocean, he was a broken man. The medics sedated him and straightened his leg out, but the limb was already swollen to twice its size, the pain excruciating.

Connie was by his side the entire time, the sternness of her resiliency the rock that supported his life.

A helicopter was called, and Gerard was airlifted to San Rafaél Arcángel Clinical Hospital in Liberia. At the hospital, the hope of a simple cast fled. Lying in the hospital, marinating in pity and self-flagellation, he listened to the doctor.

"You're lucky. The way you hit that reef..." The doctor looked down and sighed. "You could easily have ended up in a wheelchair. So as bad as it is, it could've been a lot worse."

Gerard thought maybe ending up in a wheelchair was his destiny. He lost his concentration, and the ocean punished him for this delinquency.

"I can't feel my right foot," he said.

"Your leg shattered, Mr. Noll," the doctor said. "You've got a broken leg, a dislocated knee, two snapped ligaments, major nerve damage, and an artery that tore lengthways, which filled your leg with blood."

It was a rough twenty-four hours, but thanks to an incredibly skilled surgeon, Gerard's leg didn't have to be amputated, but it was a very close call.

The nerve damage he sustained was significant, but his shredded ego just wouldn't let him go out this way. Gerard designed a custom brace to keep his leg steady, but it was more mental than anything else.

He competed in three competitions after the accident, but his performance was dismal. Fear and worry gnawed at the edges of every wave, and it caused him to make bad decisions or no decisions at all. He was bounced from the circuit, and Gerard never competed in a big wave competition again.

The aftermath had been a brutal test of mental and physical toughness that had worn Gerard down to rubble. He disappeared into himself, even with Connie and his infant children. That was what burned his stomach most in those alone moments when he was trapped with thoughts of the past and wondering what he could've done differently. He had let his family down and his commitment to never do that again had pulled him from the abyss.

Connie screamed, and Gerard was ejected from his memory.

"What is it?" he asked.

"Something bit me!" Her flashlight played around on the sand, nubs of boulders, clumps of seaweed, and broken shells staring back at them.

"A crab?" Gerard asked.

Pain, like a nail being driven into the bottom of Gerard's foot, surged through him. It was ten times worse than a bee sting, and Gerard jumped as he yelped.

Connie's flashlight beam illuminated his foot, trickles of dark blood dripping onto the beach.

A sand lance protruded from the beach like an ancient spear, its form weathered and covered in red pustules. The lance's long, slender body appeared ghost-like, its slick skin adorned with intricate patterns of erosion and sedimentary layers, its large black eyes covered in milky white. Its shaft bore the scars of disease, and at the creature's tip where the lance narrowed to a sharp point a tiny mouth flexed open, black stained teeth therein.

# 13

A field of tiny, pointed heads sprouted from the rock-encrusted seashore all around Gerard and Connie, moonlight shimmering off the creatures' silver scales. Whitewater frothed over stones and tugged on broken shells as waves crashed and gulls screeched. The scent of low tide carried off the water, and the surface of the Pacific glowed with an otherworldly light.

"Sand eels!" Connie shouted as she danced around as if the beach sand was red hot.

Gerard knew the creatures by their proper name, sand lances, but he'd never seen a variant like these before. The creatures were typically bottom dwellers, not ambush predators. They burrowed into the sand to avoid tidal currents, but these creatures... He knew sand lances didn't have pelvic fins and didn't develop swim bladders, and he'd never seen one with teeth. Both adult and larval sea lances primarily fed on copepods, though there were many different types and recently other species were discovered in the deep which hadn't been named.

Pain stinging his foot, Gerard loped away from the water and Connie fell in alongside him. He ran toward K2, tufts of beach grass and the crests of boulders rushing past in the darkness.

"Here," Connie said.

Gerard looked back to find his wife perched atop a stone. The woman was always one step ahead of him, well, in this case, one behind. He pivoted in the sand, changed direction, and jumped onto a boulder.

When he searched the shoreline, all was quiet.

Connie played her flashlight around, and tiny holes and bubbles appeared on the beach as the creatures receded into the sand.

Waves crashed, lines of white rolling over the inky Pacific.

Gerard looked down at the wound on his foot to reassure himself he wasn't going crazy. The bite was much smaller than the one he'd seen on Glenda's leg, but sand lances weren't supposed to bite at all! "Are you O.K.?" he asked.

"Yeah. You?"

Truth was, he didn't know, and he said nothing.

"Gerard?" Connie's voice was shaky and unsure.

"I'm fine," he lied. He'd learned early in life that sometimes, as a leader, either appointed or perceived, it was important to project strength, confidence, and knowledge. Gerard had understood this on the circuit when he realized the younger guys were feeding off his energy. If he was down, they were down, and over the years he'd learned to temper his responses, even with his family. It all boiled down to sometimes a lie was necessary for the common good.

There were only two other cars in the parking lot, and Gerard and Connie slid off their stones and made their way to the G-wagon. Gerard's phone was vibrating non-stop, and even Connie's cell had started trilling.

"Feeding frenzy," Connie said.

Misunderstanding his wife, Gerard pulled his phone and said, "Yup. It's begun."

"Not what I meant," she said as she gazed out at the sea.

The pair got in the truck, the folks in the other vehicles paying them no attention. If they'd seen Gerard and Connie hopping around the beach like fools, they gave no sign.

Gerard felt his wife staring at him as he drove, knew the question she wanted to ask but was holding back. He said, "Hi, Sheriff, Connie and I were walking on the beach when a swarm of sand lances appeared. See my bite?"

Connie chuckled. "What about Ray?"

Gerard hiked his shoulders, but he thought calling Ray was a good idea.

"How many of these incidents can you—we overlook?"

That was the zillion dollar question. The question that had been burning a hole in his stomach since he'd seen the diseased orca carcass. He said nothing and drove on, the heat of his wife's stare fading as he navigated the twisting roads of Liigei Too.

Back at the Noll casa, the children were waiting. As was usually the case, seeing to their kid's needs, hearing about their day, and making every effort to insert themselves in their lives pushed the issue of the sand lances, their ringing phones, and the contest into the background. If Willow or Sage saw the bites on their parent's legs, they gave no sign.

**Over the next forty-eight** hours competitors, their entourages, support staff, and equipment flowed into town. This invasion was coupled with a media frenzy, and the launch of promotional campaigns, including the town's discount passes that provided tourists with free drinks and coupons for all the local establishments.

The weather looked good, the swell was building, and the money was flowing. Everything was set, and still Gerard's stomach churned with roasting maggots.

Gerard and the sheriff hadn't seen much of each other, which was a good thing, but when he arrived at Jolene's for a nightcap Derrick pulled him aside. The lawman had a list of questions, most of which revolved around logistics at the marina. A second ramp had been added, but folks were waiting over an hour to dump their skis, and that was just too long. Gerard suggested a schedule, like tee-off times, and Derrick loved the idea.

"There haven't been any reported crimes other than a couple of kids pulling a dine and dash," Derrick said.

Gerard nodded, tension massaging his shoulders. He opened his mouth to tell the sheriff about the sand lances but decided not to. The lawman would only throw the decision back at Gerard, and he'd already decided to try and forget about the incident.

"Purgatory Beach was packed and there hasn't been a single bite or any reported sea creature-related happenings," Derrick added.

"Thank you. Have one on me," Gerard said as he moved on. With the first runs of the competition scheduled for the next day and no sign of the swell diminishing, Gerard was hopeful that a full week wouldn't be needed to get in the required runs. Flexibility was built into the schedule so he could pick the best days to compete, but this year he was more concerned about getting the competition completed than he was about waiting around for an extra few feet of wave height.

It took him twenty minutes to get to the bar, where he ordered a martini. His head throbbed with questions and worries, and the first sip of vodka not only calmed the throbbing blood vessel on his forehead but also calmed the nuclear worms wriggling in his stomach.

He was on his second drink when Connie called. Gerard glanced at his watch. It was time for dinner and Connie was probably wondering where he was. Before he could hit answer call, Ray appeared at the bar's entrance. He'd called his friend, who had insisted on coming to see him rather than talking over the phone. The coastie had a series of excuses prepared, but Gerard had cut him off, knowing the man wanted a real drink, and not the crap they served onboard ship.

"Yo," Ray said as he took a stool.

Gerard held up a finger. "Just let me take this." He answered Connie's call. "Hi, honey, what's up? I'm meeting with Ray." He hoped that last part would cover for the fact that he was late and at Jolene's.

The edge in his wife's voice was understandable. It had only been a few days since he'd been knocked ass over teakettle, and here he was worrying his wife unnecessarily. "Are you eating with us?" she asked.

He sighed. "I…"

Ray was staring at him and the voices around him had dropped several octaves.

"I'm sorry. I forgot I had this thing with Ray, so no, I'm not going to make dinner. I should have told you, but I forgot."

"The office voicemail is full," she said, but some of the frustration had leaked from her tone. "Do you want me to answer the questions I can?"

Gerard knew most of the issues at this point would be manufactured. PR people pushing and grinding and trying to get the most exposure for the least amount of money. Gerard had little patience for any of it, but he'd come to accept that without sponsors, advertisers, and public support, the contest wouldn't exist. He said, "That would be a huge help. Make a list of anything I need to deal with and we'll talk when I get home. I won't be late."

"Bye." She clicked off. No, see you later. No, I love you.

Gerard said, "How do you do it? You're away so much. Doesn't your family get on you about it?"

Ray hiked his shoulders. "My wife is ex-Army, so she gets it. The kids—they're harder, but you know how it is. They want you around until you're actually around, then they don't want to be seen with you."

Gerard nodded, but he and Connie didn't have that issue—yet. Sage and Willow were just entering the always shitty teen years, and Gerard wasn't looking forward to the experience.

The two old friends drank in silence, glasses tinkling, the low chatter of the crowd like a soothing melody. Ray was nursing his second scotch when he said, "I've got to hit the road." He downed the last finger of his drink.

Gerard chuckled. "You never told me why you needed to talk to me."

"Not talk, really," Ray said. "My Zodiac is docked down at the marina. I want to show you something if you've got the time."

Gerard looked at his cellphone where it sat on the bar.

"Won't take long. I'll have you home by dessert."

"Fine," Gerard said. He tipped back his glass, caught the olive between his clenched jaws, and smiled before he sucked it down.

Ray had used RideShare to get to Jolene's, so Gerard drove. The burn of the vodka warmed his stomach, and he was a little fuzzy around the edges, but he wasn't drunk. Slightly impaired—maybe, so he took it slow, Ray silent beside him the entire way.

When they reached the marina Gerard whistled. Despite the late hour, the place looked like a beehive that had been smacked with a stick. Surfers waxed boards, crews worked on skis, and support staff, safety personnel, and judges prepared for the first day of the contest. The scent of salt, anxiety, and competition filtered over the assembled like a building storm.

Gerard parked and the duo met Ray's crew at their coastie Zodiac. It was Ray's usual vessel, and the pair took up their customary positions on the bench seat before the command console. Dock lines were tossed, and the motors hummed to life, large bubbles popping off the stern as the pumps sucked in water.

The helmsman eased the boat into gear and the orange inflatable squeaked as it eased away from the dock. Tiny waves rolled through the calm marina as the vessel powered up the channel to the open sea.

Stars blinked overhead as the boat came up on plane, engine buzzing, the hull cutting through the rolling waves and throwing thick spray. The helmsman turned the ship's wheel to the right, and the vessel arced north, running just off the shoreline in less than thirty feet of water. Moonlight shimmered off the waves beyond the breakers, painting them with sparkling diamonds of dimpled light.

The boat hadn't gone far before the whine of the motor eased, the bow dipped, and the flowing sea crashed against the transom. No commands were needed, and the helmsman brought the vessel to a crawl as he set a course for shore.

Along the shoreline a tall cliff face filled with sliding vegetation and stones towered over a field of boulders that rose from the shallows like dirty teeth. A question formed on Gerard's lips, but he said nothing.

A green glow, like a spaceship ascending from the depths, shone in the water along the shoreline. The boat's pilot brought the Zodiac in close, then shut down the engines as the boat bumped gently into a large boulder.

"Shit," Gerard said.

"Nope," Ray said. "Mussels."

Gerard leaned over the orange gunnel, staring.

Clusters of glowing mussels clung tenaciously to a weathered boulder, the luminescent mollusks casting a fragile glow that danced across the ocean floor. The mussels were varied in size, ranging from specks to substantial shells the size of a human child's hand. Each shell shimmered with hues of green, blue, and violet as if lit from within, the soft, pulsating glow reminiscent of the bioluminescent creatures found in the darkest depths of the ocean.

Despite their odd coloration, the mussels exhibited no outward signs of decay or deformity. Their shells, normally rough and dull, seemed polished to a glossy sheen, reflecting the surrounding underwater landscape in distorted patterns of light and shadow.

As the sea pushed and pulled, the mussels swayed in unison, their delicate appendages extending and retracting with each passing wave. Schools of fish streaked through the water, their scales gleaming in the light cast by the glowing shells. Crustaceans scuttled along the sandy floor, their claws searching for scraps of food dislodged by the feeding mussels.

"Before you ask, no. I don't know why they're like that. We took samples and…"

"You're waiting."

"That's what we do," Ray said. "But you can't. Get this thing done."

Gerard nodded.

# 14

**Purgatory Beach, Liigei Too, northern California, U.S.A.**
**6:32 PM PT, October 21, 2023**
*First day of The Funnel Big Wave Competition*

The day dawned bright, thirty-five-foot rollers leading the charge. A stiff offshore wind applied steady pressure, and the steep waves were clean and dominating.

Gerard sat on his ski, a coastie drone buzzing overhead, the mid-afternoon sun turning the Pacific into a desert. Tommy T floated behind him, the towrope snaking over the surface between them. Connie hadn't been pleased when he'd offered up his services, but she'd understood, and with the coastie cutter sitting offshore she had to admit every safety precaution had been taken. Gerard wore his headset and Connie was in his ear. She could patch him into Derrick, Ray, or anyone else with access to an open channel at the first sign of trouble.

Metallic grumbles from a bullhorn fought to rise above the crashing waves as the announcers on shore updated the scoreboard. Several runs had been recorded, but Tommy T had yet to catch anything of note and he wasn't on the board.

Gerard felt a little responsible for that. The kid had been ecstatic when Gerard asked to be his wingman, but truth be told Gerard was rusty. Yeah, he knew how to pick waves, but he hadn't done it under the pressure of a time limit and competition in a long time. He was still better than Tommy T's normal tow partner, so there was that, but as he focused on the incoming set, he knew he needed to do better.

The surfing community had accepted the news of Gerard's return with stoic optimism. He wasn't riding, after all. Competitors could choose any partner they wanted, so long as said partner had passed the required safety and first aid courses. When asked if he could pass the physical portion of the ocean lifeguard test, Gerard lied confidently and said yes, but he wasn't so sure.

"Nice set coming in, Gerard," came Connie's voice over the comm.

The silver tops of the incoming rollers glowed in the sunlight. He whistled and Tommy T popped into a sitting position, gripped the tow bar, and fitted his feet into the straps on his board.

Gerard goosed the throttle and the ski lept from the sea, spitting a stream of water as Tommy T was jerked to his feet. He piloted the wave runner parallel with the incoming waves, and when his wave came, he turned toward the beach and pulled Tommy T onto the face of a monster.

With a screech, the kid let go of the tow bar and disappeared down the face of the wave.

Gerard fought through the whitewater to the backside of the wave as the static crackle of the wave breaking carried over the water. He set a course for shore, running along the break, watching Tommy T and hoping he wouldn't need rescue.

Tommy T danced on the razor's edge of a forty-foot wall of water.

A sense of awe washed over Gerard, mingled with fear. The fear. It was always with him now when he was out on the water, a tumor of angst that threatened to wash him away at a moment's notice. He'd always known the risks and understood the stakes. One wrong move, one moment of hesitation, and Tommy T would be swallowed by the unforgiving ocean.

But there was no room for doubt in Tommy T's world, no place for fear. He stood resolute, a figure of sheer determination against a snarling backdrop of controlled power. With a graceful motion born of years of practice and passion, Tommy T hurtled down the face of the wave, arms leveled for balance, white foam rising around him.

Time slowed, that now familiar sensation of comfort. The wave rose higher and higher, a towering colossus of water and foam threatening to consume everything in its path. But Tommy T was unfazed, his movements fluid and precise as he navigated the bumpy slope of churning water.

In an instant that seemed to defy the laws of gravity, Tommy T reached the bottom of the wave and carved a path through the chaos, and as quickly as it had begun, it was over. Tommy T cut back into the swell, launched off the lip of what remained of the wave, and flopped into the water to wait for Gerard.

The ride had been epic, and Gerard heard the screeching of the announcer's bullhorn as Tommy T's name was put on the leaderboard. For Gerard, the moment was about more than just victory—it was about the sheer, unadulterated joy on Tommy T's face when Gerard picked him up.

The partners repeated this process with varying degrees of success until the horn sounded and their time was up. Tommy T was greeted with applause when the pair reached the beach, and Gerard faded into the background the best he could. This was Tommy T's moment, and he'd had very little to do with it. The kid had ridden like a champ, and Gerard was a little disappointed when he reached the judge's table and saw the leaderboard.

As was expected, Twiggy Barker was at the top of the list, followed by Kai Nenny, Keala Tennelly, and Bongo. Tommy T was number eight, but the kid was less offended than Gerard. There were still two more days of competition and there would be many more opportunities to build on the day's success.

Connie met him with a kiss, her cheeks red, a radio in each hand. In addition to being the wave whisperer, she had to cover Gerard's duties while he was out on the water. Gerard was shot, but the couple hung around until all the surfers were in safe and Gerard was asked to take the bullhorn and wrap the first day of the competition.

"Thank you for a great day, everyone," he said, the bullhorn crackling. "The weather looks less than stellar tomorrow, so let's plan on an off day." The crowd didn't cheer for that, but Gerard knew the business owners in town would think he was a hero. His stomach knotted. Was he taking a chance dragging things out?

He looked out at the cutter where it floated on the western horizon, the ship's communication array piercing the setting sun. What was another day?

**When he got home**, he grilled burgers and the Noll family settled in for a quiet night of popcorn and T.V. The entire family needed to get away from the chaos of the competition, especially Gerard.

When the kids shuffled off to dreamland, Gerard read his email and he was sorry he hadn't gone to bed straight away.

There was an email from Ray. The message itself was a crossed fingers emoji, and a PDF was attached. Gerard opened the file. It was an article from the Chinook Observer dated October 18, 2023. His saltwater-burned eyes stung as he read.

### RABID GREAT WHITE SHARK TERRORIZES WILLAPA BAY

SEAL POPULATION UNDER THREAT

by Sarah Thompson, Staff Writer

In a horrifying turn of events, Willapa Bay, a picturesque inlet nestled along the Pacific Coast, has become the epicenter of a nightmare. Residents and wildlife experts alike are reeling from the onslaught of a rabid great white shark that's terrorizing the local seal population and sending shockwaves through the coastal community.

The tranquility of the bay was shattered when reports first surfaced of a series of brutal attacks on seals. Eyewitnesses described scenes of chaos and panic as the enormous predator targeted unsuspecting seals with unprecedented ferocity. Local authorities were quick to respond, deploying marine patrols and warning beachgoers to stay vigilant. The shark exhibited extremely bizarre and erratic behavior. Instead of its customary stealthy approach, the beast attacked straight on with a ferocity seldom seen.

"This is unlike anything we've ever seen," remarked marine biologist Dr. Emily Alvarez, who has been monitoring the bay's ecosystem for over a decade. "Great white sharks are apex predators, but this level of aggression and recklessness is highly unusual. It's evident that something is seriously wrong."

Local fisherman Jake Thompson was one of the first to witness the carnage. "It was like something out of a nightmare," he recalled. "The shark came out of nowhere, thrashing and snapping at anything in its path. The seals didn't stand a chance."

Authorities were quick to respond to the crisis, dispatching a team of marine biologists and wildlife experts to assess the situation. Their findings were both shocking and deeply troubling. The prevailing theory among experts is that the great white shark has contracted a viral disease which caused the shark's erratic behavior and aggression.

"We suspect that the shark may have come into contact with an infected mammal, possibly a seal or sea lion," explained Dr. Alvarez. "Like a form of rabies, we think this disease can cause neurological damage, leading to disorientation and hyper-aggression. In the case of a predator like a great white shark, the consequences can be catastrophic."

"This is unprecedented," remarked Dr. Emily Stevens, lead marine biologist for the Willapa Bay Marine Research Institute. "It's as if the shark's very nature has been twisted."

As news of the shark attacks spread, panic has gripped the residents of Willapa Bay and surrounding communities. Beaches once filled with sunbathers and surfers now lay deserted, as fear of further attacks keeps people home. The once-thriving tourism industry, which relied heavily on the bay's natural beauty, has ground to a halt as visitors have canceled their reservations and fled for safer shores.

The plight of the seals has drawn widespread concern, with conservationists scrambling to assess the impact of the attacks on the vulnerable population. Willapa Bay is home to a thriving community of harbor seals, whose numbers have already been dwindling due to habitat loss and human activity.

"These attacks couldn't have come at a worse time for the seals," lamented marine conservationist James Carter. "They're already facing numerous threats, and now they have to contend with a rabid predator on top of everything else. It's heartbreaking to witness."

For the seals that call the bay home, the threat of further attacks looms large, forcing them to retreat to safer waters in search of refuge.

Meanwhile, efforts to contain the rabid shark proved to be a daunting challenge. Traditional methods of shark control, such as nets and baited traps, were ineffective. Even attempts to tranquilize the shark were met with no success, as its heightened state of agitation made it impossible to hit with a medical dart. Marine patrols continue to monitor the bay, warning fishermen and recreational boaters to exercise caution in the waters.

"The situation in Willapa Bay underscores the interconnectedness of marine ecosystems and the urgent need for proactive conservation measures," remarked Dr. Alvarez. "We can't afford to wait until crises like this one occur—we need to take decisive action to protect our oceans and the creatures that inhabit them."

As the sun sets over the troubled waters of Willapa Bay, one thing is clear: until the rabid great white shark is brought under control, the residents of this once-peaceful community will continue to live in fear of the predator that lurks beneath the surface.

**Gerard pounded the ESC** key a bit too hard, and the loud crack echoed through the room. He leaned back in his chair, tension heating his stomach and poking at the underside of his skin. A drink would be nice—but he kept his ass planted on his desk chair. Had things reached a critical level? Was there even a way to answer such a question?

The thing was, the sea was filled with things that could cut, poke, slice, impale, and kill a human, regardless of whether or not said person respected the ocean and its strength. Danger always lurked beneath the waves. Just ask Bethany Hamilton. At the tender age of thirteen, while surfing off the coast of Kauai, Hawaii, a fourteen-foot tiger shark attacked her, severing her left arm just below the shoulder. Despite this harrowing experience, Bethany refused to let it define her. She returned to surfing a month after the attack, adapting her technique to accommodate her physical changes.

Gerard straightened and tried to gather his courage, but it felt more like selfishness.

Beyond her athletic achievements, Bethany established the Friends of Bethany Hamilton Foundation to support shark attack survivors and amputees, spreading hope and encouragement through her motivational speaking engagements and charitable work.

But she never said, "Don't surf!" Even as an old woman she still surfed, and if he asked her what he should do she would tell him competitors have to compete, and that big wave surfing was insane anyway, so if a shark got you, what of it?

A sizzle buzzed through the room, and the bulb in his desk lamp winked and sputtered out, plunging the room into darkness.

# 15

The sun was hot enough to make a shadow sweat.

Tattered clouds fleeted across the sky, the dark remnants of the prior day's rain showers. A real storm was moving in, and a faint line of white clouds marched across the western horizon. The buzz of the Coast Guard drone carried over the water, and gulls shrieked and fought. With the offshore breeze nonexistent, and a strong trade wind pushing east, the waves were long, flat rollers that broke with the inconsistent suddenness of a rogue volcano. The rides were short, severe, and often tragic.

Gerard and Tommy T had already witnessed three rescues on this day, one of which was quite serious.

Twiggy Barker launched off the top of a forty-five-footer and he didn't stop falling until he hit the base of the wave. Then the monster closed-out on him, and for over two minutes rescue personnel searched as Connie and others sitting atop K2 frantically tried to spot Twiggy. When he popped up through the dirty white foam he was stunned and gasping for air. Once on the sled he waved his partner in and was done for the day.

While less dramatic, the other two wipeouts were equally as dangerous. When a wave broke in The Funnel, the surge of water was squeezed into the cove, and the height and force of the deluge increased until it hit the shallows. A dangerous proposition for a surfer caught in its violent flow.

The middle rides of a competition were normally considered foundation runs. You built on your successes of the first day, or you eliminated failures by doing better. The middle rounds also set up the finale. On the last day, those on the bottom of the leaderboard surfed with reckless abandon, while the leaders did their best to get their runs in without wiping out or making any major mistakes.

Tommy T was in the middle of the pack, which meant he needed to be careful and reckless at the same time. He needed to take chances and calculated risks, but couldn't do anything stupid and risk slipping in the standings. If he caught a good wave and had the best ride of the day, he could find himself in the top three going into the final round of competition.

But it wasn't all about the skill, conditions, and timing. Gerard had seen the pressure take down more experienced riders, and when it came to surfing competitions, they weren't truly over until Poseidon sang.

Gerard was confident in the kid, though, and as the sun baked the Pacific, the crackle of the announcer on the beach carrying over the surf, he was happy with how things had gone thus far. The decision to be Tommy T's partner had been the right one. It was good to be back out on the water, and even though his nerves still jangled, it was becoming less so each time he ventured out.

He recalled his first competition and Gerard tried to put himself in Tommy T's shoes. It was the kid's first major competition, and it was in his hometown. Money was money, and a $50,000 purse would change any of the young surfers' lives, but the bragging rights Tommy T would win could carry him for the rest of his life.

Tommy T was lying on his board, hands knitted behind his head, eyes closed as if he didn't have a care in the world. Gerard knew better than most that early success could do as much damage as good. It was a treacherous thing when the highlight of your life came at eighteen, and you spent the rest of your days scaling an unattainable peak. Some use early successes as stepping stones, like one-armed surfer Bethany Hamilton.

But others, as adversity reared its ugly head as it always did, used their past successes to justify their current actions and failures. Not a sustainable way to live. Gerard knew from personal experience.

The squawk of Connie's voice snapped him out of his daydream. "Huge set rolling in about fifteen back."

Gerard glanced at his dive watch. They might have time to come back out and get one more run, but if they got a big one here, they could call it a day and rest on their laurels until the final day of competition.

He whistled and Tommy T got into position.

Anticipation is a strong sensation. It made a person forget their situation, the odds, and the dangers they faced. With his heart racing with excitement, his nerves tap dancing on his spine, and nausea teasing his stomach, Gerard twisted the throttle, and the ski darted forward.

The ride wasn't epic, but the wave crested at almost fifty feet, one of the biggest in the competition so far. The run strengthened Tommy T's position and when the pair hit the beach, they discovered Tommy T was in third place.

As the sun went down the rain came in buckets.

Everyone ran to their cars, more in an attempt to be one of the first to hit the local food and drink establishments than to get out of the rain, which was warm and refreshing. Gerard and Tommy T rinsed off in the rain as they stripped out of their wetsuits before climbing into the back of Tommy T's van for a beer. The partners discussed the day's runs and what they both could have done better.

Gerard had shaken off the rust, and he had put Tommy T on the best waves, in the best position, with the perfect momentum that allowed the young surfer to take full advantage of the monsters The Funnel produced. The kid had surfed the break his entire life, and now it was paying off.

"I can't thank you enough," Tommy T said as he drained the last of his beer, reached for another, and then thought better of it. "I have to drive."

Gerard nodded as he smiled. It brought him so much pleasure seeing Tommy T, Bongo, and the others growing up and taking on the responsibilities of adulthood. Tommy T knew what would happen if he got a DWI or worse, hurt someone while driving under the influence, and he'd decided not to take the risk. It was almost comical. The kid risked his life regularly, but when it came to hurting the town, the competition, or his friends, the code of law was paramount.

The next day Gerard woke at dawn to the crack of thunder. The storm was raging, and it wasn't expected to peter out until noonish the following day, so he set the final day of competition for Friday.

Though it was unavoidable, the delay further cemented Gerard's status as the unofficial mayor of Liigei Too. With the beach closed, the bars, restaurants, and entertainment venues were packed, and the money was flowing. Gerard wasn't a fan of crowds, so he stayed away from Jolene's, but with the kids in school and Connie tied up with her normal tasks and routine, he found himself sitting in the parking lot overlooking Purgatory Beach, a thick layer of misty fog hanging just above the storm surf.

He sipped a beer, the windows cracked open, the thunderous roar of the sea driving out all other sounds. Large clumps of seaweed, pieces of driftwood, and mountains of white dirty foam covered the beach as the storm thrashed the Pacific and churned up its bottom. Waves broke in every direction, a chaotic jumble of huge whitecaps that even hardcore river kayakers would find unenjoyable.

Raindrops slid down the windshield, creating thin channels, and the seat squeaked as Gerard shifted position. Phantom pain raced up his leg, the memory of the incident never far away.

Why did people do this? Why had he? The angry sea pounded the shoreline with relentless force. A power that killed. There had been three deaths at The Funnel since he'd re-discovered the break, though all three had been surfers who had gotten in over their heads. True daredevils, while reckless in action and appearance, were in truth calculated individuals who knew their limits, and understood there were things they didn't know.

The G-wagon's windows were fogging, and he started the vehicle and turned on the heat. There were no answers to these questions, he knew, and yet as he stared at the sea, he thought perhaps that was the point. The unknown was part of the thrill, and when the feeling... the burn of doing something that few others can do overtook him it was like nothing he'd ever experienced.

A huge wave closed-out and the subsequent explosion jarred him into motion, and with one last glance at Purgatory Beach, he headed for home.

**The last day of** The Funnel Big Wave Competition was overcast, humid, and low energy. The sun was like a battery charger, and with it in hiding, the competitors, volunteers and spectators were sullen and downcast. Fog hovered over the water, but Gerard had assured everyone it would burn off before the day's runs started.

True to his promise, Ray had positioned the coastie cutter offshore, and he'd dropped a couple of patrol boats and the drone buzzed in the sky. Safety personnel were in position, the surfers were ready to ride, and as the opening horn sounded the first group of competitors took turns taking their final runs.

Tommy T and Gerard waited with Bongo, Glenda, and the others at the marina. The sun peeked through the clouds, and true to his prediction, the mist burned off. The group broke up when they heard the faint sound of the horn declaring the first group was done.

Gerard took the opportunity to lay some advice on Tommy T. He was fully invested now, and bringing the win home to Liigei Too was the only thing on his mind. He said, "We're going to be patient. More patient than either of us has ever been. Today isn't about quantity, but quality. If I can put you on the biggest wave of the day, you might have a chance."

As the first group of surfers straggled into the marina, the outgoing group learned that a bottom-of-the-leaderboard surfer named Amy Toth had ridden a fifty-five-foot wave to completion, and she'd jumped way up in the standings.

"Don't think about it," Gerard told Tommy T as he slipped on his inflatable life jacket and pulled free its yellow activation handle. He put on his headset and said, "This competition is between you and yourself. Stay focused and don't let the moment get in your head."

Tommy T nodded as he licked his lips. Gerard didn't think he'd ever seen the young man so serious. To win, Tommy T needed to ride loose and free. If he was nervous or thinking too much he wouldn't perform to the best of his ability.

"Listen," Gerard said as he mounted his ski. "I want you to win. You want to win. Most of the town wants you to win. But you know what? If you don't the sun will come up and The Funnel won't disappear. You're young, and you've got many shots at this. Have fun and don't think too much."

Tommy T nodded.

Gerard fired up the Honda and got in line with the other teams who were leaving the marina single file. Skis cackled and screamed as the group headed out to the break, and Connie did a radio check. All was well, and Gerard felt good.

The first sign of trouble came when Gerard saw one of the Coast Guard patrol boats leave its position and race off to the north. Tommy T and Gerard waited in line to get their shot, huge rollers lifting and dropping them on their huge swell. Gerard looked toward the beach, and all appeared well, and at the sight of K2, he thought of Connie.

"Connie, is everything O.K. out here?"

Static, then, "As far as I know. Are you O.K.?"

"Yeah," he lied as he watched the orange Zodiac appear and disappear with the roll of the ocean as it powered north.

The shriek and roar of the crowd on shore and the ensuing warble of the announcer made Gerard shift his attention. Rescue skis pulling sleds raced into The Funnel, a clear sign someone had gone down. He stood on his ski, willing himself to have super-powered vision so he could see what was happening, but there was nothing but sun-drenched walls of furious water.

A siren wailed, and the second coastie Zodiac darted north, running parallel with the waves as it headed for its partner. The drone buzzed overhead, and its shadow trailed the fleeing Zodiac.

Gerard's ski rocked. He slipped and almost fell into the drink, his breath catching in his throat like a fishhook.

The silhouette of a massive shark stained the face of the approaching wave. A tall dorsal fin disappeared into the silvery crest of the wave, a shadowy snout like the tip of a World War II torpedo. As the wave curled and crashed, the shadow shifted between light and darkness, substance and illusion, but the shark's form was unmistakable—the sleek lines of its body, the sharpness of its fins, and the ominous curve of its tail.

For a fleeting moment, the ocean held its breath, then with a thunderous crash, the wave broke, scattering the shadow and leaving behind fists of whitewater and whispers of a near-miss encounter with a formidable predator.

When the water settled the shark was gone.

# 16

Gerard gaped as each rolling wave became a canvas painted with the brilliance of a thousand nightmares.

All his angst and fears and worries surged up his throat in the form of stomach acid, and he coughed as he searched for any sign that would tell him what he'd seen was something more than a mirage, a shadow of fear manifesting in the undulating patterns of the rippling ocean.

Sparkling diamonds emerged from the depths, jewels of light mixed with bubbles that surged through the water and snapped on the surface.

The last month replayed in Gerard's mind's eye like a fast-forward montage. His doubts, worries, and fears all manifested in a shadow. His mouth slid open to say something, but he didn't open a channel to his wife. What would he say? "Hi babe, I just saw the shadow of a shark."

"Did you or did you not see a shark, Gerard?" He could almost hear the sharp bite of his wife's voice.

He sure as shit had seen a shark. Gerard opened a channel. "Connie! Connie!" he screamed.

Then she was there, her voice frantic. "Get out of the water, Gerard. Come in now!"

A gunshot pierced the haze of the crashing waves, and Gerard jerked his head toward the sound.

The two Coast Guard Zodiacs were bow to bow, coasties in bright orange life jackets hustling along the gunnels, a field of dimpled white water surrounding both vessels as silvery scales streaked from the sea.

A horn blasted, prematurely ending the round, and Tommy T sat up, his gaze shifting to the shoreline where spectators stood at the edge of the water frantically waving at the competitors.

"What the hell?" Tommy T said.

"Get ready. We're heading in."

Tommy T's gaze shifted to the west where a steady crop of thirty-foot rollers marched over the Pacific. "I don't see anything, boss," the kid said.

"We're heading in!" Gerard screamed. He gave the kid two seconds before gunning the ski.

A great white shark missiled from the face of an oncoming wave, a dark silhouette of smiling teeth.

Had it not been for the momentum of the ski jerking the towrope and lifting Tommy T, the kid might have become the world's first one-legged surfer. As the towline went taut, the tow bar slipped from Tommy T's hands, and he fell back into the drink.

The fifteen-foot behemoth breached from the sea, mouth flexed open in search of prey. Jaws filled with crooked rows of razor-sharp teeth missed Tommy T and his board and clamped down on the towrope.

Gerard twisted the ski's throttle and its engine whined, the towline taut and holding the wave runner in place.

The shark thrashed, and the towline twanged as it was severed.

With a screech, the ski punched through a mound of whitewater.

Gerard looked back, sweat dripping into his eyes, panic surging through him. Tommy T crawled back on his board, and the tall dorsal fin between them disappeared into the Pacific.

There was a moment of stunned silence and Gerard heard nothing but the beating of his heart. Slowly the world came back online: his ears ringing, the crash of the waves, the shriek of the spectators, the staticky drone of the announcer.

Then Connie was in his head again. "Are you all right? What are you waiting for?"

What was he waiting for?

There was no question about what needed to be done. Gerard twisted the ski's handlebars, made a tight turn, and the ski skidded across the rolling sea as he headed back to grab Tommy T.

Gerard's gaze shifted to the melee occurring to the northwest where the two Coastie boats had their hands full. Fish launched from the ocean and the sailors pounded them away using their bare hands, gaffs, knives, and guns. Firing in close quarters on a boat with inflatable gunnels was less than desirable, and the targets appeared to be everywhere.

Tommy T shrieked.

The tip of a dorsal fin broke the surface as a shark rose from the depths, a churning white wake behind it.

Gerard wished he had a gun, but he didn't. What he did have was a five-hundred-pound water cycle, and as he put the ski on a collision course with the shark he goosed the throttle.

Gunshots carried over the water. One of the Coast Guard Zodiacs was sagging in the water, several large fish locked on the vessel's orange inflatable gunnel, their tails thrashing back and forth as teeth sank into rubber.

Tommy T slid back onto his board, lifting its tip and using his fiberglass blade as a shield.

The dark shadow of the apex predator filled the Pacific, the five-foot dorsal fin casting a long shadow over Tommy T.

With a battle cry he didn't recall summoning, Gerard rammed the shark with the ski as it surged from the water.

The collision knocked the giant shark off course as the wave rolled through, and the shark, Tommy T, and Gerard on his ski were forced deeper into the breakers.

A knot of whitewater crashed into Gerard as he fought for control of the floundering wave runner.

Tommy T was wailing as he stroked wildly, his board dragging behind him, its leash wrapped around his leg.

The whitewater spat the ski out and Gerard was driven toward shore. He heard Tommy T's frantic cries, and he wanted to call out to the kid. Tell him to stop making so much noise, but as he watched, the dorsal fin made a sharp turn and headed straight at the kid.

Gerard brought the ski around, but he could see there was nothing he could do. He screamed, his throat stinging as he released all his frustration. His decision had led Tommy T here—the kid had trusted him. All the competitors had, and he had failed them.

Twenty feet away, under the glare of the sun, Gerard watched the fifteen-foot shark surge to the surface, its gray body glistening. The shark's eyes were hidden behind their protective membranes, but that didn't stop the beast from using its other highly-tuned senses to lock in on its prey.

As the shark's caudal fin powered the fish forward, the creature's jaws flexed open, and rows of sharp, triangular teeth met flesh.

Tommy T shrieked as the shark's jaws clamped down on his flailing legs.

Terror gripped Gerard, and he shouted, but he couldn't hear himself over the cries of his partner. A terrible dread overcame him, and Gerard dry heaved, strands of spittle hanging from his mouth as he realized that help wasn't going to arrive in time.

Tommy T fell silent as the shark thrashed and tore his leg free before sinking back into the chaotic sea. His board was shattered, and Tommy T's broken body lay half on the destroyed board, the stumps of his severed legs hanging in the water. A crimson cloud stained the sea around the kid as he passed out, his lifeless body slipping off the board into the water. He floated listlessly on the surface amidst a blood slick speckled with fat and skin.

Rage set Gerard's stomach ablaze, his vision growing blurry, his head pounding, his muscles aching with tension. He turned the ski as he manipulated the throttle, the ski kicking up spray. If he could get

Tommy T on the rescue ski, get him back to land, he could… But his hope betrayed him as the cloud of blood grew and the shark made another strafing run.

The huge predator was driven by the scent of blood lighting up its advanced olfactory senses and calling on centuries of aggression and refinement.

A smiling mouth of glowing white teeth pushed from the sea and crunched what remained of Tommy T and his board. The air hissed as a knot of whitewater obscured the carnage, gray skin, blood, and thrashing whiteness mounding above the waterline.

An arm hung from the shark's jaws as it slithered from the whitewater and passed beneath the ski.

Shock and loss paused Gerard's adrenaline-laden muscles, tears welling in his eyes, grief stinging his throat.

A shove from below catapulted Gerard from the ski.

The wave runner continued to race across the water for a second before the safety lanyard attached to Gerard's life jacket went taut and tugged on the emergency kill switch and the motor fell dead.

Gerard vaulted through the air and landed in a slick of hot oil. It covered his face as he struggled to stay above the surface, shards of broken bone, gristle, frayed flesh, and blood floating in the water around him. He sucked in a panicked breath, then gagged and spit, forcing out the blood-laden seawater, but Gerard swallowed some of the tainted water—pieces of Tommy T.

Revulsion eating his insides, muscles cramping, Gerard stroked hard for the ski. That was his only hope. He needed to get out of the water. Fast. There would be time to mourn Tommy T, to say all the things that clouded his mind. How the kid had been fearless. Determined, but how his ethics made him a good competitor and a good friend. Gerard bit his lip as he swam. He didn't know how he was going to get over this. He literally had Tommy T's blood on his hands.

Shouts and screaming engines echoed over the water, and Gerard spared a glance north.

The coastie boats were untangled, the field of tiny whitecaps was gone, and the undamaged Zodiac was racing toward him. A line of skis towing surfers trailed toward the marina, and Gerard realized he was the last one on the break. The rescue skis were gone, but it was then he noticed the drone hanging in the air above him. He pictured Ray sitting in his command chair, watching him fight for his life.

As if his friend had read his mind, Gerard heard the whine of a helicopter engine spark to life and the *womp womp* of airfoils beating the air brought hope. The coasties were experts at water rescues, and all he had to do was stay alive until they hauled him from the drink.

The shark appeared in the water before him, and Gerard stopped splashing.

*Carcharodon carcharias*, the ocean's most feared apex predator, was renowned for its formidable appearance and powerful hunting abilities. The beast's sleek, blue-gray torpedo-shaped body slid through the sea just below the surface, as if waiting for Gerard to make a move. Its massive, tapered head housed rows of serrated, triangular teeth, each meticulously crafted for seizing and tearing apart prey, its muscular jaws capable of extending forward to deliver a decisive bite. The great white's dorsal fin rose ominously from the rolling sea, its pectoral fins, located on either side of its body, hanging still. Along the shark's sides, a series of five lateral gill slits puffed and heaved, allowing the beast to extract oxygen from the water as it perpetually moved in its quest for sustenance.

As if he had some superpower he'd previously been unaware of, Gerard considered standing his ground. The ski was twenty feet away, rolling with the waves, and if he didn't reach it soon it would be washed away toward shore by a breaking wave.

But he brushed the thought away as fast as it appeared. Punching a shark in the face only happened in movies, and even if he'd had his dive knife strapped to his leg—which he didn't—taking on a fifteen-foot missile of muscle with a mouth of razor blades didn't sound like fair odds. But if he swam hard for the ski, the motion would alert the shark, and that would be game over.

Gerard tread water in the surging sea, thinking maybe he'd be washed ashore if he pretended to be a piece of trash and did nothing.

The shark would have none of that. It pushed to the surface, jaws flexing, bloody teeth bared.

Two gunshots rang out and two fountains of water sprouted from the sea between Gerard and the shark.

The great white dove.

Gerard saw his opportunity and he stroked for the ski.

The engines of the approaching Coast Guard Zodiac roared, and Gerard thought about the expensive bottle of wine that was coming Ray's way—or at least the marksman who had saved his life. Coasties weren't known for their marksmanship, but whoever had fired the rifle, from five hundred yards distant, the sea rolling beneath his feet, deserved an award and Gerard would see that the seaman got it.

After what seemed like a mile of intense swimming, but was only twenty feet which Gerard covered in seconds, he reached the ski. He crawled onto the rescue sled and pulled himself into a sitting position atop the ski.

The shark's tall dorsal fin scythed through the ocean, coming right at the wave runner.

Gerard frantically tried to fit the emergency toggle back onto the ignition switch, but the cord was tangled. With shaking hands, he untangled the cord, forced the plastic lanyard onto the ignition housing, and started the motor.

As Gerard turned the ski around, he gunned the throttle.

An all-encompassing shadow consumed him, and Gerard looked back to find a wall of water towering over him. The wave lifted the ski as Gerard fought with the handlebars, but it was too late.

The wave drove him forward and closed-out with a thunderous roar, and then Gerard was cartwheeling through the air, blue sky, dark water, and dirty foam spinning across his field of vision.

# 17

"Get out of the water, Gerard. Come in now!" Connie yelled into her radio as she bounded down the side of K2, an unstoppable knot of terror and strength that cleared a path through the crowd of spectators. The tourists practically dove out of her way, but as the panic fled, Connie skidded to a halt. She needed to see. She was a spotter. The wave whisperer.

Connie spun around and bounded back the way she'd come, the onlookers staring at her in confusion. When she reached the top of K2 she pressed the binoculars to her eyes, but all she saw was churning white foam.

Derrick appeared at her side and asked, "What is it?"

"There's a shark out there. A big one."

The sheriff lifted his binoculars but said nothing.

Connie panned her binoculars over The Funnel, searching the sparkling water and dirty foam. Then she found him. Gerard was standing on his ski staring toward Tommy T who she couldn't see, but she did see the kid's board. "What the hell?" she muttered to herself before she opened a channel and said, "Are you all right? What are you waiting for?"

The next several minutes played out like a slow-moving nightmare.

Gerard was on his ski.

A wall of water obscured him from view.

Then he wasn't on his ski. Connie shrieked a strangled cry that made Derrick put a soothing hand on her shoulder.

"Now they're both in the drink," she said.

Huge rollers marched into The Funnel, hiding Gerard every other second. Like a movie missing frames, Connie watched in horror as Gerard swam desperately for his ski, a tall dorsal fin rising from the water like the specter of death itself.

"Yes!" she screamed when Gerard climbed back onto the ski. Her eye sockets throbbed with pain as she pressed the binoculars harder into her eyes as if the pain would somehow take her closer to her husband.

Gerard's success was short-lived.

There was blood in the water, and she no longer saw Tommy T.

"Jesus," Derrick said. "Gerard is covered…"

"In blood. What's he waiting for?" she screeched.

The dorsal fin was coming right at the ski, but still her husband hadn't moved.

"Yes!" Derrick said as the ski surged into motion.

"No!" Connie yelled as a huge wall of water rose from the Pacific like Poseidon was angry and coming to destroy everything that called land home.

The massive wave lifted Gerard and the ski, and as Gerard fought with the wave runner's handlebars Connie thought he would manage to maneuver the ski over the crest of the wave, but it wasn't to be.

As the wave broke, Gerard, along with his ski, was plowed under a mountain of water that rose like a swelling river as it raced through The Funnel toward Purgatory Beach.

A chill colder than any scare she'd ever experienced washed over her and the clock in her head started ticking. It was now all about air. Gerard's air clock used to have a limit of four minutes—beyond that... She didn't want to think about what Gerard's current limit was. Two minutes? Maybe? As she searched the angry whitewater she saw no sign of her husband.

Rescue skis whined as the wave runners fought through the watery tumult, buzzing in and out, avoiding the constant barrage of the relentless sea.

Thirty seconds and still no sign of Gerard.

Images of the crash in Potrero Grande played through her head, all the doubts and fears rushing back like the tide. The kids. What would she do without Gerard? Pain and joy and fear and apprehension all rolled into a tight ball that knotted her stomach. A fresh start. Shame washed through her, but then she reminded herself she couldn't control the crazy thoughts that clogged her head, she could only control her actions.

One minute and still no sign of Gerard.

A hush had fallen over the crowd, and all the surfers who had made it in, all the fans and staff and media, stood on the beach staring at the ocean. Wave runners screamed, waves thundered, and the pounding of Connie's heart drove out the incessant squawking leaking from her radio.

Ninety seconds. Gerard's ski appeared, tumbling in the whitewater as it battled toward shore, but there was still no sign of Gerard. The Coast Guard drone streaked toward the ski, but Gerard still hadn't appeared.

Connie had once met the husband of a police officer in an airport and struck up a conversation as people do when they're forced to sit around for hours. The man's wife was an LA beat cop. Not easy duty by any measure. It had been heartbreaking listening to the man describe the constant fear he felt whenever his wife was working, the idea that every time she put on the uniform might be the last time he saw her alive.

She'd understood. Seeing Gerard race down the face of an eighty-foot wave was akin to watching an astronaut sitting atop a rocket that would vaporize said astronaut if a tiny part made by the lowest bidder decided to pick an inopportune time to fail. That's all it took when you were riding on the edge. One bump. One slip, and you were being sucked into a void so deep the darkness drove out all hope of survival.

Two minutes.

Connie's skin tingled, pain cramping her heart. She pictured the man she loved getting tossed and pulled like a pair of underwear in a washing machine. What must he be thinking as his lungs burned and stars appeared on the dark canvas of his eyelids? Was he thinking of her? The kids? The wave that got away? Or the woman?

She screamed when she found Gerard bobbing in the whitewater. He was being driven toward the jetty of rocks that lined the northern edge of The Funnel.

Connie opened a channel and started screaming instructions and describing her husband's location. Shark aside, if the rescuers didn't get to Gerard fast, he'd be dashed upon the mussel-encrusted stones.

**Derrick could breathe again** but he felt helpless. He let his binoculars fall to his chest and shielded his eyes from the glaring sun.

The Pacific wasn't part of his jurisdiction—his little department didn't own a boat—but that hadn't stopped Nayeli from successfully campaigning for a rental vessel so the sheriff's office could have some eyes out on the water. The staties offered to send a boat, but Nayeli was familiar with her family's twenty-one-foot center console. She knew its quirks, and there wasn't much difference between her vessel and the twenty-four-foot aluminum runner the state sheriff's office wanted to send.

Derrick had relented, and he had to admit not only was it a good idea, but he liked the fact that Nayeli was taking the initiative. He was getting more comfortable every day with supporting her for sheriff in a couple of years when he hung up his spurs.

Connie was fully engaged in trying to get the rescuers to her husband, so he stepped out of earshot and called Nayeli. She picked up on the first ring.

"I think coasties have got him, but I'm moving in as backup if we're needed," she said without prompting.

Derrick smiled. He'd taught her well. "What's your position?"

"We're at the end of the jetty just beyond the break."

And that's exactly where he wanted her to stay. "Get in as tight as you can, but don't go anywhere near The Funnel. No matter what happens. Do you understand?" Most boats of any significant size couldn't survive in The Funnel for long.

"Copy that."

"Keep me informed." He closed the connection and pressed the binoculars to his eyes again. "Come on, Gerard," he muttered. "Get this done."

**Lieutenant Raymond "Ray" Tantillo** was standing on the forward observation deck of the USCGC Robert Ward, watching two of his Zodiacs tangle with a field of angry fish, when Connie's plea to Gerard roared from the radio. He had two radios clipped to his belt, along with his sidearm, which he rarely carried. The lieutenant's gaze shifted to The Funnel, where Gerard and others appeared and disappeared with the roll of the ocean.

When someone shrieked that Gerard and Tommy T were being attacked by a great white shark, Ray turned tail and ran for a patrol boat. He spoke with the captain via radio as he jogged, and though there was no reason for him to be out there, the captain knew his connection to the tournament and approved the request. Ray enlisted the first two sailors he came across and Seaman First Class Linda Darcy and Seaman Second Class Wes Ropey joined the party.

The trio arrived at the stern launching ramp out of breath and panting. Both Ray's radios were chirping with people stepping on each other's transmissions as everyone tried to help. As he waited for two coasties to untether their ride from the ramp cleats, he recalled that after the attacks on the Twin Towers on 9/11 fire departments from all over the region had raced to the scene, only to be sent home sans equipment. Though it was hard to quantify, there was such a thing as too much help. Things got crowded, and chains of command were jeopardized.

Ray and his two helpers climbed aboard an aluminum response runabout. The vessel had a powerful waterjet engine and a seaable pilothouse, which allowed the boat to Eskimo roll and remain viable.

The front of the ramp lifted and tilted the vessel toward the sea as the plow-like barrier straps sang and the hydraulic arms on the sides of the ramp drove the boat toward the water.

Ray slipped on his life vest and clipped his safety line onto a cleat jutting from the side of the command console. His mates SEA1 Linda

Darcy and SEA2 Wes Ropey did the same, and when the coastie working the ramp's controls asked if Ray was ready for launch, he gave a thumbs up and said, "Hold on!"

A buzzer sounded and the boat was released. The vessel slid backward, the metal hull squeaking on the rubber launch treads as the boat slipped off the back of the cutter into the Pacific.

The boat landed with a shuddering crash within a fist of whitewater. Using the launching ramp was easier when the cutter wasn't steaming forward at twenty-five knots. Seawater surged over the gunwales and drained away as Wes spun up the motor and headed toward the fray.

A gust of reeking wind pushed over the Pacific, and the twenty-four-foot craft dipped into a valley between waves as its hull bounced, throwing thick spray. With a bone-rattling shudder, the boat jumped the crest of a wave and Ray saw that the two Coast Guard Zodiacs had separated. One was disabled and the other was assisting the competitors as they fled.

As Gerard struggled with the ski's handlebars Ray watched a wave rise and obscure Gerard from view as heat spread through him and pain lashed his stomach.

When the next wave rolled in Gerard and the ski were gone.

Ray struggled to find his friend in the churning mass of water. "Shit!" he screamed.

"Orders, sir?" asked Wes.

Ray could tell by the tone of the kid's voice he wanted to take them into The Funnel, and Ray's skin itched with the thought of it.

He looked back and found the Coast Guard Zodiac protecting a line of surfers and skis that refused to head in. They stood on wave runners and sat on boards, staring into the melee.

The surfers reminded Ray of geese. He'd been on the golf course once—he couldn't remember where, but one of the holes ran along a narrow bay. Captain Utah had hit a worm-burner, and the ball had sizzled across the tightly cut grass and smacked right into a goose. The thing fell over dead like it had been shot in the head. That was what they'd thought, anyway, and it turned out they were wrong.

Geese came from all over the course, waddling from within the water reeds and jumping from water hazards until the downed bird was surrounded by over a hundred of its mates.

Then as if the group had performed some goose-miracle, the injured bird got up and ran off, seemingly unharmed. Its work done, the army of geese had dispersed.

Those instincts ran deep in surfers. The idea that you don't leave your friends when they're down, and no surfer is ever left behind, even competitors who hated each other, and would throw elbows while fighting to race down the face of a forty-foot wave.

That's why he loved to surf, though he'd never been any good. The camaraderie and conversations while sitting out there on dark mornings, waiting for the ocean to do its thing. There wasn't much to do between sets except sit with your thoughts or talk with the other twenty fools floating in the grayness around you.

One of Ray's radios squawked. It was Connie. Gerard was up and she was telling everyone his location. "He's being pulled toward the jetty," she screamed. Ray knew Connie well, and his stomach knotted when he recognized the fear in her voice.

Ray tried to find his friend in the whiteness, but he couldn't. He rolled his shoulders and cracked his neck. Going into The Funnel could be deadly, but as he glanced at the line of surfers and skis eager to enter the fight, shame washed over him, though it fled fast. He had his family to think about. Still… He knew what Gerard would do if their places were reversed.

"Linda, come in the pilothouse so we can seal it up," Ray yelled. "Wes, take us into The Funnel."

# 18

Gerard faceplanted on the churning sea, a swarm of phantom bees stinging his face as his headset was torn off.

For two heartbeats Gerard tumbled across the face of the breaking wave, and as the white noise of tons of pressure bore down on him, Gerard squeezed his eyes closed.

He taught young surfers the key to injury-free wipeouts was to let the ocean do with you as it willed. This is a hard concept to grasp. Especially when dealing with an untamed wild source of energy that could snuff a person out as fast as dropping a lit match into a glass of water. But it was part of the religion. Letting go. Learning that the sea was more powerful than you, by an infinite measure, and if you were going to mess with it and ride its rails, you needed to give it control and trust in its grace.

He was seaweed. A twig. An old blanket. A dead body. Because that was what he would become if Gerard fought the whitewater.

As the wave crashed down on him, Gerard went totally slack, yoga style. He focused on doing nothing, being a relaxed octopus floating on a gentle current.

The sharp sound of streaming bubbles and distant thunder filled his head, and he felt himself being drawn deeper… deeper… and deeper still.

Gerard almost laughed as he released some of the air stored in his lungs. Hadn't it been just the other day that he'd asked himself how long he could hold his breath? An estimate on his mental clock as he lay in the river, staring up at the stars, lungs burning after thirty seconds.

Water blasted up his nose and fought to get into his head via his ears and mouth. His eyes were still pressed tightly closed, and tiny sparks of light appeared on the black canvas of his vision. His legs were twisted, his arms yanked and pulled, and his body contorted as it was thrashed.

As he was pulled downward the realization that his worst fear had come to pass filled him with the heat of failure. It was his fault Tommy T was dead. Nobody else's. His. He could have called off the tournament—there had been many signs of impending danger. Yet he and Connie, the mayor, the sheriff, and the coasties had ignored what was right in front of them. The contest had been considered paramount to the prosperity of the town, and now a kid was dead because of it. As the sea hammered him, he thought perhaps he was getting what he deserved.

The water pressure eased, and his arms and legs ceased being jerked around. The stars speckling his vision had grown larger, and his lungs burned with a faint reminder that his clock was ticking. Fast.

His thoughts strayed to his wife, and he thought she might be better off without him. This wasn't a new idea. It tormented him continuously, to the point he'd voiced the thought to Connie, who had stared at him for several long moments before shaking her head and leaving him alone. Thing was, whether she wanted to admit it or not, she and the kids would be just fine if he wasn't in the picture. After an appropriate amount of time had passed, there would be a line of men vying for Connie's attention, and many of those men would have money that would allow Connie and the kids to live life any way they chose. Sure, they'd miss him, maybe even put a flower on his empty grave every year on his birthday, but would they be better off?

Gerard's lungs burned, an intense tingling spreading through him as his body was deprived of oxygen and the unreleased carbon dioxide polluted his system. His muscles throbbed with distant pain as they tightened and cramped.

He hung in the water, his body righting itself as he let more air escape his reserve. When he hung straight in the water, he felt himself floating up. Gerard looked in the direction he believed to be down and saw nothing but swirling blackness.

A glow, a corpse light, a light that illuminated nothing hung above his head, but it was so far away Gerard wasn't sure if he was imagining it.

Time was running out and the realization that he wasn't a surfer hit him like a wet fish across the chops. He'd been riding the ski! Gerard found the yellow activation handle on his life jacket and pulled it.

The CO2 cartridge injected air into the vest and Gerard was yanked toward the surface. Pain knotted his head, but the thought of Connie spotting his corpse floating in the shallows of The Funnel was too much to bear. He stroked and kicked the sea, his vest pulling him up as he forced more air from his lungs, his vision filling with starbursts that frayed dark at the edges.

He saw Sage's face in his mind's eye. His son was just getting into surfing, and he felt pride, exhilaration, frustration, and an all-encompassing fear. Should kids play tackle football given what is now known about head trauma? Should you let your child barrel down the face of a thirty-foot wave, wearing no life jacket because it was safer without one? Gerard knew the real question was how could he stop Sage? Nobody had managed to stop him.

The light above grew brighter, but Gerard's lungs were on fire, and a pain akin to a nail being hammered into his head clogged his thoughts and he almost opened his mouth to take a breath.

Instead, he released the last of his air as the inflated vest propelled him upward, the churning water clouding into a haze of bubbles, black strands of seaweed, and the rush of whitewater.

If he wasn't worrying about Sage, it was Willow, but his daughter was a rock in a stream. A steady force like her mother, yet she was so different. She liked the water, but not like the other three members of the family. Her love was for the mountains. When she sat on Purgatory Beach, Gerard often caught her gazing over her shoulder at the tall hills along the shoreline, the outline of the foggy mountains beyond.

Blackness filled the water as something large moved overhead and blocked out the glow of the sun—a boat!

He stroked on, the glow growing like he was approaching the entrance to Heaven. Was he dying? Was he already dead?

With one last push, that was either going to kill him or free him of his watery prison, Gerard broke the surface. He sucked air as he floated in the dirty foam and mountainous whitewater that filled The Funnel, the sun warming him and charging his battery.

A drone flew overhead, hanging in the air as the wind pushed it around, the four propellers on each of the unit's corners buzzing as the drone's camera turned and focused on him.

There was a lull in the action as the tide pulling water back into the sea was met by the onrush of the most recent breaking monster.

The whine of a ski made Gerard jerk his head around, and a blue wave runner towing a rescue ski darted toward him.

Another wave broke, its remnants plowing through The Funnel.

The ski pilot jumped a knot of whitewater, swung the wave runner around, and put the sled right next to Gerard. The move was textbook, but as Gerard heaved himself onto the sled a fist of water bounded into the ski, and it, along with its rider and Gerard was swept away and churned under.

Gerard grunted as the rescue sled was torn from his grasp. He flailed and twisted in the furious water, and when his life vest buoyed him to the surface, he saw the blue ski, sans rider, tumbling in the surf.

Now there were two men trapped in The Funnel.

Someone screamed, and Gerard saw the gray rocks of the northern jetty reaching out to grab him. Another wave crashed through and drove him underwater. A dark shape scythed through the sea, and

Gerard's heart thumped as he recalled the huge great white that had snuffed Tommy T, but whatever had blocked out the sun was much bigger.

Gerard surfaced and a gray metal hull loomed over him. The boat was underway and coming right at him, the vessel gliding so close to his head that the sea moaned as the boat moved past him.

Horror seized him as Gerard was caught in the boat's draft, and he was sucked toward the rear of the boat where he'd be sliced and diced by the propellers. But the coastie runabout was a response vessel and was powered by a waterjet engine, so instead of being chopped up, he was spat out the rear of the boat like a bad clam.

A red life ring tied to a black rope floated in the water and Gerard grabbed it.

Hooting and cheers emanated from the boat, and through the foam, Gerard saw Ray waving at him from within the pilothouse of the Coast Guard vessel.

The celebration didn't last long.

A forty-five-foot monster closed-out and the life ring was torn from his grasp as the surf pounded the coastie boat.

Blackness became Gerard's companion again as he was tossed and beaten, salt stinging his eyes, briny water leaking up his nose and into his mouth and ears. He was pushed closer to the jetty, away from The Funnel's sweet spot.

The life vest ushered Gerard back to the surface, the chaotic snow-like whiteness of dirty foam all around him.

The Coast Guard boat was nowhere to be seen.

Gerard's heart thumped as he looked around in panic, but there was nothing but the churning sun-drenched ocean.

The Coast Guard boat breached from the whitewater like a gray metal orca, and it landed on the tumultuous sea upside-down. It bobbed in the chaos for two long seconds, then it rolled and righted itself, the seawater washing away, the vessel's windshield clearing. Through the glare bouncing off the water, Gerard saw Ray and two other coasties reappear behind the windshield. The boat's engine gurgled, sputtered, then caught, and the vessel advanced.

This time the response boat's helmsman stayed parallel to the incoming waves, and he stayed clear of Gerard as he maneuvered the boat so the life ring would drag past him. The gap between waves was seconds, and as soon as Gerard grabbed the life ring the boat's engine whined, and Gerard was jerked through the water. Seawater plowed into his face, and he turned on his side as he was dragged like a hooked fish.

A harrowing minute followed as the boat moved out to deeper water, the relentless pounding of the waves exploding into The Funnel.

When the coastie vessel knifed through the breakers, and the waves were un-sculpted rollers that lifted and dropped the boat and its passengers, the helmsman slowed and Gerard came to a stop, but only for an instant.

Ray and another coastie came out on deck and began reeling him in.

Gerard didn't try to swim or help. He was spent. Done. Kaput. As he floated, he looked down at his rash guard and life jacket. The dark stains of Tommy T's blood made Gerard sob. Not just for the dead surfer, but for The Funnel Big Wave Competition. He couldn't help but think maybe that was for the best, for everyone. Things always ended badly, or they wouldn't end.

But tourists would still come to surf The Funnel, and life would go on, whether he drove it forward or not.

He was bawling like a baby when Ray and another coastie pulled him from the drink. Voices asked if he was O.K. and the sea screamed for blood because he'd gotten away. Gerard coughed up a lung, gagging and retching, sucking in air like it was wine and he'd just crossed the desert.

Connie. He felt for his headset so he could call his wife, but it was gone. He needed to let her know he was alright, and he tried to push to his feet.

Ray gently drove him back down.

"Connie!" he screamed. "I need to—"

Ray put up a hand. "She knows we've got you. She'll meet us at the marina."

"Thanks," he sputtered. "For everything."

"Don't mention it," Ray said.

"What about the guy who tried to rescue me?" Gerard spit up water and coughed hard.

Ray dropped to his knee and patted Gerard on the back. "They got him. He's fine."

Gerard let his head fall to the deck as he stared up at the blue cloud-streaked sky.

# 19

Gerard listened to the radio traffic as the coastie boat shuttled him to the marina to be checked out by medical personnel. The Coast Guard drone hovered over the attack scene, but the video feed it broadcasted showed no sign of Tommy T other than a few blood-tainted bubbles. There was a plan in place to recover bodies from The Funnel—it had been done, but it was tricky business. He knew that inevitably parts of Tommy T would wash up on Purgatory Beach, but it could take days, even weeks.

The thought of it made the maggots in his stomach buzz. Despite Ray's supportive words, he was embarrassed and ashamed to face the crowd at the dock. Then there was Connie. She would know where his head was, and though she'd be sympathetic, she was also a realist. The Noll family was looking at dark days ahead and his wife knew just how deep Gerard could mine his vein of self-loathing.

Gulls cried, helicopter airfoils beat the air, and the sea spray blanketing the ocean as the boat bounced over the creeping waves hissed and snapped. The tip of the jetty loomed to the east, and the helmsman arced the vessel around the pile of gray stones into the channel. Big waves were building as the tide went out, but there would be no more surfing on this day. The air reeked of sea rot, salt, and anguish.

The Liigei Too Marina was packed but sullen. Skis and boats were in line to be pulled, but most folks sat on their vessels, on the spit of beach at the far end of the marina, or in the parking lot. Joints were being smoked, toasts were being made, and most of the competitors were lost in the "it could have been me and we'll never forget him" game.

Two white Jayhawks streaked overhead, their orange nosecones marking them as coastie birds. Along with the drone, the Coast Guard was putting on a show and making a good-faith effort to find Tommy T, though no units were being sent into The Funnel.

The layout of the marina had been designed with the natural contours of the land in mind. A narrow sand spit beach and the parking lot were on the southern end, and there were permanent docks around the edge of the roughly rectangular harbor. Fingers of floating docks extended into the middle of the marina and many additional docks had been added like extra appendages for the competition overflow. Brown rolling hills boxed the facility in to the north and south, Mattole Road running along its eastern flank.

A spot at the head of the marina at the center of the permanent dock had been left open for Ray's vessel. The coasties had called ahead and told the marina crew Gerard was coming in. A horn sounded as the Coast Guard boat slid into the marina, and the helmsman, whom Gerard had been told was Wes, powered down the motor, slowing the vessel to a crawl.

Like those geese on that golf course all those years ago, surfers, staff, boat captains, TV crew, and talent, Bongo, Glenda, the mayor, Kai Nenny, Keala Tennelly, Twiggy, Derrick, and Nayeli gathered. At their head was Connie, her step quick and her jaw set. The crowd moved as one as Wes docked the coastie boat. Lines were tossed, knots tied around cleats, and the vessel's engine rumbled before going still.

Gerard sucked in a deep breath and stepped out of the pilothouse onto the rear deck.

The crowd erupted in applause. People hooted and screamed, and he heard Connie yell, "I love you, Gerard."

He was growing softer as he grew older, there was no doubt about that. But he wasn't a crier, but as his stomach went supernova and his throat stung with pain, a tear leaked from his right eye. He wiped it away with the back of his hand as he stepped up onto the boat's gunnel and jumped to the dock.

Just like that downed goose, his people surrounded him, some touching him, others only murmuring wishes of hope and redemption. "We'll be back" was the common refrain, but Gerard couldn't find any hope. Not on this day.

Connie threw her arms around him and whispered in his ear, "This wasn't your fault."

But it was.

A medic fought through the crowd and the young doctor in training made Gerard sit and she took his vitals and pronounced him shaken, but otherwise unharmed.

Unharmed. The stabbing pain in his chest said otherwise.

The crowd lingered as they waited for their king to speak. Even Mayor Roxy Templeton felt words—not hers—were needed. She leaned in close and said, "I know it's a lot to ask, Gerard. But..." Words failed her, but he understood. She was the real leader of this group, but good leaders sometimes understood that stepping aside was what was best for the greater good. Gerard often thought the world would be a much better place if politicians understood that, instead of their egos driving them to overstay their welcome.

"Everyone," he yelled when he believed he'd gathered as much courage and wisdom as he currently possessed. "This day..." He choked up. "Most of you know... knew Tommy T. Those who didn't, know he would have surfed today even if he'd known there were ten sharks out there. We would have had to put him in jail."

Chuckles.

"But that doesn't mean we shouldn't mourn him, and there will be a time for that. Just like there will be a time—an appropriate time—to discuss the future of the contest and our town. But I must reiterate that day isn't today, and I don't know when that day will come, but I promise it will.

"As to now, today, this competition..." He wiped away tears, his throat on fire. "I think we all know who the winner of this tournament is, and I will announce the victor when the time is right. Normally, I would ask if there were any questions, but since I don't have answers, I ask that you hold any concerns you may have—unless they're critical—until tomorrow.

"Thank you all for being here. For supporting the competition and giving it so much of your lives. In Tommy T's case, he gave all, and for that, we will never forget him."

Murmurs, nods, and bowed heads as the crowd dispersed.

Connie slipped an arm around him and asked, "You O.K.?"

"What do you think?"

"Did you..." Her eyes shifted to the dock.

Reading his wife's mind, he said, "Yeah, I saw it. Most of it." The memory of Tommy T being torn apart by the crazed great white would forever stay etched into his brain.

"Did it look diseased?"

Gerard hadn't thought about that aspect of things because he hadn't seen red pustule-filled gashes running along the beast's smooth skin. But could he have missed it in his frenzied state? Yeah, he could have. "I don't know," he said.

"Are you up for this?" She nodded toward Ray who was working his way through the thinning crowd.

When he reached Gerard and Connie, he said, "Sorry about your friend. We didn't have an opportunity to talk on the boat." He glanced at Seaman First Class Linda Darcy and Seaman Second Class Wes Ropey where they waited on the coastie response boat.

"Thank you for rescuing my husband," Connie said.

"I wouldn't be here if it wasn't for you and your folks," Gerard added.

"I know this is the last thing you want to deal with right now, but…" The lieutenant looked sheepish.

"What?"

"Can I have a fast word?" Ray's eyes strayed to Connie.

"Whatever you've got to say she can hear it," Gerard said.

Ray pulled a folded piece of paper from his shirt pocket and motioned toward a quiet corner of the dock. "Given recent events, the captain shared something with me." He held out the note.

Gerard stared at the white rectangle but made no move to take it.

"You're going to be mad, but…" He thrust the paper toward Gerard, who took it.

Connie nestled in close as Gerard unfolded the paper. It was a photocopy of a photocopy of a printout. It read:

**MEMORANDUM**
**UNITED STATES COAST GUARD**
To: All Unit Commanders
From: Tiffany Groale, Vice Commandant, USCG
Subject: Outbreak of mutated Zombie Deer Disease in Coastal Waters
Date: 9/21/2023
Classification: Urgent

In response to an unprecedented and highly concerning development, I urgently bring to your attention the emergence of a new threat along the coasts of the United States.

Recent reports from marine biologists and coastal surveillance units indicate the spread of a mutated version of Zombie Deer Disease (ZDD) into the oceanic environment, resulting in the infection of orcas off the coast of Washington in the Pacific Ocean. This follows an earlier infestation of mutant sea spiders that destroyed a research base at the edge of the Blake Plateau in the Atlantic Ocean.

This memo serves as a comprehensive update on the situation and outlines immediate actions to be taken.

As many of you are aware, ZDD, scientifically known as Chronic Wasting Disease (CWD), has ravaged terrestrial wildlife populations, particularly deer and elk, in various regions across the country. However, recent developments indicate a distressing escalation of the crisis as the disease has now mutated and made its way into our oceanic ecosystems. Infected creatures exhibit erratic behavior, heightened aggression, and a disturbing lack of fear toward humans and other species. It is imperative that we take immediate and decisive action to contain the spread of this epidemic and mitigate its catastrophic effects on our coastal communities.

Recent reports from marine biologists at the drop off in the Atlantic have confirmed the presence of mutant sea spiders exhibiting abnormal behavior and physical characteristics. These mutated arthropods display increased aggression, voracious feeding patterns, and a disturbing resistance to traditional control measures. They pose a significant threat to commercial fishing operations, recreational activities, and coastal infrastructure. Their size has also been reported to increase significantly, posing a direct threat to smaller marine organisms, and potentially impacting the balance of the marine ecosystem.

Infected orcas can be identified via physical deterioration manifested in red pustule-filled gashes. These wolves of the sea will display signs of neurological impairment, disorientation, abnormal swimming patterns, vocalizations, and the orcas' predatory instincts become unpredictable, posing a direct threat to other marine life, maritime navigation, commercial and recreational fishing activities, and public safety.

Immediate Actions and Recommendations:

Coastal units are instructed to enhance surveillance and monitoring efforts along the western coast of the United States, especially in areas known for frequent marine activity. Collaborate with marine research institutions, universities, and environmental agencies to monitor the spread and behavior of infected marine organisms. Vigilance and early detection are crucial in identifying and containing outbreaks of the disease.

We must foster information sharing among federal agencies, state authorities, academic institutions, and local stakeholders to effectively coordinate response efforts and share critical data and intelligence related to the spread of the disease. Coastal communities and stakeholders must be informed about the risks associated with the disease and its impact on marine life and human health.

Implement temporary fishing restrictions in areas identified as hotspots for infected marine organisms. Coordinate with local fishery management authorities to minimize human exposure to potentially contaminated seafood.

Maintain a constant state of readiness for search and rescue teams in case of emergencies, especially where human life is at risk. Equip units with necessary protective gear to ensure the safety of Coast Guard personnel during rescue operations.

The emergence of ZDD in our oceanic environment is an unprecedented and serious threat that demands immediate attention. We urge all units to stay vigilant, adhere to the outlined actions, and work collaboratively with relevant authorities to mitigate the impact on marine life and coastal communities.

Regular updates will be provided as the situation develops. The Coast Guard appreciates the dedication and commitment of all personnel in safeguarding our coastal waters.

Stay alert, stay safe.

Tiffany Groale, Vice Commandant

United States Coast Guard - Western Region

Gerard's mouth fell open, rage building in him like a storm. He crumpled the piece of paper and threw it at Ray.

It hit the coastie in the face and his friend caught it as he looked away.

"You guys knew! I can't believe this shit. I trusted you. And now Tommy T is dead." Gerard balled his fists and took a step forward.

Ray raised his hands, palms out in the universal sign of 'I mean you no harm.' "Look," Ray said. "I didn't know shit for sure until this very morning. This—" He held up the crumpled memo. "Tells us nothing. As I told you weeks ago, our orders were to patrol the western coast of the United States, especially in areas known for frequent marine activity. Not just the tournament. Just like the memo said. We knew something was up. Right? There are some details here, but would they have changed anything?"

"I would have called off the contest, so yeah, something would have changed. Tommy T would be alive." Even as the words left Gerard's mouth, he knew they were bullshit.

"Really?" Ray said. "If that makes you feel better, I'm not going to poop in your Cheerios, but you're telling me you would have canceled the competition if you knew there was another disease in the sea? That a research lab in another ocean halfway around the world was attacked?"

Gerard licked his lips. "What about the orca? The one that washed up here?"

"They didn't tell me shit and the captain still doesn't want to press the panic button, because he doesn't know shit, though he wouldn't admit it. Christ, telling the world will probably bring more people to the shore."

The guy had a point there. Gerard shook his head. "Now that someone's dead, and the bigwig ass-covering assholes have their justification, what's happening?"

Ray shook his head. "The big boys pulled rank. The guard has been relegated to support status."

"Who's in charge?" As soon as the words left his mouth Gerard knew the answer. "The feds," he said as he recalled the black Chinook and support chopper that had arrived like James Bond and taken away the orca carcass.

"Yup. They're sending some special agent. Silva is the guy's name."

"Great," Gerard said. "Just great."

Ray slapped him on the shoulder and said, "Let's regroup tomorrow."

Gerard nodded. Tomorrow. He didn't want to know what the new day would bring.

Connie leaned in and whispered in his ear. "Don't look now, but check out the guy standing by the fuel pumps."

The wind whispered, and sand scraped over the docks, and a solitary gull screamed about the lack of dead crabs.

Gerard glanced toward the fuel pumps. A man stood under the lights, examining the marina as if everything was new to him. The guy wore a black coat, and he looked as out of place as a vegan at a hotdog eating contest. Gerard recognized the man's face but couldn't place him at first. Then it hit him; it was the guy he'd seen in the second helicopter. The one that had hovered and watched as the big bird took away the orca's corpse.

"He was there when they took the orca," Gerard said as he turned to his wife.

When Gerard looked back in the man's direction, he was gone.

# 20

It was a clear night, and as the dusk fled and darkness spread across Liigei Too moonlight painted the world in its ghostly glow. Twirling sand danced on the hilltops, the beach grass whispered of loss, and the scent of low tide carried into the marina. The chatter of surfers and crew, the tinkle and pop of boats and skis being secured for the night, and the faint crackle of static from the Coast Guard vessel echoed through the maze of floating docks that spidered off the main thoroughfare.

Bongo, the other local surfers, and Twiggy and some of the other pros sat on a fishing boat drinking beer, but there was no raucous laughter on this night. Ray and his crew were preparing to head back to the cutter, and Derrick was sitting in his Tahoe, waiting for the last person to clear out of the marina so he could go home and put his head on his pillow without having to worry about mutant sea creatures. At least for the night.

Ray shared the Coast Guard memo with the sheriff, and though he was frustrated, he wasn't angry. He even went so far as to admit the sheriff's office often withheld crucial data from the public for their own good.

The marina's floodlights slowly brightened as Gerard and Connie sat at the end of the main pier that marked the center of the marina. The couple sat with their feet dangling in the cool water, sipping beers, Gerard's muscles protesting with each movement, big or small. He hadn't been injured—other than his ego, but his body had been stretched, pulled, and jerked to its breaking point.

A conversation that had started with who has the children led to the difficult task of telling their children about what had happened on this fateful day.

"I'm sure they already know," Gerard said.

"Of course they do," Connie said. "The question is what do they know? And who told them?"

Teenagers peddled bullshit almost as effectively as adults, and in some cases better for their lack of experience in knowing tall tales could get too tall. The false, exaggerated information flowed as if transmitted on fiber optic cable, and he had no doubts that the shark attack and subsequent death of Tommy T had grown to JAWS-like proportions, not that the comparison was totally out of bounds. Gerard said, "What is it you always say? Stick to the truth and it will get you through."

Connie sniffed. "Actually, what I say is 'use tragedy as a learning experience.'"

"Can't both be true? We can—"

The *plop* and *snap* of a bubble popping carried over the water, and tiny ripples, like a miniature tsunami, spread out over the smooth surface of the marina.

Gerard listened hard, blocking out the background static and burying the hiss of the wind. He heard nothing unusual. He stared into the blackness, and nothing moved on the water's silvery surface.

"We can use Tommy T's death to explain how dangerous big wave surfing is," Gerard said, but the words tasted bad in his mouth.

"Do you think that will work? It's like telling a kid they can't have a beer—or anything for that matter. What's the first thing they do, your words still hanging in the air?"

Gerard nodded. His wife was right. He couldn't scare Sage out of the water. "What's the lesson then? Live life to the fullest because today might be your last day?"

"If you want them to quit school," Connie said, and they both chuckled. "I think we bring them to the memorial, let them pay their respects, answer any questions they may have, and let things be. They understand more than we give them credit for."

Neither of the kids had ever been to a funeral. He said, "Once we tell them the true story and strip away all the bullshit."

She nodded.

"What do we say when they ask about the competition? About if we're staying in Liigei Too?" he asked.

"We don't know and yes."

Gerard nodded. His wife was always better at breaking things down than he was.

*Bloop. Plop.* More rings of tiny waves.

Gerard got to his feet as he looked around. If anyone else had noticed the bubbles, they didn't let on.

A crow cawed as it landed atop a mooring pole, its shadow falling over the dock.

Bubbles surged to the surface at the center of the marina as if an airline had ruptured deep down. A white spot appeared in the dark water, the tiny waves growing.

Now the surfers noticed, and they jumped one-by-one from their boat and walked to the end of their floating dock, staring like a class of lost school children searching for their teacher. Twiggy was out front, his dark hair up in a man-bun, the others hanging back.

"What is it?" Connie asked as she pulled her feet from the water and stood.

"I don't know, but—"

A shadow stirred beneath the surface, subtle yet undeniable. Gerard's gaze snapped down just in time to catch a glimpse of movement—an undulating, sinuous motion slicing through the water. His heart thundered in his chest, the tips of his fingers and toes stinging with pain.

A thick rope-like tentacle shot out of the water, reaching for Twiggy. It was a thing of nightmarish beauty, a twisting, writhing serpent. The tentacle unfurled with eerie grace, its skin shimmering with iridescence in the dappled moonlight, the large red pustule-filled gashes unmistakable.

Suction cups of various sizes ran along the tentacle's length, puckering like miniature mouths—and were there teeth glittering within?

Gerard blinked, mouth hanging open, his feet rooted to the dock.

Connie grabbed his arm, and her vice-like grip sent daggers of pain spidering through him.

The tentacle was a mosaic of intricate patterns, shades of gray and black dominating as it slithered over the dock, leaving behind a residue of translucent slime. With each twist and turn, the tentacle seemed to come alive, its movements fluid and sinuous as it explored its surroundings with a curious intensity. It reached out with cautious deliberation as if testing the boundaries of its newfound domain.

When the tip of the tentacle was ten feet from Twiggy the pro surfer broke free of his amazement and took several hurried steps back, his eyes still locked on the tentacle as it coiled and writhed over the dock.

Twiggy stumbled backward, but the appendage moved with preternatural speed. It lashed out with uncanny precision, wrapping around his ankle. The kid screamed and a jolt of primal fear coursed through Gerard as Connie's grip tightened on his arm.

The crowd backing up Twiggy ran, a mass exodus of human panic trying to force its way down the thin floating dock. People stumbled and tripped, the dock swaying and shifting, and two people fell into the drink with a splash.

"We need to help them!" shrieked Connie, but she didn't let go of his arm.

Gerard's stomach boiled. What could they do? He looked toward the coastie boat and didn't see Ray or his crew.

Twiggy fought against the relentless pull of the tentacle, thrashing and twisting in a desperate bid for freedom. But the octopus's arm was relentless as it dragged him inexorably closer to the murky water.

Fueled by desperation, Twiggy clawed at the wooden planks of the dock, his fingers finding purchase in a crack.

The tentacle went taut as it pulled, the unoccupied suckers chomping on air and searching for flesh.

For a fleeting moment, it seemed as though Twiggy might break free, but then, with a sickening lurch, the floating dock listed hard, and Twiggy was pulled screaming into the water.

Whitewater closed in around Twiggy, swallowing him as the writhing tentacle dragged him under. As Twiggy disappeared Gerard dry heaved, specks of mustard-tinged ham splattering the dock.

Tommy T and Twiggy on the same day? That could not stand. It wasn't too late. The kid could be saved if he acted fast.

A salty breeze stung his face as Gerard broke free of his wife's grip and headed for the coastie boat. Ray had guns and would know what to do. He stopped short when an explosion of bubbles and foam erupted from the water.

Twiggy appeared, hands clawing at a second tentacle that was wrapped around his neck.

Ray stood on the gunnel of the Coast Guard response boat, staring at the spectacle. One of the vessel's searchlights snapped on, and it was trained on the center of the marina where Twiggy fought for his life.

Ray drew his sidearm as he vaulted off the boat and hit the dock at a full run, his gun out before him. He fired into the air, but that didn't discourage Twiggy's attacker.

With a hollow gasp and a surge of whitewater, the tentacle jerked Twiggy beneath the surface again, the guy leaving nothing behind except a strangled cry.

Ray cut through the crowd fleeing the dock, and when he reached its end, he aimed his gun down at the turbulent water but didn't fire. Twiggy was down there.

The water settled, someone cried out in anguish, and Gerard's concern turned to Connie, who was still at the end of the pier, staring at the commotion as it unfolded.

A horrible dread leaked through Gerard. Where there was one tentacle, there were more.

Gerard felt time slow, that comfortable feeling that gave him his superpowers. Heartbeats became seconds, and seconds became minutes. Everything settled; the water, the wind, the panicked screams of the fleeing crowd.

Ray stood at the end of the floating dock, staring into the white-clouded water. Blood bubbles snapped in the boiling water, a field of smaller bubbles spreading out around the attack scene.

A hollow wail, like a cow screaming, thundered over the marina as numerous tentacles, short and long, thick and thin, surged from the water, a coordinated attack with one intention.

Gerard couldn't count how many tentacles there were as they flailed about, but as a large one speared from the water and wrapped around Connie's waist, he lunged toward his wife in a desperate attempt to get to her.

Twiggy hadn't surfaced, and the heat of failure washed over Gerard. As he ran to help his wife, he scanned the docked boats. He came across a filleting table, its white plastic top stained crimson, a knife holder at its base. Knife handles protruded from the holder, but Gerard didn't pause as he ran past the butchering table. He grabbed the largest handle and yanked the knife free. It was a twelve-inch curved blade perfect for filleting fish, its dirty plastic handle scarred by many years of use, its blade narrow from being sharpened hundreds of times.

Connie screamed as she struggled, the thick cable-like tentacle gripping her waist and lifting her off the dock.

More tentacles writhed over the dock, searching, a tangle of sinewy appendages filled with sucking mouths searching for flesh.

Heat burned his chest and even in the insufficient light raining down from the dock lights, Gerard could see that Connie's face was a light shade of purple. She clawed at the tentacle as she dangled like a marionette, but her movements were slowing.

Gerard skidded to a stop, dropped to his knees at the end of the dock where the tentacle holding Connie knifed from the water, and went to work with the blade.

He hacked at the tentacle like a man possessed, and even in his madness he knew that he was indeed possessed. Fate had dealt him this hand, and he had to play his cards. Everyone in Liigei Too had been dealt a crappy hand on this day, but there was no way he was losing Connie. No way.

The blade rose and fell, but the tentacle was rubbery and flexible, and the knife was doing little damage, so Gerard switched his approach.

He sawed the blade across the slick flesh, the sharp knife cutting into the tentacle, red blood-filled pustules exploding and leaking viscous fluid. He drew the knife back and forth, and then as fast as the tentacle was there, it was gone.

Connie hit the dock in a tangle as the wounded tentacle retracted into the water.

The beast beneath the water gurgled, and a mountain of whitewater, bubbles, and foam erupted at the center of the marina.

Yelling and screaming, and a gunshot rang out.

Gerard dropped the bloody knife and went to his wife's side.

Connie lay prone on the dock, unmoving.

"No. No. Noooooooo!" Gerard screamed as he pumped on his wife's chest, years of CPR training paying off. "You can't leave me. Not like this." He bent over to give his wife mouth-to-mouth, but she spat water in his face and rolled onto her side.

Relief flooded through Gerard as he fell back onto his ass, pain and exhilaration momentarily blinding him. "Are you O.K.?" he forced out.

Dots of blood marred her torn shirt where the tentacle had bitten into her, but she said, "I'm alive."

Ray was yelling, but Gerard couldn't understand what he was saying. His vision cleared and through the haze of light filtering over the marina, Gerard saw Twiggy's broken body swaying in the air at the end of a long tentacle.

The kid was still thrashing—his breathing clock was much longer than Gerard's, and for a sunny heartbeat Gerard thought the kid was going to make it.

A loud *crack* reverberated over the marina, and Twiggy's body went limp as his spine snapped.

Another tentacle wriggled over the dock and Gerard squished it under his foot as Connie jumped out of the way. In that moment he wished he hadn't dropped the knife, but as he considered diving for it a new horror presented itself.

The owner of the tentacles was rising above the knot of water building at the center of the marina, but that wasn't what drew Gerard's attention.

Twiggy's broken body floated in the turbulent water, his clothes torn, an arm and a leg twisted in directions they weren't meant to be twisted. Though he couldn't see the surfer's face in the gloom, Gerard felt Twiggy's eyes watching him and heard the dead man's admonishments.

"Let's go," Gerard said as he grabbed his wife's arm.

The couple escaped down the dock but skidded to a halt when a massive tentacle broke through the dock's floorboards, blocking their way forward.

# 21

Connie grabbed a gaff pole from a rod holder on a nearby boat and spun it like a baton. She had a black belt in Taekwondo, and she'd won several metals in the staff category. The dots of blood on her shirt where the tentacle had bitten into her had grown, but the wounds weren't affecting her movement.

Gerard thought of the knife again. He couldn't undo the past, but he could try to remedy the situation as his wife had.

The tentacle that wormed through the dock was creeping over the wooden planks, searching, the sharp pops of its many sucking mouths carrying over the chaos.

There was a filleting table, but Gerard didn't see any knives. Fishing poles stuck from holders, surfboards lay stacked, and deck chairs and coolers were strewn along the dock, but he saw no weapons.

Ray screeched something about needing a bigger gun, and Gerard saw the coastie turn tail and bolt down one of the long floating docks toward his boat. There was an M240 machine gun mounted in the bow of the coastie response boat, though there was a tangle of docks and humanity between it and the beast.

A loud pucker resounded over the marina, and as Gerard and Connie were pressed back the mutant made its appearance.

The Giant Pacific octopus emerged from the depths of the harbor, its gargantuan, rubbery mantle shimmering in the moonlight. Its eyes, unusually large and intelligent, gleamed with an unsettling intensity as the beast scanned its surroundings with predatory awareness. The creature was marked with intricate pulsating ribbons of red blood-filled pustules, and its skin pulsated with a tapestry of deep grays and shimmering black that glistened under the moonlight.

As the colossal Kraken broke the surface, the air filled with a deep, resonant hum. Its enormous, suction-cupped tentacles raged across the docks, each arm writhing with a life of its own. One of the longer appendages was bleeding from Gerard's knife strokes.

The monster was easily ten times its normal size, and as it hovered on the surface at the center of the marina, the water around it churning and foaming, the beast moaned.

Most folks had escaped the docks and retreated to the parking lot, but several people still staggered and slipped as they fled, the dock swaying and shifting beneath their feet.

Tentacles found the two people who had been tossed in the drink, and the man and woman shrieked as they were tossed around like marionettes.

More gunshots, the coastie response boat rumbled, and a jet of water sprayed the dock as Ray brought the boat about in a tight, stationary turn. Ray maneuvered the vessel through the chaos, Wes manning the forward gun and waiting for a clear shot.

The tentacle searching the dock behind Gerard and Connie could go no further. It had become too thick to fit through the gap in the dock boards, and with a hiss and the slap of meat, the arm disappeared back into the water. The pier swayed, the boards creaking and groaning as water surged up through the gaps between the planks.

Connie stopped running and Gerard almost slammed into her as he skidded to a stop. The filleting table he'd stolen the knife from sat under a floodlight to his right, and he jerked another white plastic-handled knife from its rack. This blade was smaller and caked with blood, but it was better than his bare hands.

A tentacle inched over the edge of the dock and wriggled toward Gerard and Connie, searching, its suction cups flexing open. Giant Pacific octopuses normally have eight legs. Gerard couldn't get a count with all the movement, but the creature had more than eight legs. Smaller secondary appendages branched off the larger tentacles that disappeared under the monster's huge mantle.

The Kraken oozed back, exposing the mouth on the underside of its body, at the center where its arms converged. A hard, sharp beak, resembling a parrot's, opened, its tongue-like radula lolling out. Under the marina's harsh light, Gerard saw that the creature's radula was covered with tiny, tooth-like structures that helped grind its prey.

Two people still dangled from the ends of tentacles, screaming and wailing as the barbed suction cups bit into flesh.

A tremor of fear and anxiety raced through Gerard. He knew a thing or two about Giant Pacific octopuses and his blood boiled as the beast utilized its legs to drag its prey toward its open maw. Normal Giant Pacific octopuses had salivary glands that produced venom and digestive enzymes. The venom was injected into prey to immobilize it and begin the digestion process, while the enzymes further broke the food down into a soupy consistency, making it easier to consume. Gerard could only imagine what the mutated creature's venom would do. The Great Pit of Carkoon came to mind.

Connie shrieked as she spun, striking out with the gaff, and hitting the advancing tentacle dead-on.

The fleshy snake veered away from Connie, right at Gerard.

Without the reach of the gaff pole, Gerard was forced to work in close. He swung the knife, and it slashed across gray undulating flesh, opening a thin wound.

As blue blood leaked onto the dock, all the appendages raged with a newfound fury.

The tentacle before Gerard reared back, rose like a King Cobra, and lunged at him.

Gerard lashed out with the blade again, but the dock was wet, he was tired, and the sinewy arm was stronger than Gerard's on his best day.

The tentacle slammed into him, a bone-rattling thump that made Gerard's vision dance with tiny starbursts. He was knocked from his feet, and as he sailed off the dock he twisted in midair like a cat and managed not to land face first in the chaotic water.

As darkness wrapped him in its cold cocoon Gerard couldn't help but embrace the irony of his situation. It was all happening again, and he hadn't even gotten a night's sleep. The day that just wouldn't end kept on coming and wouldn't let him be. He'd already tumbled in the ocean's washing machine, an apex predator on his heels, and now a Cthulhuian nightmare had appeared to test his metal.

He wanted to give up, and as he sank into the abyss, he let the last of his air escape his lungs. But then Connie's face was there, Sage's and Willow's. If he did nothing else on this day, he needed to survive for them. To help them deal with what was becoming the destruction of their world.

A tentacle coiled around his calf, the teeth-like serrations in the suction cups biting into skin. He wanted to scream, but he had no air left, and his heart just wasn't in it. He remembered the knife was still in his hand, and he lashed out with it, slicing water and cutting through the bubbles, but finding no flesh. Supernovas appeared on the underside of his eyelids, and a weak burning sensation, like a dying flame, heated his lungs.

The muffled pop of gunshots penetrated the water, three staccato blasts.

Something huge rushed by Gerard in the darkness, and the tentacle wrapped around his leg released its grip and slithered away. Gerard stroked up, the marina's floodlights showing him the way. He broke the surface and gasped for air.

The Coast Guard response boat was caught up in a tangle of boats that had been dislodged by the floating docks, many of which had broken away and were floating freely across the marina. There were people stranded on several of these iceberg-like docks, but he couldn't help them. He couldn't help himself.

Gerard swam for the dock, Connie battling a tentacle with her gaff like a ninja, swinging her pole and hitting the arm that attacked her with measured strikes that kept the appendage at bay. He reached the side of a boat and swam along its hull, looking for a ladder or a dive platform. He found neither, but he was able to grab hold of a mooring line. Frustration burned his stomach as the water raged about him, a maelstrom of tentacles worming through it. Gerard couldn't carry the knife and climb, so he tossed the filleting knife over the boat's gunnel and climbed, using the last reserve of energy to pull himself onto the fishing boat's deck.

He snatched his knife and stood, the marina a churning hive of chaos.

The sheriff was working his way toward Connie, gun up.

A tentacle rose behind Connie as she fought off the arm before her, the owner of the appendages huffing and chuffing as the monster surged toward the docks, its huge mantle like a plow as the creature poured over the inky water.

Derrick and Gerard screamed a warning at the same time.

Connie spun an instant before the second tentacle grabbed her. She swung away, the pole connecting with the thick rope-like appendage and knocking it aside.

As he jumped from the boat onto the dock, Gerard spared a glance for the Coast Guard boat as it picked its way through the chaos, moments away from having a clear shot at the monstrosity.

Would bullets hurt the thing? It was a valid question, though irrelevant at the moment. The M240 was their only chance, and all he needed to do was make sure he and Connie survived the next three minutes. He came up behind the tentacle at Connie's back and impaled it with his knife.

The octopus wailed, a hollow whimper that ended in a high-pitched wail that sounded like a scream of pain. With a snap, the tentacle retracted and slithered away.

Gerard went to Connie, but she was a master and didn't need him.

Connie twirled and hopped like a dancer, swinging the gaff pole and hitting the tentacle before her with steady, powerful strikes.

Like a boxer without eyes, the appendage shifted and writhed, swaying in the air, its tip searching for a target, its extrasensory perception alien-like.

Derrick arrived on the scene and wasted no time. He stepped past Connie, took aim at the heaving tentacle, and squeezed the trigger.

The shot severed the end of the tentacle and plunked into wood as the arm retreated, the gigantic octopus bellowing as it drove out of the water. Thunderous whitewater washed over the dock and Gerard, Connie, and Derrick were swept down the pier like trash along with the writhing tip of a tentacle.

Gerard's calf throbbed as the water rolled him under and he lost sight of Connie. The deluge drained away, the octopus's massive shadow obscuring the moonlight. A deep cold settled in his chest, and it turned to pain when he couldn't find his wife.

Derrick rolled onto his hands and knees, still clutching the Glock as he spit out water.

"Connie!" Gerard shrieked.

"Here!"

Gerard jerked his head around, searching, but he couldn't find his wife. Then he tracked movement out of the corner of his eye, and he turned to see Derrick racing toward the edge of the dock.

Connie was in the drink.

The Coast Guard boat coughed as Ray worked the controls. People hid in their vessels, and still, Wes couldn't fire. Thirty more seconds…

Gerard joined Derrick, who said, "Hold my ankles."

With the gargantuan mutant Giant Pacific octopus pulling apart the dock, its many tentacles curling over the wreckage of the marina, Derrick lay flat on the pier and extended his arms over the edge to help Connie.

Gerard dropped his knife and barely got hold of the sheriff's feet before Derrick was tugged forward, Connie's weight yanking on him.

The trio struggled for several long moments as Connie tried to claw her way onto the dock. Whitewater mounded over the pier, the octopus thrashing, its tentacles whipping about wildly, its huge bulbous eyes wet with palpable primal rage. The beast's two captives hung in the air at the ends of tentacles forgotten, all the monster's attention focused on Gerard and Derrick as they helped Connie.

A sharp pain knotted Gerard's side.

Derrick screamed as Connie slipped from his grasp.

A tributary of a thick tentacle poked at Gerard's shoulder, the thing a wiry abnormal growth on one of the octopus's main branches.

Gerard scooped up his blade and pushed to his feet.

Derrick rolled and avoided the stabbing strike of a tentacle.

The rank stench of decay wafted over the dock as Gerard attacked, knife up, the cutting edge facing away from him. He punched with the knife—one, two, three, four times as he slashed the blade across the writhing gray appendage, its suction cups mumbling, the gray and black skin rippling as if small creatures crawled beneath it.

Gerard had never been in a knife fight, but suddenly he was dancing on his toes, swinging the blade back and forth, the tentacle hanging back.

The massive octopus huffed, and as the coastie response boat pulled free of a knot of boats and brought its main gun to bear on Cthulhu's mantle, Gerard smiled.

# 22

The mutant octopus thrashed, the marina a bubbling cauldron of seawater, tentacles, debris, and blood.

Gerard's skin itched with tension as he felt Connie's time running out. He slashed and fought his way forward, driving back the thick slimy appendage that blocked his path.

A horn sounded, and the loud click of metal tapping metal carried over the marina.

Then Derrick was next to him, gun out in a two-handed grip. He fired the Glock twice, and both bullets tore into the writhing tentacle.

Blue blood sprayed the dock as the arm fell back.

Connie climbed onto the gunnel of a fishing boat, the craft listing as she flopped over the side onto the deck.

"Let's go!" Derrick said, and he grabbed Gerard's shirtsleeve as he ran full tilt toward the edge of the dock.

Gerard jolted back as Derrick let go of his shirt. It took a second for his stress-addled brain to realize what the sheriff was doing, and another second for his bean to give the order to run. Run as if your life depended on it because it just might.

Derrick leaped from the pier onto the fishing boat Connie was on and the sheriff disappeared as he hit the deck, the boat's sidewalls obscuring the sheriff from view.

The loud ratatat of heavy arms fire erupted over the marina.

Gerard reached the edge of the dock and jumped for the safety of the fishing vessel. He hit the deck hard, and Connie gathered him in as the couple, along with Derrick, hunkered down in the boat.

The snap of the M240 continued, the crack and pop of the belt-fed ammunition discharging and traveling at twenty-eight hundred feet per second echoing over the marina. Each successive gunshot was followed by squishy thumps and hollow bellows.

Blue blood and pieces of the creature rained down on the trio where they hid, the rank scent of rotten eggs driving out the smell of gun smoke and blood.

Gerard peeked over the boat's sidewall and stared at the unfolding battle which played out under the floodlights like a poorly lit movie set.

Ray was at the helm of the Coast Guard response boat, and he had the vessel's nose on the creature as the craft listed and bounced in the whitewater churned-up by the beast.

Wes stood behind the M240, the tripod-mounted gun shaking in his hands as it spat bullets. The general-purpose, open bolt machine gun chambered 7.62 NATO rounds that packed a punch, especially at close range. Loved by soldiers and sailors alike, the M240 was designed to withstand the rigors of combat, though Gerard doubted its designers had foreseen the current enemy. The gun utilized a gas-operated system with a rotating bolt that ensured reliable operation under extreme conditions, and it was equipped with a quick-change barrel system to prevent overheating during sustained fire.

A loud high-pitched shriek pierced the night, and the massive creature bucked as bullets smacked into its bulbous mantle.

The water heaved, a wave crashed over the bow of the coastie boat, and Wes and the gun were momentarily consumed by whitewater. As the water drained away the M240 continued to fire, the shots thwapping into the monster, pieces of flesh flying in the air like bloody ash.

Wes leaned back as he depressed the trigger, his head aligned with the weapon's iron sight.

Blue blood streamed down the beast's bulging mantle, and with a final heave of desperation the gigantic beast surged from the water, waves rolling over the docks, boats listing and smacking dock posts. All the tentacles fell limp, their unanimated forms floating on the chaotic water as the creature's body floated listlessly on the surface.

But even as the giant beast deflated and lobster-like meat seeped from its wounds, the dying mutant lashed out with one of its tentacles. The appendage wrapped around Wes's legs and jerked him away from the gun, but the coastie screamed and managed to grab hold of a safety rail.

The tentacle went taut, the suction cups tightening, giant bubbles popping on the surface of the marina as the massive monster sank and a foul rush of air pushed over the chaos as the creature's mantle sagged like a deflating balloon.

Wes managed to hang on for several seconds before losing his grip and disappearing over the side of the boat into the churning water.

Gerard's leg wound throbbed with the beating of his heart, and he turned when he felt a presence next to him. Connie and Derrick were watching along with him, their faces painted in shades of horror. His gaze shifted to his wife's midriff and her shirt was fully stained with blood.

Connie felt him looking at her and said, "I'm fine. It looks worse than it is."

A primal scream of rage broke the stillness as Ray bounded out of the pilothouse, gun in his hand.

Wes emerged from the water at the end of the creature's only moving appendage. The tentacle spasmed, the mutant's brain giving out its final commands. Like a floundering fish, the tentacle flopped about, slamming Wes against the roof of the Coast Guard boat's pilothouse.

Once. Twice. Three booms as Wes was smashed into the boat's unforgiving metal. Bones cracked, and a hallow thud carried over the water as Wes fell still, his lifeblood splattered on the coastie pilothouse roof, thin lines of blood that looked black under the harsh lights inching down the windshield.

Ray screamed again as he got behind the machine gun, spun it on its tripod, and pumped bullets into the tentacle holding Wes's broken body. The weapon rattled him as he screamed, the tap and crack of gunpowder expanding and the hiss of the bullets streaking through the air driving out all other sounds.

The tentacle released Wes and the sailor's corpse fell to the roof of the pilothouse as the appendage flopped onto the deck and slid back into the water. Clouds of gun smoke hung in the air, the sharp stench tickling Gerard's nose.

Derrick stood up and holstered his gun. "Well, shit."

Out on the marina, the dead gargantuan octopus's corpse floated in the churning water, a blood slick speckled with gray and black shards of skin and gobs of fat undulating on the settling water.

Yelling, weeping, and the murmur of voices carried over the marina as folks emerged from their hiding places. People climbed from boats and the crowd that had fled to the parking lot inched onto the docks as they gaped at the carnage.

Gerard saw Bongo, Glenda, the mayor, and several of the pro surfers standing arm in arm, comforting each other as they gazed out upon the devastation. The marina would need significant repairs, but did it matter? He thought of Twiggy, Wes—what would the body count be when this day finally came to an end?

Connie put an arm around Gerard. "Are you O.K.?" she cooed.

He nodded in the affirmative, but he was anything but O.K. He'd spent the last ten years of his life building something, a future filled with prosperity, purpose, and fun. Yet it had all been taken from him in one day, and as the heat of shame washed through him—there were at least four dead, and he was thinking about himself—he didn't know how he could move forward. He'd given everything he had, and the thought of starting over made his stomach go sour and his neck muscles pulsate with pain.

Connie squeezed him.

At least he had Connie and the kids, and nobody, other than himself, would blame him for what had happened. On the contrary. He'd be praised as a hero, one of the people who had tried to save others when most people ran. They'll say, "When trouble comes, some people stand, and some people run. You, my friend, stood your ground."

What a joke. What had he done? Saved his own ass and tried to help his wife?

It was then that he noticed the wail of sirens and the distant *womp womp* of airfoils slicing the air. Gerard's leg wound stung, and his thoughts turned to the injured.

The trio climbed from the fishing trawler and set about helping those in need.

Ray and Linda were working on getting Wes's corpse off the roof of their boat, and Gerard took command as he reached the end of the dock where the king was met by his subjects.

Questions, concerns, pleas for aid, and information were thrown at Gerard with the reckless abandon of people who have been through a great trauma.

Without saying a word Gerard calmed the crowd by patting the air with his hands. Then he gave out instructions and answered whatever questions he could, but as an ambulance arrived his adrenaline fled, and he had to sit down. His muscles were knotted, his throat dry as paper, his clothes soaked through, and he had to dig back to the incident to find a time when he'd felt worse.

Sensing his unease as only she could, Connie slipped an arm around his waist again and said, "It will be alright. Everything will be O.K."

Gerard forced a smile. He knew she was trying to relieve his stress and help him understand that he couldn't carry Liigei Too on his shoulders, but still, a wave of anger surged through him. He beat it back. Nothing was going to be O.K., he knew that, but taking it out on the person trying to ease his pain was the height of callousness. He pulled Connie close, kissed her, and said, "You're right, honey."

**When the state police** arrived, several fishermen had already used their boat hoists to haul the corpse of the dead mutant out of the water. The huge monstrosity hung from the competition fish hook at the end of the main pier, its tentacles dragging in the water. Eyes glazed white stared out at the darkness, the floodlight above the dead beast creating a freakshow-like image, the monster's skin mottled black and white.

The monster hung by its mouth, its beak broken, and most of the pustule-filled wounds were broken open. Blue blood trickled from the many gunshot wounds, and the creature looked like a busted open bag of garbage. Its mouth-like suction cups no longer searched for flesh, and its oozing mass no longer expanded and contracted.

Shadows danced out on the water, and the distant sound of crashing waves played second fiddle to the gusting wind. Medical personnel treated superficial wounds, but the corpses had yet to be removed from the scene.

Twiggy, Wes, and three others had been pulled from the drink, their bodies trashed, broken, and missing pieces. The corpses were laid out on the main pier covered in a tarp, and there were wildflowers from the surrounding hills spread atop the covered remains. Other offerings were laid at the feet of the deceased, and though the bodies hadn't started to deteriorate, the air was putrid with the stink of death and rot.

A marina worker sprayed down the main dock, clearing it of the octopus blood, but it couldn't take away the stink. There were still a few folks taking pictures, and there was no question that the cat was out of the bag.

Connie sat alone, gazing at the dead octopus as if not believing what she was seeing. She'd changed her shirt and the medics had bandaged her up. The tiny mouth-like bite marks around her waist hadn't gone deep, but the doctor said she'd most likely have a thin belt of scars.

The wound on Gerard's leg was smaller, but the serrations along the edges of the suction cups had bitten deep into his flesh and he had to promise the doctor he'd come to the clinic for stitches.

Derrick and Ray gave updates to the staties, and when they were done Derrick sauntered over and said, "Ray was just informed that they are to stand down. The feds are—" He stopped talking as a large gray boat with a black stripe around the upper portion of its hull powered into the marina.

The ship had a tall conning tower, its roof packed with antennas and rotating dishes. The bow of the vessel had tall sidewalls that tapered down to nothing when they reached the rear deck, leaving an open platform with a folded boom arm at its center.

Everyone—the staties, the coasties, the locals, the tourists—all stared as the boat glided gently to the dock. A man with dirty-blonde hair wearing black pants and a black shirt leaped from the ship onto the dock.

Someone gasped as the man slipped on the freshly mopped dock, but didn't fall. Gerard saw it was the guy he'd seen the other night watching him at the marina. The same man who had been in the second chopper when the orca's corpse was taken away. This must be the mythical Silva, but Gerard didn't voice his opinion. He simply watched like all the others as the boat's crew went about cutting down the octopus and laying it out on the rear deck of the newly arrived ship.

Moonlight painted the water silvery white, and Gerard was weary to the bone, yet he knew he had one more task to perform on this day.

Connie got to her feet and stood next to her husband, who was flanked by Ray and Derrick. All four of them stared at the man in black as he worked his way through the shadows and the harsh stares of the floodlights.

# 23

The man in black stopped before the four companions, eyeing them each in turn. "My name is Silva. I'm here to help. I work for the federal government."

"What branch?" Ray asked.

"All of them," Silva said as he leaned in and made a show of examining the coastie's chest salad of ribbons that was still pinned to his dirty blood-speckled uniform shirt. "Lieutenant Tantillo. Your captain tells me you're a good man." He shifted his attention to Derrick. "Sheriff."

Derrick nodded but said nothing.

"That leaves surf legend Gerard Noll and his wife and wave whisperer, Connie Noll." He bowed to all four of them. "Sorry about the entrance."

"A bit late," Gerard said, not knowing if the bowing thing was mocking or genuine.

"That's fair. Can we talk in a more…" The agent looked around at the lingering crowd. "Where it's more comfortable? Are you hungry? Do you have to get back to your children? Sage and Willow, right?"

"What do you do for the government, Agent Silva?" Connie asked, her tone prickly. "Before we start answering your list of questions."

The agent nodded emphatically. "I investigate anomalies."

"And that's why you're here? Because of this." Gerard dug in his pocket for the copy of the Coast Guard memo but pulled free a clump of white, black-streaked, waterlogged pulp.

Silva said, "I am sorry to impose, really, but I do need a word with all of you."

Ray and Derrick were already nodding their heads in agreement. In their worlds, when the feds came calling, you answered.

Gerard said, "I haven't seen my children yet today, Agent Silva. Six people are dead, two of whom were close personal friends. I'm exhausted and starving. It can't wait?"

Silva did that nodding thing like he understood, and Gerard thought maybe the guy did. "What can I say, Mr. Noll? Everything I do, time is of the essence."

Connie said, "Let's get this over with. Where?"

Silva gazed down the length of the dock at his boat. The stink of the dead octopus pervaded the air, and it stuck in Gerard's nostrils like stale smoke. "Perhaps you're right," Silva said. "I didn't mean to be so inconsiderate, but… Can we reconvene at first light?"

"That would be better," Gerard said, and the others nodded.

Derrick said, "We can meet at my office."

"Why don't I pick you up here?" Silva said. "You can come out to the boat. I can show you a few things that might help you understand."

To that, nobody had anything to say. If Gerard didn't understand the threat yet, he thought perhaps he never would.

The fed said, "3 AM?"

"Make it 8:30. We need to get the kids off to school," Gerard said. Truth was, there were many shitty tasks that needed to be performed at first light.

"Until the morrow, then," Silva said as he turned on his heel and walked up the dock toward his boat without looking back.

**The next morning Gerard** and Connie had the dreaded conversation with their children and told them the truth about what had happened the prior day. The couple fielded questions, got the kids off to school, and moved on to the preliminary arrangements for a memorial to honor the dead. Next, Gerard crafted a press release to be sent out on behalf of The Funnel Big Wave Competition.

It read: The surfing community is devastated today at the deaths of surfers Tommy Tulane and Twiggy Barker, Coast Guard Seaman Second Class Wes Ropey, jet ski pilot Kris "Santa" Cronkle, fisherman Dee Landry, and deckhand Lisa Romaro. Our condolences go to the families who have suffered such a tragic loss.

In light of these unfortunate deaths and the incidents that caused them, the Competition Committee is deferring all decisions regarding future competitions until further notice. The winner of this year's contest will be announced at the memorial, which is set for tomorrow at St. Patrick's Mission Church in Petrolia. See the competition website for further information.

Connie finished reading the draft and said, "Short and sweet. I like it."

Gerard sent the message out over the internet to the news agencies and the competition listserv. With that done some of the stress knotting his chest eased, but he knew from experience the pain wouldn't be going away any time soon.

The drive to the marina was a quiet one. Gerard and Connie marinated in their thoughts, and Gerard knew his wife was wondering about what the next step was, just like he was. The kids had school, so until the year was out there would be no talk of leaving Liigei Too.

That wasn't a real possibility anyway. There was no way he and Connie could leave town, not after they'd helped rebuild the place. But without the competition, what would he do? Waste away in some little surf shop in town that sold more t-shirts and Sex Wax than boards? But that was a question for another time.

Unlike the prior day, the Liigei Too Marina was dead. No shiners jumped in the shallows, no fishermen prepared to leave for the day, no skis waited for riders, and no surfers gathered in the parking lot. Purgatory Beach was closed until further notice, and Gerard knew that Bongo and the others would honor the closing, at least for a day, maybe two.

The marina lot was almost empty, but Derrick's police Tahoe was there, and Gerard parked next to it. Silva's black boat with the gray stripe around the top of its hull was docked at the end of the main pier, a Coast Guard Zodiac tied to its rear dive platform.

Derrick greeted the couple as Gerard and Connie headed for Silva's vessel. "Doing O.K. today?"

Connie shrugged.

Gerard said, "The best that can be expected. Any intel on what this fed is going to tell us?"

Now the sheriff shrugged.

The trio was greeted by Ray and Silva, both men standing at the head of the gangway that led up onto the main deck of Silva's vessel. Under the light of day, Gerard saw that Silva was of medium build, and on this day his dirty-blonde hair was neatly coiffed, and he'd shed his ninja black outfit and replaced it with blue work duds.

An army of whitecoats poured over the octopus carcass like ants, and Gerard saw that the beast had already been partially dissected. Clouds of fog caused by giant chunks of dry ice hung over the deck, a series of tables running along the dead creature's length holding scientific equipment and a variety of octopus pieces.

As the group walked up the gangway, Silva said, "Not that it needs to be said, but like the orca—and other specimens, our top scientists are doing their best to understand the ZDD mutation."

"Who?" Ray asked.

"Top people," Silva said.

"Are these top people trying to find a cure?" Connie asked.

"In a perfect world," Silva said.

"A perfect world?" Gerard said, his hackles rising. People were dead, the future of Liigei Too was in doubt, and this guy was talking about a perfect world?

"Poor choice of words," the fed said.

"I'll say," the sheriff said. "It would have been nice if you guys had been a bit more communicative before the shit hit the fan."

"True enough, but—"

"But nothing," Gerard said.

Silva appraised him before responding. Clearly, the agent wasn't used to being addressed in such a derogatory manner. "You're an ocean boy, right? Do you know what percentage of the Earth is covered in water?"

As it turned out, Gerard did. "Seventy percent," he said smugly.

"Seventy-one, actually. What are you suggesting? We should have tried to close seventy-one percent of the world? I'm sure you understand the panic and economic chaos even an attempt would create."

"So, we're doomed?" Connie said.

"We'll see."

"You must have a plan," Ray said. "One that goes beyond the basics of the Coast Guard's current orders."

"We'll get to that," Silva said.

The group spent a few minutes examining the dead octopus before heading for a less smelly meeting place. There wasn't much left of the beast except a bag of rancid skin, but samples of flesh were being collected from every part of the corpse.

Silva undogged a hatch and held it open for the guests as the group passed through the bulkhead into the ship where they were directed to a conference room. Coffee and a box of donuts from Barb's Bakery in Liigei Too sat at the center of a scratched conference table, and everyone helped themselves to refreshments before taking seats around the table.

"Before we get to the purpose of our meeting..." Silva sipped coffee, "I think I'll fill you in on some of the science. Stuff that wasn't in the memo you saw."

Nobody responded and the murmurs of voices and the cry of a gull filled the silence.

"I've been tracking odd mutations in sea creatures. You may recall the incidents at the drop off in the Atlantic and the situation with the sea wolves up north from the coastie memo."

Nods and general agreement.

"First," the agent said, "you all know the legal spiel about confidentiality?"

Nods.

"And you're prepared to keep your mouths shut? I mean, I don't see what you could do with the information, but protocol is protocol."

Ray said, "There were rumors that the research station in the Atlantic burned to the sea, and nobody knew what caused it."

"That first part is true, but the second..." Silva sighed. "The base was overrun by mutant sea spiders. Normally, sea spiders are harmless arthropods, not predators. But as it turned out, the creatures were infected with a mutation of chronic wasting disease."

Silence filled the room, the air moving through vents and the distant static of voices the only sounds.

"The bigheads have been running tests, looking for cures, but they haven't had much luck," Silva said. "They say what they've found so far doesn't make sense."

"Why's that?" Derrick asked.

"For starters, the infected sea spider and orca DNA doesn't match anything in the known records." Silva paused to let that sink in. "The only connections they've found so far aren't possible."

"Not possible? After everything I've seen recently you can still honestly say something's not possible?" said Gerard.

"The bigheads found odd macrophages in sea spiders and infected orca. Stuff that shouldn't be present in the ocean, especially four hundred miles offshore," Silva said.

"Macrophages?" Ray said.

Silva sighed. "I've got this spiel down." He looked at the ceiling as if recalling a conversation. "They're a type of white blood cell. Part of the immune system that engulfs and digests cellular debris, foreign substances—anything that doesn't have the type of proteins specific to healthy body cells of the organism it's in. The process is called phagocytosis."

"There are macrophages in most living tissues?" Ray asked.

"Yes, but the type found in the mutant sea spiders and orca is commonly found in salamanders," Silva said. "The scientists believe this specific macrophage is responsible for limb regeneration."

"Salamanders in the middle of the Atlantic?" Gerard said. It sounded too fantastic to believe.

"Like I said, the facts don't add up."

"You said connections. Plural," Connie pushed.

"The other is the scientists found prions," Silva said.

Silence pressed on the room.

"Prions are misfolded proteins. They cause chronic wasting disease and play a role in each mutation," Silva said.

"So now what?" Connie asked.

"The first thing I need—we need, is to keep Purgatory Beach closed, and everyone out of The Funnel until further notice."

"That's going—" Gerard started to say, but Silva put up a hand.

"I know the situation enough to understand. That's where I need your help, Gerard."

Connie and Gerard exchanged a worried glance.

"I need you to keep an eye on Bongo and the others. Make sure they don't do anything stupid like try and surf The Funnel."

Derrick and Connie chuckled.

"That's like asking a little kid not to touch a shiny new toy," Ray said.

"But Gerard is tight with them, he can keep an eye out from the inside."

"Like a spy?" Connie asked.

Gerard considered his words carefully because he knew what was at stake. To save surfers' lives he'd have to betray their code. The code that built the town. "I think you're overestimating how much they trust me," he said. "I'm a father figure, if that, and they won't tell me if they're getting wet."

"But you know their secret access points, and you can—"

"I won't betray their trust," Gerard said, a little too loudly. "It took too long to earn, and I... I just..."

"It's not him," Connie said.

"This isn't the time to be honorable. There are people in our government..." He sighed. "Do you want to see Purgatory Beach closed for good? The sea dead and The Funnel nothing more than rough water?"

"You know I don't but—"

"But nothing," Silva said. "The higherups are considering using a Chytridiomycosis bioweapon to kill the mutants, but the collateral damage could be catastrophic."

"They want to use what?" Derrick asked.

"Chytridiomycosis is a disease that affects amphibians."

"Like salamanders?" Gerard asked.

Silva nodded. "The disease is caused by the chytrid fungus Batrachochytrium *dendrobatidis* and Batrachochytrium *salamandrivorans*. It is considered one of the most devastating wildlife diseases known."

"And they want to introduce it into the marine environment to kill the mutants?" Gerard said.

"If I can't buy some time and find another way..." Silva threw up his hands. "The bigheads have another plan."

"Don't they always?" Ray said.

"Good point."

# 24

**Purgatory Beach, Liigei Too, northern California, U.S.A.**
*11:58 AM PT, November 1, 2023*

Tommy T's crab-ravaged torso rolled onto Purgatory Beach three days after he was declared the 2023 winner of The Funnel Big Wave Competition. Gerard announced the champion at the memorial honoring those lost on what had become The Day in the town's vernacular, and after a final silent prayer for the fallen, the residents of Liigei Too went about picking up the pieces of their torn apart town. Tommy T would be buried in his family plot after the feds got done with his remains. Gerard couldn't imagine what the feds could learn, but he was no scientist. So far there was no evidence of the disease spreading to humans, but surely that was the concern driving Silva's decision to take what was left of Tommy T's body.

Gerard had reluctantly agreed to do his best to keep Bongo and the others dry. So far there had been no attempts to surf, but it had only been a couple of days. Gerard figured in another day or two the itch would be too great, and Bongo, Glenda, and the others would have to hit the water, and they'd use "that's what Tommy T would want" as justification. He'd been staking out Bongo's house, and all the kid did was sleep and go into town for food.

Tommy T had been a central figure of the local surf community, and his legendary status was cemented when he died surfing in The Funnel. As winner of the 2023 competition, Gerard had decreed that the purse of $50,000 would be paid out to his family, though there were no provisions in the competition bylaws for such a decision. Gerard didn't care, and neither did anyone else.

In the meantime, the coasties were heavily patrolling the area, and the mutant shark hadn't been seen. Specialized personnel were brought in to install a containment system that would turn The Funnel and Purgatory Beach into a holding area where diseased sea animals could be corralled and dealt with. What that meant exactly Gerard didn't know, but he guessed the beasts would be observed, euthanized, and dissected.

What was it the wise said? Doing the same thing over and over and expecting a different result was the definition of insanity?

Gerard sat on the bench forward of the pilothouse, watching the coastie work crew lay out the containment barrier.

Using the tips of the long rock jetties that extended outward from Purgatory Beach to the north and south, two teams were working their way toward each other, closing off ocean access.

It had been explained to Gerard that installing a containment ring in the ocean was a complicated process that involved careful planning, design, precise execution, and continuous monitoring.

Normally, an environmental impact assessment would be conducted to understand the local marine ecosystem, weather patterns, and ocean currents. Then a feasibility study would be done to determine the technical and economic viability of the project. Permits and approvals from local, national, and international regulatory bodies were required, and environmental groups, local communities, and industry experts would be consulted, but the feds were the feds.

Before deployment of the ring—which Gerard noted wasn't a ring at all, but a line that would connect the tips of the north and south jetties—divers and remote ROVs conducted a detailed survey of the ocean floor where the containment barrier would be anchored. Plans were adjusted to account for major obstacles or hazards that could interfere with the installation process.

The top part of the containment ring floated on the surface. It was made of yellow high-density polyethylene, and netting made of corrosion-resistant materials reinforced with strands of Kevlar were attached to the floats and hung to the ocean floor where it was anchored.

The containment rig itself was assembled on the rear deck of the fed boat, the mutant octopus carcass having been dissected and what was left removed. The modular sections were transported and joined together in the water, and each section was tested to ensure its integrity, including pressure tests, buoyancy tests, and structural strength assessments.

Hoist arms moaned, winches rattled, and there were divers in the water to position the barrier accurately. Bubbles churned over the rolling surface as the divers screwed the containment anchors into the sea floor, being careful to unfurl the netting and secure it to the bottom to prevent movement due to ocean currents or other forces.

Underwater cameras and sensors were placed by the divers to inspect the anchoring system, and the overall health of the containment equipment, and to monitor the sea creature's movements and behaviors. These systems would be calibrated and watched, and they provided real-time data on the containment zone's status to the coasties and the feds.

Someone yelling orders snapped Gerard from his reverie and he pushed up from his seat and went to the port side gunnel.

The boats installing the southern section of the barrier had stopped working, and a new section was being moved into position to be deployed. Gerard saw that the next section didn't have netting attached to it.

He gazed north. The work crew there was chugging along, and Gerard calculated that the two teams would most likely meet at some point the following day, and The Funnel and Purgatory Beach would be contained.

As the coasties to the south dumped the next section of barrier into the drink, Gerard rolled his shoulders. Something wasn't right. Even he could see that. But the workers didn't appear to notice, which meant they were doing exactly what they'd been ordered to do. He went in search of Silva who was back on the command boat.

Seaman First Class Linda Darcy, who'd been assigned as Gerard's detail, transported him to the command boat where he found Silva on the phone pacing up and down the rear deck between the workers assembling the final pieces of the barrier. He saw no netting and sea floor equipment or anchors. They'd all been deployed.

When Silva saw him coming, he made a circular motion with his finger next to his head and mouthed bigwigs. "Yes, sir. I will, sir." Silva rolled his eyes. "Yes, sir." He tapped his phone and let it fall to his side. "Goddamn brass. The world would be a better place without them."

"I don't know," Gerard said.

Silva's eyebrows lifted and he said, "Everybody serves someone. Am I right?"

"I suppose you are."

"What brings you?"

"Why aren't nets being attached to the center of the barrier? The part at the head of The Funnel?"

An odd smirk Gerard had never seen the likes of before leaked over Silva's face. "You paid attention at the briefing, I see."

Gerard said nothing.

"Think about what a funnel does, Gerard," Silva said.

Confusion twisted Gerard's face.

Silva chuckled as he nodded toward the bow of the ship. Two men walked along the starboard side of the vessel, huge rolling waves jostling the ship like it was a toy in a bathtub. When the two men were alone again, Silva said, "You remember what I said about confidentiality?"

Gerard nodded.

"I'm telling you this row because I trust you, Gerard. Do you trust me?"

Gerard let a stream of air escape his lips.

"O.K., I get it. Do you at least believe I'm trying to do what's best for everyone and everything? Even the creatures who call the sea home?"

"I do."

"The barrier is mainly for show. While it will serve as a containment tool, its main purpose isn't only to keep the diseased creatures in, but to use The Funnel to corral mutants. You understand the currents here better than anyone alive, Gerard. Why do you think I asked you to look at the plans for the barrier?"

Gerard's face twisted. He was stunned. His beach. Purgatory Beach was being turned into a literal hell.

"As of today, no other specimens have washed up elsewhere that we're aware of. This is ground zero. Here and up north. This…" He pointed at The Funnel. "This could save the world's oceans and we'll be monitoring everything bigger than a sand lance…" He smiled at Gerard. "We'll be monitoring everything that enters and leaves The Funnel."

Gerard mentally wrestled with himself, his ethics, angst, and basic logic mixing in a toxic brew that left him confused, disheartened, and angry. Mostly angry. Not only had he been asked to spy on fellow surfers, but now he was in the know about how the feds planned to kill Purgatory Beach and use it as their private laboratory.

"Tell me why I shouldn't go to the sheriff and the news people?" Gerard asked. The words sounded stupid, and he was sorry he'd spoken, but still… His concerns weren't without merit.

"You could do that," Silva said. "Do you have proof? Do you have any way to obtain proof? Look around," he said as he spread his arms expansively. "We don't have a choice here, Gerard."

Gerard balled his fists, took a step forward, but then shook his head and flexed his fingers. None of this was Silva's fault, or his—it was nobody's fault, and the fact that his beach was the center of attention was unavoidable, yet still he felt betrayed. "You should have told me."

"Why? So it could eat you alive? These orders come from way up, Gerard. You—we, are bugs."

"Ask Linda to take me home," Gerard said.

On the trip back to the marina, Gerard was bombarded with thoughts and decisions that needed to be made. His superpower of slowing time failed him, and not only didn't he get an extra few minutes to think, but time sped up at a precipitous rate. Before he'd even made a mental checklist of what he needed to do he was back at the marina.

Thankfully, there was no one waiting for him, and he wandered out to the rock pile west of the parking lot, which had a good view of the sloping cliff that ran down to the boulder-filled shoreline and the ocean beyond. Hazy clouds hung in the sky as if unsure whether they intended to come together or scatter to the winds. He felt like those clouds. Thin. Confused. Pressed by time and circumstance and ethics.

He could blow the whistle, despite what Silva had said. What that would get him he didn't know. What would the town get? Again, he didn't know. But he did know his decision would most likely have negative ramifications for himself, and for the town and everyone who lived in it or near it, so he put that option to the back of the line.

Another alternative was to apologize. Tell Silva he'd been an ass and ask that he be given more responsibilities. He heard himself in his mind's eye. "Silva, I'm going crazy sitting out on these boats watching your guys dump shit into the water. Give me something meaningful to do."

He genuinely felt that way, and the agent would most likely respect his plea. Then Gerard would be on the inside, in the know, and maybe impact decisions and plans. The thing was, the feds didn't need him. Gerard had figured out some time ago that the mission to watch Bongo was actually just a mission to keep track of him.

Not that Silva was worried Gerard would get wet, but... What?

His father used to say there was no problem a night's sleep wouldn't solve. Gerard didn't know about that, but his old body was done with the stress. Maybe it was time to head back to Hawaii when school let out, at least for the summer? More and more he felt the need to get away, to escape the nightmarish reality that had tainted his masterpiece.

Even as the thought pranced through his head like a golden goose, he knew that wasn't an option. He didn't run from challenges, he ran toward them. He'd take things one day at a time—as if he had a choice in the matter—and when it came time, he'd do what he always did. Press into a standing position and ride the wave he'd been given.

A large set closed-out beyond the breakers, a cacophony of crackling static, hissing air and angry water pushing over the shallows. The sun touched the horizon in the west and the day faded into the ashes of twilight.

# 25

The next morning's stakeout was a bust. Bongo didn't even go out for breakfast. Either the kid knew Gerard was watching him—which he didn't think was the case—or Bongo was dealing with the loss of his friend and the fears that strike a surfer's heart when someone dies riding. "It could be me" thoughts lead to fear, and there's no place for fear when surfing big waves.

Gerard was starting to worry that Bongo's boys were looking for a new entry point to the Pacific. The surfers all saw the cutter anchored at the head of The Funnel, the beach patrols, and they knew if they were going to get wet, they'd need to find a creative way to do it.

All that made it easy for Gerard to convince Ray to take him on a tour of the coast so he could check for potential entry points from the sea where he'd have a better view of the cliffside. Gerard knew the coast from Eureka to Shelter Cove like the back of his hand, but he was bored. He didn't know what to do with himself, and Tommy T and Twiggy's ghosts were always riding shotgun and asking when Purgatory Beach would be open.

Seaman First Class Linda Darcy was at the helm of the coastie Zodiac. She'd refused to take bereavement leave after her fellow coastie was killed at the marina.

Ray and Gerard sat on the bench forward of the pilothouse. Eddies of wind pushed around the flat waves that pounded the shoreline, the Pacific a blown-out mess. The surf was crappy. At least Gerard had been lucky there. Bongo and the boys probably wouldn't have gone out anyway, regardless of the closing.

As the twenty-four-foot boat plowed through the sea, the shoreline appearing and disappearing as the Zodiac rolled into the deep valleys between waves, Gerard asked himself what the hell he was doing out on the ocean. But he knew the answer. Guilt. The need to do something.

The Zodiac was on a northern course churning at fifteen knots, a light sea spray blowing back across the boat as Gerard used binoculars to scan the coastline. Huge boulders littered the shallows beyond the breakers, the sheer cliffs a patchwork of dirt and falling foliage. He saw no paths. No newly cut vegetation. If Bongo and his crew had constructed a new entry point, he didn't see it, and they'd completed the task in the dark.

When the trio reached Centerville Beach Linda arced the ship's wheel and turned the vessel around.

As the Zodiac zipped its way south, Ray leaned in and said, "If you need to talk, I'm here."

Gerard said nothing. What was there to say? But suddenly he wanted to say something. "It's just... You know. We knew on some level. We knew something bad was gonna happen."

"We didn't know anything, Gerard. Something bad is gonna happen today. I guarantee it. That doesn't mean we can stop it. That doesn't mean we can stop the world from going forward."

"But we probably should've kept the world out of the water at Purgatory Beach. At a minimum, we shouldn't have held a damn surf contest."

Ray stared wistfully out at the sea, and Gerard saw the young man he'd known, the surfer with long hair, narrow features, and scruffy stuff on his chin. "I guess you're right. But I doubt you would've felt that way a few years ago," Ray said.

"You got me there. Oh, to go back."

"But since we don't have a time machine, we need to get beyond this." Ray shook his head and repeated, "We need to get beyond this."

Gerard nodded to appease his friend, but he had no idea how he was going to get beyond it.

The trio passed the Coast Guard cutter, the thunderous roar of The Funnel drowning out the arguing gulls. Silva's black boat sat beyond the coastie vessel, but Gerard didn't see Silva or anyone else up on deck.

To the south the coastline turned east, the Punta Gorda Lighthouse marking the southern edge of Mattole Beach. Bright rays of sunlight arced through the thin cloud cover as the sun started its drop to the horizon. Gerard scanned the shoreline, but the coast was much more open than to the north. Rolling hills ran away to the road, but getting into the water wasn't the issue down this way. It was getting by the beach patrols.

Gerard asked, "Has there been any more talk about using Chytridiomycosis to kill the mutants?"

Ray sighed and ran his fingers through his short hair. "One of the things I hate about the service—any military service—is every room you enter has a warmonger in it. Now, I understand. I do. I've never been in battle. Shit. Never even sniffed it. The worst things I've had to deal with are fishing dead bodies from the ocean and gunfights with drug runners." He looked out at the sea again as if the answers to every question were there.

Gerard said nothing but noted that his friend hadn't answered the question… yet.

"Those warmongers. They don't give a shit about the sea. It's creatures. All they care about is keeping Americans safe. A noble cause, for sure, but one that often creates collateral damage that exceeds the damage caused by the potential threat."

"The 'we have to do something' approach," Gerard added.

"Right. Got to show we're not sitting on our hands. There is order. A plan, and for some that revolves around destroying the problem, rather than fixing it."

"Who's winning? Fix or destroy?"

Ray chuckled. "That implies there are two sides to debate the issue."

"Great."

"That's why we're out here. Come on, Gerard. You know these waters better than anyone. Give me some ideas. Think outside the box as the kids say."

"I'm no scientist, but it seems to me that trying to eliminate a disease by introducing another disease is akin to trying to stop gun violence by giving out more guns. Doesn't seem very smart, though I guess live vaccines aren't far off. But what the hell do I know?"

"I have to agree, but until I've got some ammo to fight back with I—"

"Sir," came Linda's voice over the exterior comm system. "Can you come in here, please?"

Gerard and Ray pushed to their feet and made their way into the pilothouse.

"What is it?" Ray asked as he took the seat beside Linda, Gerard hovering over his right shoulder.

"I just got a call from the cutter," Linda said. "Look at this." She pointed at the SONAR screen. In the bottom right corner on the black background, there was a cluster of bright, multi-colored dots.

Linda adjusted the SONAR and said, "Whatever they are, they're pretty big."

"Full stop," Ray said. "Call the cutter and tell them to get some containment vessels out here. If these things are mutants we'll drive them into The Funnel."

Gerard slid open the pilothouse door and he and Ray stepped outside.

To the south, a patch of the ocean's surface was broken by the rhythmic undulations of tiny whitecaps. Flickers of movement stirred the water, followed by silvery flashes that caught the last rays of the falling sun. The Pacific shimmered, a dazzling interplay of light and shadow.

Gerard pressed the binoculars to his eyes as a swordfish broke the surface, leaping into the air in a graceful arc. The sunlight caught its body, creating a dazzling display of shimmering blues and silvers, its sword-like bill extended forward.

The school of swordfish was approaching fast.

Gerard knew that normal swordfish didn't travel in schools, but he also knew the disease infecting the ocean caused all types of abnormal behavior. Swordfish are solitary creatures, although juvenile swordfish are often seen in groups.

As the fish approached the Zodiac, their long, slender bodies undulated in perfect harmony, leaving a trail of bubbles that quickly dissipated.

Swordfish are among the ocean's most formidable predators. Their torpedo-shaped bodies, designed for speed, narrowed down to pointed snouts with sword-like bills, ancient weapons perfectly suited for slashing through schools of prey.

Several tall, crescent-shaped dorsal fins broke the surface all around the boat, the thump of the fish hitting the bottom of the hull echoing up through the vessel.

Another swordfish propelled itself out of the sea in a magnificent leap, and droplets of water scattered in all directions creating a momentary rainbow. The fish's scales glinted and all along its length there were the telltale signs of the disease; gashes packed with blood-filled pustules. As the fish re-entered the water, another jumped, and then another—a ballet of powerful leaps.

The ocean came alive, a mosaic of swirling currents and splashes, and several fish sped up in unison, a sudden burst that caused a ripple through the school. Gerard had seen this type of thing before. Synchronized bursts were often a prelude to an attack.

A massive blue-gray missile breached from the sea, its sword straight, tiny pectoral fins fluttering, its caudal fin powering back and forth. The fish hung in the air for an instant as it appraised the coastie vessel, then came down with the instinct of half a billion years of evolution, its sword piercing the Zodiac's front port side chamber.

Hypalon ripped and air shrieked from the puncture as a section of the sidewall deflated and seawater surged through the gap into the boat. Bilge pumps snapped on and drainage holes pissed water as the vessel was swamped, but Zodiacs are very hard to sink. Though the craft was hard to handle with one of its compartments deflated, the boat would function.

The swordfish flopped to the side and landed on the deflated gunnel as its bill pulled free.

Fish jumped from the sea all around the boat.

Ray found his voice. "Linda, take us back. Now!" He turned to Gerard and added, "Kreger is going to be so pissed. This is a new hull."

Gerard hardly heard his friend. He was still focused on the surface of the Pacific.

Out in the deep blue, the fish were dancing, their weaponry on full display, as if saying, "See what we can do? Best be moving on." A field of crescent-shaped dorsal fins and smaller tooth-like dorsal fins knifed through the churned-up sea, and Gerard estimated that at least twenty swordfish had come together.

Linda set a course for the cutter and powered up the vessel until waves of water were pouring through the gap in the bow. Then she eased back on the throttle until the bow was lifted and pushing through the dimpled whitewater like a raised plow.

Swordfish arced through the air, and one flopped onto the deck. The fish tossed and jerked, and Ray grabbed a gaff and secured a specimen for the bigheads. Thrashing and fighting, the fish's blood-filled pustules broke open and stained its iridescent skin crimson.

Ray held the fish up, the hooked end of the gaff pole through the fish's shoulder forward of its dorsal fin, blood dripping onto the deck.

Gulls hollered as the school of swordfish zigzagged and turned, and the Zodiac left them behind.

Gerard sucked in a deep breath, the air tainted with a metallic-like scent. The Coast Guard boat's deck looked like it had survived a massacre.

The sea was becoming more dangerous by the minute, and Gerard heard Ray's words echoing inside his head. "That's why we're out here. Come on, Gerard. You know these waters better than anyone. Give me some ideas."

But Gerard was… had been, a surfer. He had no idea what the hell he was now, but as he watched the ocean pour through the gap in the Zodiac's hull, he decided it was time to find out.

# 26

Three more days slipped away, and a storm in the northern Pacific created a medium-sized swell that brought nice thirty-five-foot rollers into The Funnel. The school of diseased swordfish had been corralled into the containment area, and Silva said there had been no other reports of abnormal sea creature encounters in the area. Life in Liigei Too had begun to return to non-competition normal, and that meant Bongo and his ilk would get the itch.

Gerard sat in the fading darkness, his old G-wagon tucked into the vegetation at the side of the road where he would see any vehicle that came out of Bongo's cul-de-sac. There was a trailer park of a kind at the end of Remy Road where some of the young local folks fled when they left their mom and dad's place and couldn't afford to pay high rents but wanted to stay in Liigei Too.

Though no headlights blossomed through the trees, a car motor rumbled through the morning's grayness, and Bongo's van appeared, lights off, cab dark. The vehicle crawled to a stop at the head of Remy Road where it met Mattole Road. Several minutes faded away and the van didn't move as the darkness slowly marched toward dawn.

The vehicle inched forward, and for a heartbeat, Gerard saw Bongo's haggard face in the dashboard lights. Bongo made a left on Mattole Road, which would take him toward town, and the van's headlights didn't come on until the vehicle was a quarter of a mile up the road.

Gerard had a pretty good idea where Bongo was going to attempt his entry because he knew the perfect spot to sneak into the Pacific. But before he went there, Bongo would go through a series of pick-ups and collect the brave few willing to defy the man.

Bongo was obviously looking out for watchers. This had been proven by his patient pause at the end of his street. That meant tailing him was going to be impossible on the deserted single-lane roads at dusk. But Gerard had a plan... or rather, he could intuit Bongo's.

Gerard headed to Glenda's house. He knew from experience that she got picked up last so she could sleep the latest, and there was no way she wouldn't go out if Bongo was.

In line with his habits, just as rain must fall and the sun must shine, ten minutes later Gerard sat up the street from Glenda's house and watched as Bongo quickly pulled to the curb and picked up his final passenger.

Gerard hung back, headlights off, the dark winding road to the coast so well known to him he could drive it with his eyes closed. Part of him was proud of Bongo, but another part, the part that had grown larger than all the other parts, his callus of experience, resentment, and pessimism, was angry.

When surfing was his life, Gerard would have done anything to get wet and ride big waves, regardless of its impact on his body, his life, and the lives of those around him. He respected that drive. The will to sacrifice everything to catch the big one.

But if life had taught him anything, he'd learned that when people who knew more than him spoke, he listened. He'd asked Bongo and the others to respect Tommy T. Respect the fact that another death in The Funnel might close Purgatory Beach for good. Was this wisdom? Or was he just an old fart?

Taillights bloomed in the darkness ahead and Bongo turned off exactly where he'd suspected the kid might.

There was a natural grotto—a sinkhole-type formation that had been created when a section of the cliff face had given way millennia ago, leaving an inaccessible soup bowl with a narrow opening to the ocean. Gerard had never done it himself, but he'd watched others jump from the seventy-five-foot cliffs into the cove. From there, surfers could swim through the inlet to the sea, where a narrow boulder-encrusted channel cut through the breakers.

Gerard, Connie, and the kids hiked the surrounding forest on occasion, and he knew a way down to the ocean. Even if Bongo had known about the route, the trail was very difficult carrying boards and they'd be seen from the road. Also, there was no place to launch a wave runner, though skis could be put in at Mattole Beach and meet the surfers. Gerard didn't think that was the plan on this day. No, he didn't think Bongo would be stupid enough to try and get into The Funnel. Not when there were plenty of smaller breaks around Purgatory Beach, and with The Funnel raging at thirty-five feet, the secondary breaks would still be pushing twenty feet. More than enough for Bongo and his crew to get their fill.

Shame washed through him. Today he had to be an adult.

As Gerard parked dusk painted the world in shadows that danced beneath every bush and under every tree limb. Traversing the path was difficult in the gloom without a flashlight. There were several very steep sections, but he made it down without falling.

Gerard positioned himself atop a boulder along the edge of the narrow gap that led out to the sea where he was partially hidden from view by thick clumps of beach grass that dotted the mounds of sand between the rocks. The tide was going out and a steady current of water flowed from the cove. Voices echoed off the grotto walls... laughter and shrieks of excitement. Gerard peered up at the cliffs surrounding the hollow, but all he saw were vague shapes standing beside surfboards that looked giant in the grayness.

He counted five boards. Bongo, Glenda, Tasmin, Joey, and... Gerard wasn't sure who the fifth person would be, but he'd bet a week scrubbing toilets he was right about the other four.

A flashlight briefly illuminated the cove but quickly winked out. Jumping from a seventy-five-foot cliff in daylight was crazy enough, but doing it in the semi-dark? Gerard was happy to see someone had at least checked the water below.

Against the black-gray stone of the cliff side and the deep green of the vines clinging to its face, Gerard didn't see the first plunge, but he heard it. Someone hooted—Bongo, he thought—and that was followed by the slap of a surfboard hitting the water and a splash.

Screeching, laughter, and thrilling screams filled the grotto as the other four surfers jumped.

The sun inched over the horizon in the east, casting pale light over the stark landscape as Gerard waited. He heard the group talking and laughing as they swam, apparently no longer concerned about being watched.

Bongo was the first to materialize out of the gloom. He lay flat on his board stroking for the cove's outlet, four others trailing behind him like eager ducklings.

Heat burned Gerard's stomach, but he tamped it down. He was about to ruin their fun, and on many levels that crushed his spirit in ways he didn't want to think about. The thought of letting them pass entered his mind, but he'd seen enough death and he didn't want any more blood on his hands.

As the surfers approached the inlet Gerard whistled. A sharp, steady call that brought the swimming caravan to a standstill.

"Who's there?" said Bongo.

"Batman," Gerard said. He stood on the boulder and revealed himself as the first light of day fell over the shoreline. The sweet scent of salt and honeysuckle carried on the breeze. Gulls shrieked, the wind whispered, the beach grass sighed, the rushing water tinkled, and the faint static of crashing waves filled the void.

Glenda said, "So you've been spying on us?"

"No, not you, Glenda. Just Bongo," Gerard said. "Everybody out of the water. Now!" Bile crept up his throat and he felt nauseous.

As predicted, Glenda, Bongo, Tasmin, Joey, and a younger boy Gerard didn't know climbed from the water and balanced themselves atop stones around Gerard. He had his speech prepared, a litany of his disappointment, anger, and worry for their wellbeing, but all he said was, "I'm sorry about this. I am. I understand you want to go out, but maybe it's a good time to take a trip. Go surf somewhere else for a bit."

"With what money?" Glenda asked.

There was that.

"I want to surf here," Bongo said. "They can't keep the ocean closed forever."

They can, and they just might. Gerard said, "Look, there are more important things than surfing."

A crow cawed as Bongo and the others stared at him open-mouthed, and Gerard wasn't surprised to discover his own mouth was hanging open.

"Safety," he sputtered. "I know you want... No, need, to be out there. But it's just not safe."

"Is it ever?" said the new kid.

"No. It isn't. But these aren't normal times." Gerard jumped from stone to stone until he stood before Bongo. "Do you promise not to try this again?"

"Why should I?"

"I'm asking. Me. I think you owe me a little leeway," Gerard said.

Bongo pushed air through his pressed-together lips, then said, "Fine."

Gerard explained the path, and how to get back up to the road. "How did you plan to get back up?" he asked.

Bongo waved a hand. "We were going to walk out onto the beach... after we surfed."

"If you made it back in one piece and were caught you would have been arrested and I wouldn't have been able to help you."

Bongo said nothing as he examined his feet.

"Get out of here. I'm going to sit for a bit," Gerard said. The sun was up, the morning fog teasing the ocean's surface as gentle sea spray carried over the shoreline.

"Don't trust us?" Glenda said.

Gerard said nothing. He was counting the seconds between the crashes of closing out waves and wondering how the hell he had become his father overnight. Connie would make it all better. She'd tell him he'd done the right thing, though he already knew that, and it didn't make him feel any better.

Some minutes later, when the squawking and whispering of Bongo and the others was gone, and Bongo's van was rumbling down Mattole Road, a male voice called out from the cover of the forest.

"I know that was hard for you."

Gerard jerked his head around and found Silva inching from the vegetation onto a large stone. He leaned his head back and sucked in a long breath. "I could do that every day."

"What are you doing here?" Gerard was a bit miffed.

"I needed to know for sure if I could trust you," Silva said.

Gerard's stomach stirred like when Connie said she needed to talk to him about something important.

"I want you to come out to the boat tomorrow. Can you trust Derrick? I mean really trust him? And Ray? I know I've given them the confidentiality speech, but things have changed."

Gerard wanted to say yes. To state unequivocally that he trusted both men. Instead, he said, "Trust? At this point, we're talking about trust?"

"The information you might glean tomorrow..." He paused and rubbed his hands together. "Well, let's just say it's not good news. For anyone, and if it were to get out..." He spread his hands in the universal gesture of 'then it's out of my control'.

Gerard put himself in Ray and Derrick's shoes. Both men knew the seas contained dangers, and that the new dangers were beyond anything they'd ever seen before. Could they do anything about it? No, so what would burdening them with a ton of new horrible information accomplish? He could always tell them after the fact, even though he wasn't supposed to.

"Your pause tells me everything I need to know," Silva said. "No need to answer. I understand loyalty. And friendship. And I respect both."

Relief flooded through him. Gerard didn't fully trust Derrick, but he'd rather leave that fact in the locked vault of honesty. Ray... He told himself he could trust Ray because if he couldn't, he didn't know how he'd be able to trust anyone other than Connie.

"I'll pick you up at the dock at 9 AM after you get the kids off to school," Silva said. The agent didn't wait for an answer, or a protest, but simply jumped from his stone and stalked off into the vegetation, leaving Gerard alone with his thoughts.

That was a dangerous place to be these days, with his thoughts. If there was a way to forget the last two weeks, he supposed that would be the option he'd take. Avoid the memory of the pain, the death, and disaster. But even as that thought set up camp in his head, he knew rain was coming and the campers would be heading home, because if there was one thing he was certain of, it was that he would never forget. He couldn't. And trying to would be to dishonor the memory of Tommy T and all the others.

He sat there a long time, the wind hollering, the waves mumbling, and the gulls arguing. When the sun was overhead Gerard pushed to his feet and started his climb back up to the G-wagon.

# 27

Gerard couldn't help but feel that the beautiful weather was nothing but the calm before the storm.

The ride through the hills down to the sea eased his jumping nerves. Bright sunlight cast an intricate mosaic of shadows across the road, the gently swaying trees, and the rhythmic chirping of the birds a relaxing melody that stirred his heart and made him want to stay in Liigei Too.

That's what he and Connie had decided to do. At least for the next couple of years. Sage and Willow were both at critical points in their education. They had friends, favorite teachers, hangout spots, and to pull them away from all that would create unnecessary stresses in their delicate lives. Being a kid these days wasn't easy. The constant barrage of peer pressure. The relentless pull of the cellphone and everything that meant, for better or for worse.

Gerard was on autopilot, and he concentrated on trying not to think about his decision to exclude Derrick and Ray from his clandestine meeting with Silva, but he was failing miserably. His reasoning, which centered around sparing their feelings, hadn't stood up under the light of day, yet he kept telling himself he was doing the right thing.

Derrick was an extension of the invisible hand of the law. A hand that could reach out and crush anyone that threatened its power. The same went for Ray, despite his best intentions. Orders were orders, and in the end, Ray would do what his superiors told him.

Gerard thought that might be why Silva wanted him under his wing. Not just because of his connection to the town, or his knowledge of The Funnel, its currents, and the underwater mounts. No. It was because he had once been a maverick. Someone who questioned authority, but was loyal to a fault, and maybe that's exactly what Silva needed at the moment.

He made a left off Mattole Road into the parking lot at the south end of the marina, parked, and shut down the G-wagon as he stared through a gap in the hills at a blue patch of ocean beyond. Clouds settled low over the water, the early morning dew still clinging to the muttering beach grass. He closed his eyes and sucked in fresh air.

Gerard's eyes snapped open when he heard the crunch of gravel under rubber.

With a squeak of brake pads slipping on metal, Derrick's Tahoe pulled in beside the G-wagon and came to a stop.

Guilt washed through Gerard like scalding water had been poured over his head.

Derrick got out of his truck and leaned in so that he could see Gerard through the half-open window. "Hey, what's up?" The sheriff looked over his shoulder at a black Zodiac with a gray stripe across its bow waiting at the end of the main pier.

Gerard was momentarily speechless. If he and Derick weren't friends, they sure as hell were teammates, and his decision to cut the sheriff out was sure to rankle the lawman. Since Derrick probably already knew exactly what Gerard was up to, he went with the boring and always vilified truth. He said, "I have a meeting with Silva."

"About?"

Gerard hiked his shoulders. "It's Silva."

"No mayor? No guard? No law?" Derrick was doing his best to keep the edge out of his voice, but it didn't take a trained conflict negotiator to know the sheriff was angry.

"What do you want me to say?"

Derrick let a long breath of air escape his lips like a leaky tire. "I get it, and I don't blame you. You should have been at the briefing I had with the County Supervisor and the staties this morning." He shook his head.

In California, sheriffs operated with a significant degree of autonomy, though the County Supervisor played a large role in helping direct law enforcement's principal goals and activities. The voters of Humboldt County were who Derrick had to please, but the blue religion is practiced at all levels of law enforcement, regardless of local reporting structures and red tape.

"He doesn't trust me," Derrick said as he jerked his thumb in the direction of the black Zodiac.

It was me, actually. Gerard said, "You know the feds." Seeing his way out of the pickle he'd created, he added, "You're here. Why don't you come with me?"

"Do you think Silva will allow it?"

"If he doesn't, he doesn't. What do we have to lose?"

Derrick nodded.

Gerard got out of the G-wagon, and the two men walked down to the docks and threaded their way to the main pier.

Some of the damage had been repaired, the chaos ordered, and many of the floating docks had disappeared along with the media vessels, extra jet skis, and supplemental safety boats. Gulls wept, and shiners jumped from the silver-flecked water, but Gerard saw no fishermen or charter captains as he strode down the main pier.

Silva's face twisted into a smile as the duo approached. "Sheriff. I didn't know you'd be joining us." He shot a sideways glance at Gerard, who found a particularly interesting dock plank to examine.

"Is that a problem?" Derrick said.

"Of course not," Silva said. "All the normal disclaimers about confidentiality and going to jail for chirping notwithstanding." He put on a wide fake smile.

"Certainly," the sheriff said.

"Shall we?" Silva waved toward the fifteen-foot dinghy.

As he stepped aboard Derrick said, "Looks a bit small for a man of your stature."

Silva chuckled but said nothing.

The fed took it slow, the dinghy gliding in and out of the valleys between waves. Gerard strained to see the Coast Guard cutter, but the vessel had moved out to deeper water and its white hull appeared and disappeared within the flickering gleam of the ocean. The outboard whined, the boat throwing a light spray that blew back into the trio's faces. It felt good—the sting of the saltwater on his face, the sun reminding Gerard that it had in fact risen as the prophets promised it always would.

Silva docked at the rear dive platform, and the trio worked their way up to the bridge. The mutant octopus and containment barrier no longer littered the rear deck, and the vessel looked barren without some oddity heaped upon it.

The bridge appeared to run the world. Gerard couldn't get a count of the number of monitors, because several of them were laced together and contained one large image. Three coasties sat in chairs with castor wheels, and they slid up and down their workstations, monitoring gauges, twisting dials, flipping relay switches, and listening to communications, all while accepting orders and monitoring the containment zone.

Silva motioned toward seats at the front of the room before the main screen and the three men sat. He addressed the coastie sitting at the forward control panel. "Get that series of video images together, will you Darla? The ones we were looking at yesterday and put the first one up on the main screen."

The coastie nodded and went to work hitting buttons and tapping on her keyboard.

As she worked, Silva said, "As you know we've got cameras, sensors, and I've had divers in the water twenty-four-seven."

The main screen filled with a closeup of a diseased great white shark. Gashes filled with red pustules covered the beast's slick gray skin, and its eyes were a fine spiderwork of red blood vessels. Gerard wondered if this was the creature that killed Tommy T. Half the beast's dorsal fin had been severed, and a clump of its caudal fin was missing.

"I think that's your boy, though he's taken a beating since he got Tommy T," Silva said, reading his mind. "But I didn't bring you here to see things you've already seen. Next one, Darla."

The screen pixeled for an instant and a fish Gerard didn't recognize materialized from the rainbow of dots.

"You'd never be able to tell but that's a tuna," Silva said.

The normally sleek and robust fish was bloated, and its skin was covered with ulcers and pustule-filled wounds that were red and inflamed and oozing a dark viscus fluid. As the image jerked into motion, the abnormal coloration of its skin shifted, and patches of red and black cycled over the creature's body. Its fins were frayed and discolored, and a yellow fungus grew around its mouth. The fish moved sluggishly through the water, sticking to the bottom as it swam in an erratic pattern devoid of its normal vigor.

"Do you see its swollen gills, the cloudy eyes," Silva said.

Gerard and Derrick both nodded.

Silva said, "Next one."

A brightly colored sea slug with a translucent body striped blue, orange, and red appeared on screen.

"Opalescent nudibranch, known commonly as Horned Nudibranch. See those red lines? They shouldn't be there. Sea slugs love kelp forests and are a critical part of the marine environment," Silva said. "Next."

A Red Abalone clinging to a rock among a field of sea urchins materialized. The tips of the urchin's spikes were red, their main bodies covered in pustule-filled gashes. The Red Abalone's thick, rounded shell had a rough exterior and a series of respiratory holes that spit out crimson fluid.

The next diseased specimen was a Top Snail, its smooth, rounded shell, which was usually reddish-orange, was black.

"The disease is devouring everything in The Funnel," Gerard said.

"That's not the half of it," Silva said. "The virus has mutated further and is now infecting fauna. Darla."

The image on the main screen shifted to a shot of a Giant Kelp forest. The tall green seaweed swayed gracefully with the ocean currents as they reached for sunlight.

"Kelp is a crucial habitat and food source for a diverse array of marine life," Silva said. "The imposing seaweed can reach lengths of up to one hundred feet or more, making it one of the fastest-growing and longest seaweeds on Earth. See that red algae covering it? It's supposed to be yellow."

Derrick grunted.

"Why do we care, you might ask? The algae have long, flexible fronds, which are buoyed by gas-filled bladders called pneumatocysts. These bladders keep the fronds afloat, allowing the kelp to reach towards the surface to maximize sunlight exposure for photosynthesis. If that algae doesn't do its job, the kelp will die. See how it's hanging over already?"

Gerard did.

"We're seeing the same thing with Rockweed and Sea Lettuce."

The main screen split into two. On the right, tree-like Rockweed swayed in the current, its normally olive-green color black with outgrowths of red. The left side showed a patch of Sea Lettuce clinging to a boulder as it danced, its light green leaves black and red at the edges, its veins black.

Silva said, "No need to lecture you if fauna starts dying off. It could also spread the disease as it mutates."

"The coasties don't know any of this?" Derrick asked.

"They've got pieces, but not the whole," Silva said and sighed. "I'm not sure even I have the whole of it yet."

A cold dread seeped over Gerard. He loved and respected the sea. Knew its greatness and its foibles. The Funnel and Purgatory Beach had become an apocalyptic stew. Anger rose in him, but he didn't know where to direct it. God? Any lower power, including Silva, wasn't worthy of such condemnation. "You're saying we've got a mess now that the cove has been mostly sealed off from the open ocean? I could have predicted that," Gerard said.

"Thing is, we haven't seen anything like this anywhere else. Not in fauna," Silva said.

"What does that mean?" Derrick asked.

"It means that the high concentration of diseased animals in the containment zone is helping the disease proliferate and spread to other organisms. As that happens the disease mutates further."

"So by creating the containment zone you're effectively killing Purgatory Beach?" asked Gerard. Not a new idea and one he'd thrown at Silva before, yet now it seemed more real than ever.

Silva said, "We've been down that road, remember? It ends in a bioweapon that could kill everything in the sea."

"What does all this mean?" said Derrick.

"It means that The Funnel could be a microcosm of the future of our oceans," Silva said.

# 28

That gem sat out there like a fart in church, the words "microccsm of the future of our oceans" like a toxic cloud.

"You're saying the disease could wipe out all the world's oceans?" Gerard said. It sounded too James Bondian to be real.

"Worst case scenario, yes," Silva said. "But many marine organisms have an amazing ability to adapt, and maybe herd immunity will kick in and knock the disease out."

"Is that what you think will happen?" Derrick said.

Silva said nothing.

"Sir, you should see this," came a harsh male voice from the opposite end of the room.

"Put it on the main screen," Silva said.

A bobbing picture, as the camera taking the shot shifted and dipped with the roll of the ocean, showed a black bag inching down the side of a cliff like a snail.

"Zoom in," Silva muttered.

It was a surfboard bag, and as the camera zoomed in the word 'Billabong™' became visible in white block letters.

"Look at the brown rope," Gerard said. "It blends into the cliffside."

"Premeditation. Awesome," Silva said.

When the board bag hit the shoreline, someone inched over the cliff edge and started climbing down. The climber's hair was tied back in a man-bun, and the surfer wore tattered red swim shorts.

Gerard said, "It's Bongo. Son of a bitch."

Bongo made fast work of the climb, and when he reached the bottom, he perched himself atop a boulder and took up the end of the rope, anchoring it as the next surfer crept over the edge and started their way down.

"They waited for the morning mist to burn away, and for everyone to move on with their day," Derrick said.

Silva chuckled. "More premeditation."

Gerard said nothing. This failure was at his feet, and he didn't need to be told that.

"Darla, get me setup on a patrol boat and notify all units that there has been a breach of containment in zone six," Silva said. Then he turned to Gerard and Derrick and said, "Let's go."

Silva sprang toward the bulkhead door and one of the coasties bolted up from his workstation and opened it, and Silva left the room.

Gerard and Derrick exchanged glances.

"He did say let's go," Derrick said.

"I was hoping you didn't hear that," Gerard said.

The two men followed Silva, and when they exited the bridge, the fed was already climbing a ladder at the end of the passageway.

Gerard and Derrick ran down the hallway and when they reached the ladder Gerard started down, Silva's face staring up at him as he climbed. Cold steel chilled his hands and sweat ran down his forehead into his eyes. Tiny starbursts winked and he saw the faces of his children, Tommy T's ravaged torso, Twiggy's torn-up body, and his wife dangling at the end of an octopus tentacle. Flashes, snapshots, light, dark, and then he felt sunlight on his face.

Seamen pressed themselves to bulkheads to let the trio pass and the partners arrived at the rear dive platform to find it swarming with activity. A twenty-eight-foot Interceptor, black with a machine gun mounted in the bow, stainless steel pilothouse with a tall conning tower with more antennas and dishes on its roof than the president's private yacht, was being prepped to launch. The pilothouse was currently open at the rear, two large folding doors pulled back, and a helmsman stood at the control console, the boat's engines gurgling gently.

Silva didn't pause as he untied the bow line, and Gerard instinctively took the stern. Ropes were tossed and the trio jumped aboard.

As the boat pushed away from the dive platform, Silva tossed Derrick and Gerard life jackets and put on his own. Not the fancy inflatable kind, either. The old-school vests that had been used for years.

Gerard was half done snapping his chest buckles when the helmsman roared, "Grab onto something."

The engines cycled up; twin diesels that powered jet pumps that propelled the boat to speeds upwards of forty-five knots. There were self-bailing slots between the sidewalls and the deck, making the vessel essentially unsinkable, and an array of handholds and cleats ran all along the gunwales and the sides of the pilothouse.

As the boat hissed through the sea, sunlight painting the ocean white, Bongo and his companions could no longer be seen scaling the cliff face. The surfers had disappeared into the tangle of boulders and debris that separated the shallows from the shoreline.

The rock jetty that marked the northern edge of Purgatory Beach was off the starboard bow as the vessel plowed over the rolling hills of water north of The Funnel, heading for the shoreline.

Two coastie Zodiacs raced toward the scene, one from the cutter and the other cutting across the containment zone just beyond the breakers.

Attempting to sneak into The Funnel was next to impossible, so Bongo and his friends were doing the next best thing. The surf up the coast from Purgatory Beach was nothing special, but none of that would matter if a nasty grabbed hold of one of the kids and dragged them down to see Poseidon.

Ahead mountains of whitewater poured over the silvery sea, and the helmsman brought the vessel to a stop just outside the breakers, large hills of water lifting the boat like a leaf.

"I don't see them," Silva said. He had his legs braced against the sidewalls, binoculars pressed to his eyes.

Tension leaked over the boat like sewage in clear water, the stink of the sea filling the air. Gerard stared beyond the breakers, the Interceptor rising and falling. Derrick joined the search, and the three men gazed east, the glare of the sun almost blinding, the roll of the boat making it difficult to focus on any particular spot for long.

"Got them. Ten o'clock," Silva said.

To the northeast, the shallows were deeper than in The Funnel due to the pull of the tide being less severe, and as he shielded his eyes from the sun Gerard saw a head appear above a breaking wave as someone caught a ride.

"That's Glenda," Silva said.

Several minutes ticked by as the surfers caught rides and the tension in Gerard's stomach eased. Bongo and the others were staying close to shore, taking the small stuff and having fun. It was hard to see the harm in it, and apparently, Silva agreed because he made no move to intervene.

Derrick said, "We could bring in skis."

Silva nodded. "You should see the ones I've got." He addressed the helmsman. "Can you get us in closer? Maybe at the head of where the break they're surfing peters out? We'll have a better view from there and we can keep an eye on them."

"Yes, sir," the helmsman said.

"You can tell those two approaching vessels to stand down and stand by."

"That's a 10-4, sir"

The helmsman cycled up the motors and the boat jerked into motion. Sea spray pelted the starboard side of the Interceptor, the wind gusting out of the west, and the helmsman used the flat water in the valleys between waves to track north.

"This is good," Silva said.

The helmsman slowed, the following sea smashing into the transom as he dropped the boat into neutral, the craft rocking and listing.

Three surfers floated just beyond the wave break, bobbing in the rolling sea, doing what surfers do best. Waiting.

"They must see us," Silva said.

Gerard nodded. "They know we wouldn't go beyond the breakers in this boat unless it was absolutely necessary."

"Smug little shits," Derrick added.

Maybe, but they're wet and we're sitting around watching. Gerard said, "Would they hear the external comm?"

Silva shrugged. "Maybe, but do you think they'd listen?"

"Good point," Gerard said. "I think—" He felt like he'd been punched in the gut.

Out on the ocean, one of the surfers had disappeared, but there'd been no wave to catch.

"What ju—"

"Something's got Glenda!" Silva shrieked. "Son of a bitch. I knew it. I knew it."

The shriek of screaming rose above the pounding waves, and the two surfers sitting on their boards were waving their arms and yelling for help.

Glenda broke the surface for an instant. She was thrashing and struggling but Gerard couldn't see what she was fighting with. Then she was gone again, pulled beneath the surface.

Bongo surged off his board and dove, chasing after his girlfriend.

The third surfer, Joey, sat on his board as if in shock, staring at the dimpled whitewater frothing all around him.

Glenda reappeared, but she was fifty yards away from Bongo and Joey. This time she managed to stay on the surface as she was dragged toward deeper water, her board trailing behind her by its leash.

Bongo lurched onto his board and swam after her, though Gerard could see there was no way the kid would reach his girlfriend.

Joey, realizing the situation had gone off the rails, started swimming for the shoreline.

"Intercept her," screamed Silva.

The helmsman brought the boat up on plane as he set course for Glenda, who was still being dragged toward deeper water.

"What the hell has her?" Derrick asked.

"I don't know!" Silva shrieked.

Gerard saw no dorsal fin, no tentacle wrapped around the struggling Glenda.

Joey was halfway to shore before his wail of pain carried over the raging surf. The kid's board floated freely in the dirty foam that covered the shallows like icing on a birthday cake, but there was no sign of the kid.

Decision time. Turn back and help Joey and let the coastie Zodiacs deal with Glenda, or stay on the current course and condemn Joey to death. At that moment Gerard didn't envy Silva, not that he ever had.

"Helmsman, bring us about," Silva said as he darted into the pilothouse and pulled the radio handset free. "Put me on the emergency channel."

The helmsman's hands strayed from the ship's wheel just long enough to adjust the radio.

"Coastie vessels, do you copy?" Silva said.

Both boats responded in the affirmative, and Silva gave orders to intercept Glenda. The captain of the Coast Guard cutter had informed all coastie personnel on the USCGC Robert Ward that Silva was in charge, and if he said jump, the response should be how high.

The heat of failure that had become so familiar to Gerard filled him with anger, frustration, and worry. There were three kids in the drink. Three kids it was his responsibility to look after. His charges.

To that the rational side of his brain reminded him that he'd done everything he could. Staked out the kid's house, dressed them all up and down more than once, and relayed the danger, the concern, and the effect another death might have on the future of the town. It had all gone in one ear and out the other, and the pull of the ocean had been too strong.

That pull might cost the young surfers their lives, and it wouldn't matter whose fault it was. When everyone was standing at yet another memorial, all eyes would stray to Gerard, the leader of the town and its former savior. The townsfolk would look to him to fix things, to make everything right, but he was getting ahead of himself.

The day could be salvaged, and the kids saved, but as he peered at the churning whitewater and didn't see Joey, doubt crept in.

Joey appeared within a knot of whitewater, a narrow black head attached to his forearm.

Gerard heard the kid's screaming. His hands shook, and when the wail ceased, he realized he had been the one screaming.

# 29

Silva's voice burst over the comm and it sounded like he was gargling sand. "Ray, get Glenda and have your other vessel help Bongo. We'll move in and rescue Joey," the agent said.

"10-4," responded Ray.

Seaman First Class Linda Darcy adjusted the ship's wheel and changed course, putting the nose of the coastie vessel on Glenda, who struggled to stay above the surface half a mile to the northeast. Something was dragging her through the water, an unseen menace that was determined to get her into deeper water.

The Zodiac launched off the crest of a wave, and the boat landed in a fist of whitewater that sent shards of pain running up Ray's legs as he issued orders to the second coastie vessel. Three boats. Three people in need of rescue. Ray liked those odds. The Guard had been rolling into impossible water to make saves since the service was created in 1790 when the United States Congress authorized the construction of ten vessels to enforce federal tariff and trade laws and to prevent smuggling. These ships, known as "revenue cutters," were the forerunners of the modern Coast Guard.Linda kept the boat on course, the breakers looming ahead, a watery cliff that was pushing twenty feet high, the sea floor rising to meet the bottom of the hull.

"Slow us up," Ray said. Though the waves were much bigger and more powerful in The Funnel, a twenty-foot wave requires respect no matter the size of the vessel. Ray peered through binoculars. "We need to get to her now or she's done. Take us in."

Glenda disappeared beneath the water again and as Ray counted the seconds his heart beat faster and harder. He gasped when she broke the surface, treading water. Whatever had been attacking her was gone, at least for the moment.

"Sir," said Linda as she pointed off the port bow.

Ray shifted his gaze, binoculars pressed to his eyes, the scene shifting and bouncing with the roll of the ocean.

The second coast guard vessel had come to a full stop, and Bongo was nowhere to be seen.

"Do they have him?" Linda asked.

"I can't see," said Ray who was still trying to use the binoculars despite the movement of the boat.

The ocean around the second coastie Zodiac churned violently as an unseen force stirred it from below. A hum echoed over the water as the boat shuddered violently, and the sailors on deck clung to anything they could to avoid being tossed into the drink.

All at once a series of massive, sinuous tentacles burst from the sea, each as thick as a python and covered in a forest of suckers. The snake-like arms wrapped around the hull with terrifying speed, the powerful suction cups clinging to the Zodiac and holding it in place.

A tentacle coiled around the stern, and the boat lurched violently, tilting at an alarming angle as panic erupted among the crew.

The helmsman gunned the engine, but the Zodiac was caught in the colossal beast's vice-like grip. With a rush of whitewater, the vessel's bow dipped sharply, pulling the stern into the air as the coasties scrambled to hold on, their shouts swallowed by the wind and crashing waves.

A hollow moan, as cold and alien as the abyss below, carried over the ocean as the tentacles tightened their grip, silencing the boat engine's desperate roar. The Zodiac tipped precariously, water rushing over its sides as the Giant Pacific octopus flexed and pulled, determined to drag its prey into the abyss.

The sea frothed and bubbled around the boat, creating a whirlpool that tugged the vessel downward. Gunshots rang out, but the crew's efforts didn't deter the beast.

In the heart of chaos every second is a test. The sea churned violently, and the bow disappeared beneath the surface, followed by the stern, the tentacles wrapping tighter, pulling the vessel into the depths as fiberglass creaked, rubber squeaked, and metal wailed.

The coasties fought as they were dragged into the icy water, the octopus's massive body undulating as it descended back into the depths, the sailors' cries for help lost in the maelstrom.

With a final, inexorable pull, the Zodiac was dragged beneath the surface and engulfed by the ocean. Water geysered from a knot of water on the surface, the hiss of the turbulent sea like the sound of frying bacon.

The rolling surface of the ocean grew calm, the occasional bubble popping amidst the forlorn debris of the lost vessel.

Ray stared, his mouth hanging open.

The sea, indifferent to the drama that had just occurred, continued to pound the shoreline.

Linda, who was still at the helm and powering toward Glenda, looked back and blinked. "What? Where?"

Ray shook his head as if trying to dislodge the thoughts that clogged his head. More dead to add to the growing list.

"I still don't see Bongo," Linda said.

Ahead, out on the choppy sea, Glenda tread water as she waited to be rescued, but there was no sign of Bongo.

Ray looked back toward the debris field where the second coastie boat had just been sucked into the depths like a water bug. He didn't see any of the coasties, but that didn't mean they were dead. He looked back to Glenda. They could still help her. "There's nothing we can do for them right now," he said. "Stay on course."

Linda said, "Copy that."

**Glenda and her screams disappeared** again as a hill of shimmering water rolled towards Bongo.

A calamitous roar of crunching metal, cracking fiberglass, ripping fabric, gunshots, and panicked screams rose over the pounding surf.

Bongo was overcome with regret as he paddled harder than he ever had in his life. Days of Sex Wax encrusted with sand covered his board, but he didn't care as the specks of quartz and iron dug into his forehead. He deserved the pain. It was his fault he was out here. It was his fault Glenda and Joey were out here.

Gerard had done everything he could, and they just had to be spoiled little brats. "We'll just get wet in the shallows," he'd said. "Some little rollers. Who's gonna care?"

He pushed the thoughts away as he stroked. Glenda wasn't dead yet. Nobody was dead yet. But unlike every other mistake he'd made, this one was too big to push aside.

Bongo crested the top of a wave and saw Glenda in the watery valley below. She was floating freely as she tread water. She looked to be unharmed.

Relief washed through him like a fever. A coastie Zodiac zipped across the valley between waves, but Bongo couldn't see the second Coast Guard vessel that had been coming in from the direction of the containment area. He stopped paddling and let his board glide down the back of the wave he'd just climbed, the momentum jetting him into the valley where Glenda waited.

A bloody and broken dorsal fin scythed through the water ahead, its top torn off. In the face of the oncoming wave, Bongo saw a massive shark. The creature's caudal fin swayed back and forth as it swam against the tide just beyond the breakers, its slick skin covered in long gashes filled with red pustules.

There was no textbook for surviving a shark attack. No secret is passed down by surfers from generation to generation. It was pure survival. A fight he was ill-equipped for, a battle against an ancient beast that had reigned as the sea's unmatched apex predator for thousands of years. He had his board and his wits… And did he really have his wits? If he did, he wouldn't be in the water.

The monster was big, fifteen feet if it was a foot, and as it surged to the surface it flexed open its jaws as it prepared to strike.

Bongo saw his entire pathetic life flash before his eyes, the blink and pop of a bottle rocket. There were worse ways to go out, right?

He looked over his shoulder and saw the black fed boat racing towards the shallows, and he tried to find Glenda again, but the next wave obscured her from view. He thought perhaps that was for the best. Bongo didn't want her to have nightmares for the rest of her life.

The broken dorsal fin disappeared along with its owner.

Bongo slipped off his board, hoping the shark would take a bite out of it thinking he was on it. He lay flat in the water next to his sled, legs on the surface, nothing but his fears dangling below him.

A gray nosecone inched from the water as if the great white was sticking its head above the surface to survey the world for the first time. Its eye membranes protected the creature's eyes from the sunlight, but the beast sensed him. Bongo was certain of that. He felt the monster's stare, felt it appraising him.

The shark smiled at him, pink skin inching back over rows of crooked teeth. Then the beast slid back into the sea without a sound.

Bongo stayed motionless for a sixty count, his heart pounding in his chest, his head ringing. He pretended to be a twig, a piece of seaweed, a leaf—as he waited for the bite, the surge of pain, the end.

But no bite came.

Bongo opened his eyes and heard Glenda calling his name. With the exuberance of a man who knows he's been given a second chance, he rolled onto his board and paddled like the hounds of hell were on his tail.

**The bow of the Interceptor** dove down the face of a twenty-foot wave, engines whining, the wind from the movement scouring the vessel with spray. When the boat crashed into a fist of whitewater and started its way up the back face of the next wave Gerard almost fell on his ass. His life jacket had a safety lanyard and it was attached to a cleat affixed to the pilothouse wall. He might get knocked on his ass, smashed and thrown and beaten, but he wasn't ending up at the bottom of the ocean. Bank on that.

"Derrick, help me, and Gerard," Silva said. The fed unhooked his safety lanyard, darted out the rear of the wheelhouse onto the deck, and began peeling a life ring off the boat's sidewall.

Gerard undid his safety line and he and Derrick followed Silva without a word.

Silva pointed and yelled, "Get that rope there!"

Gerard grabbed a length of line hanging next to the life ring. He quickly untied the knot holding the rope in place, unspooled the coil, and tied one end around a rear cleat.

Derrick handed the other end to Silva, who tied it off on the life ring.

Then the men waited like eager fishermen, half hanging over the gunnel as they stared into the sea.

Linda brought the boat in close to Joey, who was bobbing listlessly in the dirty foam just inside the breakers.

A Moray eel as thick as a snake had hold of Joey. The sinuous beast bucked and heaved, the beast's thin dorsal fin just behind its head wavering like a sail that's lost its wind. Crimson lines stained the creature's black skin, its protruding snout ending in wide, powerful jaws that were clamped down on the kid.

Joey screamed, but Gerard was happy to hear vigor in the surfer's voice. He wasn't done yet.

Even as that thought fluttered through Gerard's exhausted brain, the Interceptor was pounded by a breaking wave, and the boat listed sharply to port as water swamped the deck. Silva and Derrick managed to hold on, but Gerard was swept from his feet, the surge of whitewater pushing him down the deck like trash.

Gerard reached out in desperation and managed to grab hold of the line affixed to the life ring, and Derrick stopped his slide with a tug of the rope.

Out on the water Joey emerged from a knot of whitewater, the eel thrashing, its jaws still attached to the kid's shoulder.

Seawater drained from the deck as the helmsman worked the ship's wheel, the boat rocking and swaying in the wave wash.

Gerard worked his way back to the bow, where Silva waited for a chance to throw the life ring to Joey.

Another wave closed-out, but the ship's pilot managed to keep the vessel's bow into the wave, and the boat skipped over its top.

The water settled as the Interceptor glided down the back of the wave and Silva took his shot. He tossed the life ring like a frisbee and came up short.

Joey swam toward the ring but stopped when he saw Derrick reeling it in for another throw.

A wave rolled through, the hissing crack of its crest breaking carrying over the chaos.

The Interceptor dipped again as Derrick frantically reeled in the life ring.

Another wave rolled in, and Silva almost fell into the drink as he leaned over the gunwale to fish the ring from the sea. This time he didn't wait, take aim, or line up his throw. He tossed the life ring with the desperation of a man who knew this was his last chance.

The ring sailed through the air and landed ten feet from Joey. Close enough for government work, and the kid stroked hard as Gerard watched, worms devouring his stomach.

A big wave closed-out and drove the Interceptor toward shore, and the safety line went taut. The sea churned and frothed, and Joey disappeared within the dirty foam.

Silva hooted.

The kid had hold of the life ring. His shoulder was a bloody mess, his rash guard torn and hanging from his torso, his surfboard gone, his broken leash trailing from his ankle, but he'd managed to get his arm hooked through the ring.

"Go! Go! Go!" yelled Silva as he and Derrick hauled Joey in.

The helmsman cycled up the engine and slowly brought the boat about, setting course for deeper water.

When Gerard and Derrick hauled Joey over the side onto the deck, Silva yelled, "Punch it!"

The helmsman dropped the hammer and the Interceptor jumped from the sea.

For the first time in minutes, Gerard scanned the western horizon and saw only one coastie Zodiac dipping in and out of the waves.

# 30

The sun in the western sky looked like a bloodshot eye.

Ray stood in the bow, life ring at the ready as the Coast Guard Zodiac zipped over light chop, mountains of water towering over the vessel on both sides. Two hundred yards ahead Bongo was in the water holding Glenda.

The tang of salt filled the air, the deep blue sky free of clouds. Ray peered through the mist, then back over his shoulder as he searched for the fed Interceptor. It was coming on hard and would be on the scene in sixty seconds. "Linda, did they get the kid? Is he O.K.?" Ray shouted.

Linda stared at him through the pilothouse windshield and put a hand to her ear.

Ray pointed to the northeast and gave her a thumbs up and then a thumbs down.

She nodded and picked the comm handset up from its cradle.

The Zodiac bounced and listed as a wave rolled through, and for an instant Bongo, Glenda, and the coastie vessel were in the same trough of water.

Fifty yards.

"They got him," yelled Linda. "He's hurt, but it looks like he's going to be O.K."

One down and two in his sights. Ray gripped the lifesaver so tightly his knuckles hurt, mist blowing in his face, the bite of the salty spray stinging his eyes.

Linda brought the boat parallel to the incoming wave and used its momentum to get close to Bongo and Glenda. Gulls shrieked and argued, and the wind hollered, the crack and pop of snapping bubbles rising above the gurgle of the motors and pumps.

"Hurry!" Linda yelled.

Ray tossed the life ring.

Bongo snagged it on the first try. He quickly looped his arm through the life preserver and held on to Glenda as Ray pulled them in.

"Hold on!" Linda screamed.

A monstrous wave rolled in and broke at the head of the shallows.

The life ring was jerked away from Bongo as Linda spun the ship's wheel and gunned the engines in an expert maneuver that drove the Zodiac up the face of the incoming wave, through the whitewater on its crest, and onto the other side. The twenty-six-foot boat came down with a horrendous slap, and water sprayed and gurgled over the sides.

Linda brought the vessel about, but Bongo and Glenda were gone.

The icy fingers of fear and worry massaged Ray's neck and maggots feasted on his stomach as he searched the dirty foam, water slapping and shifting, the sea a chaotic mix of whitewater, seaweed, and popping bubbles.

"There!" Linda shouted. She pointed off the port bow where Bongo's surfboard floated in the churning surf. Was his leash still attached?

Ray struggled to see through the frothing water, but when the board surged up on an incoming rush of water he saw that there was no leash attached to the leash cup.

Then he saw them. Bongo had Glenda in a bear hug as he tried to keep his unconscious girlfriend above the furious water. Whitecaps crashed into them as another wave rolled in, lifting the pair and then dropping them into the valley between waves.

Linda didn't need to be told what to do. She brought the coastie Zodiac up to half speed as she tracked south at the top of the shallows. When Bongo and Glenda were due south, the coastie twisted the ship's wheel and went in to get them.

Ray's nerves danced just beneath his skin. With the bow facing land, the stern of the boat was vulnerable to a breaking wave, but as Ray peered back over his shoulder, he saw that the next few sets weren't huge. He braced himself against the sidewall and reeled in the life ring.

A broken dorsal fin sliced through the water, its top red and infected, pustule-filled gashes running the length of what remained. The shark swam between the Zodiac and Bongo and Glenda, but the beast didn't appear to notice the Zodiac.

"Ram it!" Ray screamed.

Linda shifted course slightly as the boat picked up speed.

Ray wedged the life ring between himself and the sidewall as he drew his Glock. He held it in a doublehanded grip and aimed at the dorsal fin, the boat heaving and listing, the sea bouncing and rolling.

Bongo held on to Glenda as the pair rolled in the surf.

Ray smiled. The kid was trying not to draw the shark to him. As far as he knew there was no blood in the water and the mutant was probably confused. Sharks used sound to navigate and locate prey in the ocean and are particularly sensitive to low-frequency sounds, but with the sea a chaotic stew, Ray didn't think the fish would be able to track much.

The shark dove and faded into the deep blue.

Another wave broke and drove the Zodiac further into the shallows, land getting closer with each push, the situation getting worse with each passing second. Water sprayed over the boat as a wave broke behind them and the deck was swamped.

Ray holstered the Glock, grabbed the ring, and tossed it.

The lifesaver landed twenty feet from Bongo and Glenda. Fear and uncertainty sent bolts of pain rushing to the tips of Ray's fingers and toes. Reel in the rope and try again, or…

Ray recalled that the largest wave Bongo had ever surfed—on record—was a sixty-eight-foot monster in The Funnel. The kid—young man—was an expert swimmer, a licensed ocean lifeguard, and he was trained in water rescue. With one arm tucked under Glenda's arm and wrapped behind her back, he stroked with his free arm and kicked with his legs, driving through the water as he headed for the life ring.

Another wave washed over the boat, but it wasn't particularly big or powerful, and Linda used its momentum to get closer to Bongo and Glenda.

Ray's heart threatened to escape his chest as he watched, each second an hour, his head pounding.

A horn sounded and Ray looked back.

Silva's black Interceptor was seconds out and coming on strong.

Bongo snatched the life ring, placed it over Glenda's head, and pulled through the unconscious woman's arms. Then he gave the thumbs up.

Ray pulled, the wet rope slipping through his hands, but with Bongo swimming it only took a few seconds for the pair to reach the boat.

"Are you alright?" Ray screamed.

The kid said nothing. He looked spent and the fear painted on Bongo's face almost made Ray feel sorry for the kid. Almost. Bongo was the leader of the local surfers—especially now with Tommy T gone, and he was no doubt the driving force behind Glenda and Joey being in the water. He made a note to cut the guy some slack, though, at least until everyone was on land safe.

Ray leaned over the side and clutched Glenda's shoulders as Bongo did his best to drive her upward, but without any leverage, it was a losing battle. Water lashed him as Ray snapped his safety lanyard onto a safety line attached to a cleat and leaned out further, his feet leaving the deck as he tried to haul Glenda up.

Linda gunned the motor and put the bow of the boat into an incoming wave, and the mountain closed-out on the Zodiac, burying it under a knot of violent water.

Ray pushed off the sidewall with his legs, using his leverage to pull Glenda aboard. He tugged with everything he had left, and the unconscious surfer flopped over the gunnel.

The boat rocked, Ray slipped, and Glenda was torn from his grasp as his momentum sent him skidding across the deck. He slammed into the opposite sidewall and pitched over the side into the drink, the safety line jerking on his life preserver as he hit the water.

**Gerard watched the remaining** coastie Zodiac get folded under a wave, the entire vessel disappearing in a cloud of water.

Derrick was tending to Joey, who was conscious, but squeaking and moaning, every shift of the boat aggravating his injuries. A huge mound of red-stained gauze and bandages were assembled on his shoulder, and it appeared as though the bleeding had stopped. The boy kept asking about his friends, how he said they shouldn't have gone out.

Silva was in the bow, staring at the coastie boat as it popped through the whitewater like a cork, sans Ray.

"Ray is in the drink!" Silva yelled, "But it looks like they've got Glenda."

The radio blared—something about reinforcements being on the way and two coasties in the water by the destroyed Zodiac. Gerard bit his lip as he realized the other coastie boat had been destroyed. What could have destroyed a ship like that? And so quickly? He could think of several creatures, the one that destroyed the marina, though dead, immediately coming to mind.

Gerard knew that small coastie Zodiacs normally ran with a crew of three or four, but Linda and Ray had been out as a twosome. So it was that Linda and the unconscious Glenda were the only ones left aboard the Zodiac and Linda couldn't leave the helm for fear of getting destroyed by an incoming wave.

"Get us in close. Now!" Silva yelled.

Bongo disappeared under the Zodiac as Ray struggled in the water, his safety line tangled around his torso as he fought to grab one of the handholds that ran along the Zodiac's gunnel.

Derrick drew his gun, but Gerard didn't know what the sheriff planned to do with it.

A wave rolled through and lifted the chaos and then dropped it to the bottom of the valley beyond. "There's a large set coming in!" Gerard shouted. They had a minute, maybe less, before larger waves started breaking at the top of the shallows.

The Interceptor bumped the coastie Zodiac and Linda gave Silva a thumbs up. Bongo was still lost in the churning water. Ray's safety line was twisted around his arm, and his entire body was jerked and stretched with each rise and fall of the Zodiac.

Silva darted across the deck as he pulled a utility knife from a pocket. Gerard saw the flash of metal as the agent flipped it open, and then Silva was hanging over the side of the pitching vessel, slicing at the safety line that ensnared Ray.

Gerard's insides went supernova as he caught motion out of the corner of his eye. He turned to see Bongo, struggling in the Coast Guard Zodiac's motor wash, the vessel's powerful water-jet engines spitting the kid out like green apple-flavored bubblegum. Bongo swam for the Interceptor, the kid fighting through the whitewater.

The sheriff holstered his gun and headed to the stern to help Bongo.

Indecision gripped Gerard. Help Silva? Ray was seconds away from being cut free. Or he could go help Derrick? Bongo was an expert swimmer, and when he arrived at the boat, he would climb onboard like a spider retreating when the lights came on.

Ray was dazed and confused, his eyes rolling in his head as he clawed at the safety line holding him tight against the Zodiac's hull. He was needed right where he was, but doing nothing just wasn't in Gerard's DNA. His nerves crawled as time slipped away, and despite his constant criticism of the often ineffective approach of doing something is better than doing nothing, he waited, breathing gently, letting the salty mist cool his face.

A large wave rolled through. Then another, the large set getting closer.

Ray's safety line twanged as it was severed, the tension in the rope giving way as he tumbled toward the sea.

Silva grabbed Ray's life jacket, and then Gerard was there, and the two men were yanking and pulling the concussed coastie aboard.

Ray heaved himself over the gunwale and the three men hit the deck in a tangle.

Derrick was hardly needed in the bow. When Bongo reached the boat, the sheriff helped the young surfer climb aboard as if they'd practiced the process.

With everyone out of the water, Linda dropped the hammer, and the Zodiac pulled away, jumping waves as it headed for deeper water.

Derrick helped Bongo to the bow where Ray was spitting up water and Silva was smacking him on the back as Gerard knelt next to his old friend.

"You O.K., partner?" Gerard asked.

"Yeah," Ray said. "I think I am."

"Sir!" the helmsman screeched. "There's something beneath us!"

As the group high-fived and celebrated, a tentacle speared from the sea and coiled around Derrick's waist. The scene froze, as if for a picture, Derrick's mouth falling open as his eyes grew wide.

The tentacle retracted and jerked Derrick over the side into the churning sea.

"Full stop!" wailed Silva.

The Interceptor was beyond the breakers, the waves nothing but hills of rolling water, everyone staring at the spot where Derrick had been sucked under.

Silva was the first to recover and the fed braced himself against the port gunnel as he searched the ocean for Derrick.

A mound of bubbles gurgled to the surface as if a giant leviathan was ascending. Thirty seconds drifted away, Gerard's head pounding. The boat rocked and Gerard's stomach burned. "We need to do something!" he yelled, but he didn't know what that something was.

Silva had his gun out, but there was nothing to fire at. Time spooled out. Two minutes. Three. When Derrick didn't reappear, and it became clear he wasn't going to, Silva went into the pilothouse and called the cutter. They needed medical help. Divers. More searchers.

As Gerard listened to the fed spew orders—doing something was always better than doing nothing—he said a silent prayer for Derrick. He looked at Ray, then at Joey and Bongo, his thoughts drifting to Glenda who was safe on the coastie Zodiac.

The surfers that had caused the day's chaos had survived, and the town's lawman had paid the ultimate price. What that would mean Gerard didn't know, but he felt the sweet release of knowing it wasn't his responsibility or his decision. That relief brought little comfort. There were dark times ahead and Gerard wasn't sure he'd be able to weather the storm.

# 31

**Purgatory Beach, Liigei Too, northern California, U.S.A.**
*5:01 PM PT, November 12, 2023*

It is often darkest before dawn, but light always overcomes.

Three days after Derrick's death helicopters came in the night, the thunder of their airfoils beating the air echoing through the hills and carrying up into the mountains. The air armada deployed a doctored version of the disease chytridiomycosis, which had been linked to dramatic population declines or extinctions of a variety of amphibian species. Using samples obtained from various infected sea creatures and plants, the bigheads claimed to have created a new strain of chytridiomycosis that would only kill the flora and fauna infected with the mutated strain of ZDD.

Gerard, Silva, and all the rest had their doubts, but the situation was no longer in their control, if it ever had been.

As the helicopters dropped their payloads, tiny pellets, like gerbil or fish food, pelted the containment zone. As the pellets fell through the water they broke apart and dissipated, filling the sea with the contagion.

In an effort to contain the disease and attempt to control the disbursement of the bioweapon, a second containment ring was added beyond the original barrier wall, extending the treated area to double its original size. Designed to contain oil spills and the like, a private subcontractor was employed, and a mile of secondary containment barrier was installed before the deployment of the bioweapon. The opening in the original containment zone that used the currents to draw in diseased animals was permanently sealed.

Liigei Too and the surrounding area were on full lockdown, with the Guard doing water patrols and the staties monitoring the shoreline from Eureka to Shelter Cove. The official story was there was no story. The feds were tightlipped, as were the staties. Nobody wanted to draw conspiracy theorists, amateur scientists, and those looking to make a career of a nonexistent news story that would sensationalize things to the point of trouble. Rumors were spread of an oil leak, though the locals knew the truth, as did all the surfers, so the entire world knew what happened, but that didn't mean it needed to be put in writing.

Silva and his boat had disappeared—no goodbye, no thank you, but Gerard had a feeling he'd be seeing the guy down the road.

Regardless of the rumors and news releases, ninety-nine point nine percent of the U.S. population had already moved on and forgotten about the blip off the northern California coast.

Gerard and Connie sat atop K2 watching the drones plow over the ocean's surface, collecting the dead. Purgatory Beach smelled like a fish store's dumpster, the surface of the containment zone covered in an undulating oozing mess of dead sea creatures and vegetation. It was a depressing sight, but there was hope on the horizon, and as the last rays of the setting sun knifed through the thin clouds and cast God-like beams of light on The Funnel, Gerard felt like he'd dodged another bullet.

"Do you have any meetings tonight?" Connie asked. She had an arm around Gerard's shoulders, and she held his hand.

"Naw," Gerard said. "I'm done for the night."

Gerard was acting mayor. After Derrick's death, Roxy Templeton came to Gerard and informed him she was stepping down.

"I think the town needs new leadership," Roxy had said. "And I think you are that leadership."

Gerard initially balked, but he soon discovered that sometimes he didn't get to choose his own path. Sometimes fate had a say. He'd said, "I'm not sure everyone will agree."

"They already have," Roxy said. "The town council has met. The vote was unanimous to elect you as Interim Mayor until the next election cycle."

"Elections. Speeches, I don't know."

"Unless something dramatically changes, you'll be running unopposed," Roxy pushed. "Try it, and if it's not for you don't run."

Gerard had reluctantly agreed, but his hesitation was just for show. He suddenly had a purpose, and even if being the real mayor and everything that meant wasn't his final destination, it was an excellent respite. He asked, "Did you get your school schedule yet?"

Connie shook her head no. With the kids getting older, and Gerard taking on a respectable job, Connie wasn't the only one in need of a purpose. Her path had proved easy to find, and she'd also decided what to do with her second life, and it turned out to be an obvious choice, at least to her. She enrolled in Eureka College up the coast, and she was pursuing a two-year program that would allow her to sit for the state teacher certification exam. Her goal was to teach in Liigei Too's small school.

Gerard's first order of business as mayor was to appoint Deputy Sheriff Nayeli Stonetree as Interim Sheriff. This decision was met with widespread praise, and she was also expected to run unopposed in the next election cycle.

The day after the events that took his life, Derrick's corpse was found floating in the shallows. His back was broken in two spots, and the state coroner's office said there was water, mud, and algae in his lungs, pink foam in his airways and mouth, his lungs showed signs of pulmonary edema, and there were hemorrhages in his middle ear and petechial hemorrhages on the inner surface of Derrick's eyelids and face. All this led to what everyone already knew; Derrick had drowned, sucked under by a mutant octopus that by all accounts was still alive and on the loose.

Connie said, "Have you been in touch with Bongo and the others?"

Gerard nodded. "I'm having lunch with the three of them the day after tomorrow."

"Good," she said. "I know you're angry with them, but they're just kids, really."

He nodded. That was no excuse, but still…

Like a drunk driver who survives a crash that kills others, Bongo, Joey, and Glenda would have to live with their choice to go surfing. A decision that had contributed to Derrick's death. But that storyline was in the past. Bongo and the others were alive, and they needed to get on with their lives, and he intended to help them.

Joey's wound was healing well, and other than some bumps and bruises, Glenda recovered fine, though she'd given up surfing, at least for a bit.

A horn sounded, and Gerard and Connie shifted their gazes to the Coast Guard cutter as it inched north. Ray and the Guard were playing a large part in what had become known as The Purgatory Beach Revitalization Project.

Ray had gone to battle not only for Liigei Too but for The Funnel Big Wave Competition. With Seaman Second Class Linda Darcy's help—she'd been promoted—Gerard and Ray successfully argued that funds be allocated for a clean-up, and it was decided that the containment barrier would remain in place indefinitely.

Once the cove was dead, and everything had floated and been disposed of, a cleansing chemical would be introduced, and the hope was that the sea's flora and fauna would re-emerge. With the barrier in place, Gerard announced that the town's premier event would return the following year to a cleansed and contained environment that was more secure than it had been before. A channel from the marina to the surf site would be created, and it would be protected and guarded, and everyone would be safe, except from the waves.

Though a date hadn't been set, the announcement that The Funnel Big Wave Competition would return let the air out of a balloon that was filled to its breaking point. This allowed the entire town to take a deep breath, and if there was any place on Earth that needed some fresh air, it was Liigei Too.

Gerard pressed to his feet and helped Connie up. The couple dusted themselves off, took one last look at Purgatory Beach, and turned their backs on the desolation with the knowledge that their beach wouldn't always be dead, and might end up being better than it had been before.

Connie pulled Gerard to her and kissed him. "Thank you."

"For what?"

"For being you," she said. "For holding it together when most other people would have crumbled. I guess riding those big waves wasn't for nothing. It made you strong... no, stronger, you were always strong."

Gerard laughed, full and hard. "Thanks, but you know without you I'd be picking fruit down southward way."

Now it was Connie's turn to laugh, and the sound was like music to his ears.

Gerard didn't know if he'd ever surf again, or even if he'd agree to be someone's tow partner. The ocean still called, but it was a different song, a different voice, a different language, and he no longer understood or wanted to accept what it was trying to tell him because the sea didn't always have his best interests at heart.

Still, Gerard didn't see himself straying into the mountains just because he knew his daughter would. But perhaps he'd find a new love there when he went to visit her? Maybe there was a new thrill in his future?

But all that would have to wait. There was damage control to be done, things to be straightened and fixed, and there was a learning curve to being mayor that even someone like Gerard, who knew the town and its bureaus of barnacles well, would have to suffer through. He was confident he would have a lot of help, and as the daylight faded, he thought—no, he knew, tomorrow held the promise of something better.

The setting sun kissed the western horizon and miniature sand tornadoes spun and twisted across the empty parking lot. As Gerard and Connie headed for home, an old saying worked its way forward from the dusty corners of his mind.

Last one out of the sacred gin mill please turn out the lights.

# 32

**Cape Adare, Victoria Land, East Antarctica**
*10:07 AM NZST, February 21st, 2024*
Silva planted his hiking poles in the snow, pulled up his gloves, and adjusted his goggles. The glare off the snowpack was blinding, and the wind gusted, cyclones of ice and snow twisting and swirling over the barren terrain, the sound like sandpaper rubbing on wood. Waves crashed in the shallows, the clean, frothy whitewater bubbling and gurgling onto a frozen rocky beach. Sheer cliff faces one hundred feet high boxed in the cove that was created over the millennia as the softer rock was worn away by the sea.

Dr. Bernard "Bernie" Krestler had called a halt as he examined a marker attached to a stake sticking from the snowpack. "We've got another half a mile to go," the doctor said. Bernie was a professor of geosciences at UC Berkley and a glaciologist who had traveled to Antarctica using grant funds to study the movement and composition of Antarctica's ice masses. He'd been on a field research trip when he came across an odd series of corpses while taking ice core samples.

The trip to the bottom of the world had been slow and arduous, but with the world's oceans hanging in the balance Silva knew he had to see what the doctor had found with his own eyes. Pictures, samples, and videos—they just weren't enough. Too much was at stake.

Two support agents waited at the Zodiac ready to move in and help if needed. Silva's radio was off, and the desolate silence of the barren shoreline was broken only by the loud shrieks of the snow petrels and the breaking waves, the stone walls magnifying each sound like a megaphone.

The pair passed two more markers before they reached the site. A red pole taller than all the others stood at the center of a small snowdrift. Without a word, Bernie dropped his pack, unfolded a shovel, and went to work clearing the drift.

Silva grunted as he pulled his shovel and got to work.

Twenty minutes later a frozen, preserved penguin corpse appeared beneath the ice. The beast was an Adélie penguin, and the professor had told Silva there were millions of the creatures crawling over the bleak terrain, particularly around the Ross Sea and Cape Adare.

Adélies are small and have a distinctive appearance. Though dulled by the ice, Silva noted the penguin's sleek, black head, back, and tail, which contrasted sharply with its white belly and chest. Its beak was short and black, with a subtle reddish hue at the base, and striking white rings encircled the creature's eyes, giving it a wide-eyed look. The penguin's flippers were black on the outside and white on the inside, and its legs and feet were pale pink and ended in sharp claws.

What caught Silva's eye were the wounds he knew all too well. Gashes covered the animal's slick skin, and red pustules spilled from within, like the most intense case of poison oak ever seen. The beast's dark eyes were clouded, and they melted into the white rings around its eye sockets. Half the penguin's right flipper was missing, and the tip of its beak was broken.

"Was it a fresh corpse when you found it?" Silva asked.

"That's tough to tell," said Bernie. "It was covered in snow, but it wasn't frozen yet. It's hard to see now, but there were splatters of blood on the icepack, but not like it had been attacked. It was more like drips or a puddle than splatters."

Silva licked his lips, his eyes going wide.

"CSI: Crime Scene Investigation," the doctor said. "It's one of my favorite shows."

Silva chuckled.

"This was the first one," Bernie said. "Come on and I'll show you the others."

The pair climbed a mound of rocks as they trekked deeper into the cove, the cliffs getting taller, the shoals filled with the thunder of breaking waves. Out on the bay tall black dorsal fins scythed through the water as orcas hunted for their next meal.

With the snow petrels urging them on, the pair passed three more markers and climbed over a boulder bigger than Silva's childhood home before arriving at what looked to be a field of battle.

A sandspit filled the tip of the cove and spilled into the churning shallows. Penguins of all sizes lay strewn about on the snowpack, their bloody carcasses frozen under a light covering of snow. The stink was unbearable, and Silva pulled up his balaclava to cover his nose, but it didn't help much.

"Is this where you took the samples?" Silva asked.

The doctor nodded.

Those samples and their processing were how Silva became aware of the doctor's discovery. Silva's people did a background on the professor and discovered the scientist had performed tests and experiments on the samples he'd obtained. He'd also given samples to two colleagues in the biology department, both of whom ran a series of tests on the disease only to come up with the same thing everyone else had. It was a mutation of ZDD.

But how had the disease found its way to Antarctica so fast?

As Silva stared at the carnage that question kept repeating over and over in his head. He was two thousand miles away from civilization, and the most expansive and unforgiving ocean on the planet separated him from the rest of the world, and yet....

The duo moved in closer as birds chattered and protested, and the coppery stench of blood mixed with salt and rotting fish permeated the air. As Silva walked through the corpses, he estimated that half the dead had been infected, the other half killed by their kin. Claw marks marred many of the dead beasts, a product of the disease causing an over-aggressive prey instinct.

"I've never seen an Adélie penguin attack one of its own," Bernie said. "And I've seen A LOT of penguins."

"This is what will happen everywhere. Species feeding on species," Silva said.

"What?" the professor asked.

Silva said nothing. He'd heard the doctor's story several times, he'd seen pictures and videos, but now that he stood there amongst the corpses, he had to admit he'd never seen carnage on this level.

He set about doing his own documentation; taking samples, and pictures, and walking the perimeter of the massacre as he counted the carcasses. He was almost done when a loud splash echoed off the cove's walls and Silva's gaze was drawn to the sea.

A crowd of penguins waddled through the shoals, and a cacophonous series of rapid, and rhythmic squawks that sounded like a cross between a donkey's bray and honking horns carried over the cove.

Out in the deeper water, an orca rose from the depths, its dorsal fin swaying as it left a wake of whitewater.

Penguins fled for shallow water, their sleek black bodies missiling from waves, but there were many, and some were sickly and slow.

An orca breached, its nosecone driving from the water as it nudged a penguin into the air. The beast cartwheeled as it tried to get control, but as the penguin crashed into the sea the orca attacked.

Silva pressed binoculars to his eyes.

The orca could have been one of the beasts from the San Juan Islands. Its black skin was covered in gashes, its eyes engorged, and as the sea wolf tossed the penguin around Silva noticed that the orca's movements were sluggish and erratic. It wasn't unusual for orcas to hunt seals and penguins, and it was common practice for the beasts to play with their prey before consuming it.

Killer whales are highly skilled and strategic predators known for their sophisticated hunting techniques. The beasts created waves by swimming in unison, which boxed in their prey. Once contained, the orcas moved in, using their powerful jaws and sharp teeth to seize and kill the unfortunate creature—in this case, a penguin.

Silva watched the pod share their bounty, the sea wolves tearing the penguin into manageable pieces. The orcas ripped at the penguin's flesh, tossing chunks of meat in the air and swallowing large chunks whole.

When the frenzy was over Silva stood in silence, staring out at the cove filled with diseased sea creatures. What would he do now? He didn't know. Containment was out the window, and though the bioweapon used at Purgatory Beach had worked as designed, releasing the doctored strain of chytridiomycosis into all the world's oceans made his stomach hurt and set the invisible ants marching down his spine.

The wind hollered and sang, the penguins barked and hooted, and Silva was pulled from his reverie by the sound of footsteps crunching through ice. He turned to see Bernie heading back the way they'd come, camera in hand as he documented the scene.

Silva dug in his hiking poles, rolled his shoulders, turned his back on the ocean's end, and started his long journey home.

Other Severed Press novels by Edward J. McFadden III: Time's Claws, Landfill Lizards, CRICS, Terror Lake, TRAGIC (#1 Amazon Bestseller Tag), Predators & Prey, Wolves of the Sea, Fortune's Cypher, Crimson Falls (#1 Amazon Bestseller Tag), Hell Creek, Barracuda Swarm, The Cryptid Club, Dinosaur Red, Drop Off (#1 Amazon Bestseller Tag), Jurassic Ark, Keepers of the Flame, Throwback, Sea Tremors, Primeval Valley, Shadow of the Abyss (#1 Amazon Bestseller Tag), Awake, and The Breach (#1 Amazon Bestseller Tag, Amazon #1 Hot New Audio Release Tag). His other novels include: Just Beneath the Skin, Terror Peak (#1 Amazon Bestseller Tag), the Theo Ramage Thriller series: Quick Sands, Sandbagged, and Too Much Grit, and Dogs Get Ten Lives, The Black Death of Babylon, and HOAXERS. Ed lives on Long Island with his wife Dawn, their daughter Samantha, and their cats Snoop and Skittles.

THE END

 SEVERED**PRESS**

 facebook.com/severedpress
 twitter.com/severedpress

## CHECK OUT OTHER GREAT DEEP SEA THRILLERS

### THE BREACH
by Edward J. McFadden III

A Category 4 hurricane punched a quarter mile hole in Fire Island, exposing the Great South Bay to the ferocity of the Atlantic Ocean, and the current pulled something terrible through the new breach. A monstrosity of the past mixed with the present has been disturbed and it's found its way into the sheltered waters of Long Island's southern sea.

Nate Tanner lives in Stones Throw, Long Island. A disgraced SCPD detective lieutenant put out to pasture in the marine division because of his Navy background and experience with aquatic crime scenes, Tanner is assigned to hunt the creeper in the bay. But he and his team soon discover they're the ones being hunted.

### INFESTATION
by William Meikle

It was supposed to be a simple mission. A suspected Russian spy boat is in trouble in Canadian waters. Investigate and report are the orders.

But when Captain John Banks and his squad arrive, it is to find an empty vessel, and a scene of bloody mayhem.

Soon they are in a fight for their lives, for there are things in the icy seas off Baffin Island, scuttling, hungry things with a taste for human flesh.

They are swarming. And they are growing.

*"Scotland's best Horror writer"* - Ginger Nuts of Horror

*"The premier storyteller of our time."* - Famous Monsters of Filmland

# CHECK OUT OTHER GREAT
# DEEP SEA THRILLERS

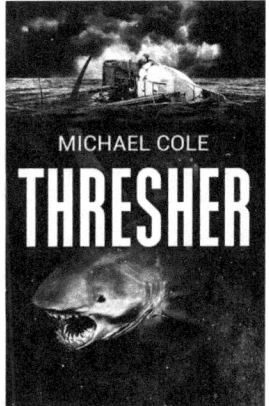

## THRESHER
## by Michael Cole

In the aftermath of a hurricane, a series of strange events plague the coastal waters off Florida. People go into the water and never return. Corpses of killer whales drift ashore, ravaged from enormous bite marks. A fishing trawler s found adrift, with a mysterious gash in its hull.

Transferred to the coastal town of Merit, police officer Leonard Riker uncovers the horrible reality of an enormous Thresher shark lurking off the coast. Forty feet in length, it has taken a territorial claim to the waters near the town harbor. Armed with three-inch teeth, a scythe-like caudal fin, and unmatched aggression, the beast seeks to kill anything sharing the waters.

## THE GUILLOTINE
## by Lucas Pederson

1,000 feet under the surface, Prehistoric Anthropologist, Ash Barrington, and his team are in the midst of a great archeological dig at the bottom of Lake Superior where they find a treasure trove of bones. Bones of dinosaurs that aren't supposed to be in this particular region. In their underwater facility, Infinity Moon, Ash and his team soon discover a series of underground tunnels. Upon exploring, they accidentally open an ice pocket, thawing the prehistoric creature trapped inside. Soon they are being attacked, the facility falling apart around them, by what Ash knows is a dunkleosteus and all those bones were from its prey. Now...Ash and his team are the prey and the creature will stop at nothing to get to them.

SEVERED**PRESS**

facebook.com/severedpress
twitter.com/severedpress

# CHECK OUT OTHER GREAT DEEP SEA THRILLERS

## SHARK: INFESTED WATERS
by P.K. Hawkins

For Simon, the trip was supposed to be a once in a lifetime gift: a journey to the Amazon River Basin, the land that he had dreamed about visiting since he was a child. His enthusiasm for the trip may be tempered by the poor conditions of the boat and their captain leading the tour, but most of the tourists think they can look the other way on it. Except things go wrong quickly. After a horrific accident, Simon and the other tourists find themselves trapped on a tiny island in the middle of the river. It's the rainy season, and the river is rising. The island is surrounded by hungry bull sharks that won't let them swim away. And worst of all, the sharks might not be the only blood-thirsty killers among them. It was supposed to be the trip of a lifetime. Instead, they'll be lucky if they make it out with their lives at all.

## DARK WATERS
by Lucas Pederson

Jörmungandr is an ancient Norse sea monster. Thought to be purely a myth until a battleship is torn a part by one.

With his brother on that ship, former Navy Seal and deep-sea diver, Miles Raine, sets out on a personal vendetta against the creature and hopefully save his brother. Bringing with him his old Seal team, the Dagger Points, they embark on a mission that might very well be their last.

But what happens when the hunters become the hunted and the dark waters reveal more than a monster?